Gary Corbyn-Smith lives with his teenage son in Shrewsbury, Shropshire. Forced into early retirement by ill health, he took to writing and painting full time. He divides his time between both loves and regularly exhibits his work. Born in London's East End, he was first married at age 21 and after 10 years as a plumber, moved with his wife and two sons to Norfolk to set up a successful meat processing business before moving on to Pubs and restaurants, being awarded runner up position of "Entrepreneur of the year 1997." Remarried to Lily in 1998, he now has another son Alfie, plus two stepsons.

For Lily and Alfie, who never doubted.

Gary Corbyn-Smith

PEACE FOR THE WICKED

AUSTIN MACAULEY PUBLISHERS™
LONDON • CAMBRIDGE • NEW YORK • SHARJAH

Ordering Information:
Quantity sales: special discounts are available on quantity purchases by corporations, associations, and others. For details, contact the publisher at the address below.

Publisher's Cataloging-in-Publication data
Corbyn-Smith, Gary
Peace for the Wicked

ISBN 9781643787039 (Paperback)
ISBN 9781641822343 (Hardback)
ISBN 9781645364221 (ePub e-book)

Library of Congress Control Number: 2019937092

www.austinmacauley.com/us

First Published (2020)
Austin Macauley Publishers LLC
40 Wall Street, 28th Floor
New York, NY 10005
USA

mail-usa@austinmacauley.com
+1 (646) 5125767

The Prologue, 1877

The young girl stepped lightly from the shallow stream, shivering despite the warmth of the sun. The lush grass of the bank felt soft and yielding on her bare feet after the rounded roughness of the pebbles beneath the gently flowing water. A slight breeze, cold on her damp body, moved the slender hanging withies of the overhanging willow, making the light dance pleasingly about her. It was a good day, an important day, probably the most important day of her young life.

Hurriedly drying herself with her threadbare petticoat, she pulled on a shabby cotton pinafore, patched and washed so many times that the original color could only be guessed at. It had once belonged to her elder sister Ivy and would in turn be passed on to baby Mary, born only six weeks earlier and now happily feeding at her mother's breast, oblivious to the excitement caused by the Baron's visit the previous night.

Shaking her wet hair in the warm breeze, allowing the morning sun to dry it, she wondered what the coming day held in store for her. In the space of just a few hours, her life had been turned upside down, her future changed, mapped out and arranged by this strange night-time caller.

She recalled once again the tearful conversation that morning, seated on the steps of the gypsy caravan in which she had been born fifteen years earlier.

"Your true life begins this very day," her mother had said. "God has smiled on you, a poor uneducated gypsy child."

Alice had tried hard to look happy at her imminent change of circumstances, but she knew it was pointless trying to fool her mother, who was, after all, renowned in Romany circles for possessing the gift of foresight, of sensing what will be and what may come to pass, many even suspecting that Alice herself may have inherited the gift.

Now the Baron had come out of the night and chosen Alice, her amongst all the young girls he could have picked. This was the moment she had been waiting for since she was a child. Mother had told her long ago of this day. Mother knew. Mother had the gift.

Soon dry, she gathered her damp petticoat, shoes and stockings into an untidy bundle and tucking them under her arm, strode barefoot across the common, back to the gaily-painted caravan.

Her mother was perched on the driving seat, still attending to baby Mary. The infant seemed absurdly small, her face crushed into the fleshy breast showing white from among the folds of a dark woolen shawl.

Ivy climbed from the rear of the wagon calling excitedly to her younger sister "Hurry Alice, you haven't got all day. Your dress is all ready for you."

Alice dropped her bundle onto a growing heap of soiled clothing piled high against the front wheel as Ivy handed her an old but spotlessly clean, white cotton frock which she quickly pulled on, smoothing down the sides with her small hands. Stepping away from the shade of the van she held herself erect, awaiting her mother's inspection.

The gypsy woman, baby now falling asleep in her arms, looked down wistfully at Alice, realizing not for the first time that her precious little girl was fast becoming a beautiful young woman, perhaps too fast? Her dark, sun-tanned skin seemed to glow through the thin fabric of the dress, her mass of curly hair falling thickly about her shoulders, still damp and so black it almost appeared to shine with a dark blue iridescence, and her eyes, rich dark hazel, gypsy eyes, huge almond shaped pools of liquid, staring up at her unblinking. For a moment she was reminded of the eyes of a deer startled by some strange sound.

Clearing her throat, she spoke sadly, "Finish getting dressed and Ivy will brush your hair for you. We must have you looking your best for His Lordship."

Turning her face away to attend to the baby she could feel the tears swelling behind her eyes.

Ivy looked her younger sister up and down appraisingly, "It seems such a shame that father isn't here to see you looking all grown up."

"Be quiet, Ivy," snapped her mother, climbing from the seat. "If your father were still alive, there wouldn't be any reason for Alice to be leaving us at all."

How she missed her dear Walter, his dark good looks and his strong arms, taken from her so cruelly by pneumonia barely six months ago. She had tried so very hard to keep her three daughters fed and clothed, but it was almost impossible for a woman to survive alone in a man's world. Ivy would one day find herself a husband who would take on the responsibility of the whole family, as was the gypsy way, but until that day came there was only one way for a woman like her to earn a shilling… the oldest way in the world.

In the last three weeks she had been with seven men, shepherds, tinkers, even a policeman, but never other Romanies. She would have begun sooner,

but her pregnancy had prevented it, a farewell gift from Walter, she thought lewdly to herself. It was only a matter of time before her daughters too, would be forced to join her in this loathsome occupation which she despised but which kept them all fed. Now maybe…just maybe, it was going to be different for young Alice.

The previous night as they lay in their narrow cots, the fat-lamp turned to its lowest, the sickly sweet smell of warm goose fat filling the interior of the small wagon, she had been awakened from her light sleep by the drunken calls and laughter of men coming towards the van from the direction of the village tavern situated behind a short row of cottages that skirted the common, by the sound of their shouts it was a good bet that they had just vacated the public-house after supping a good deal more ale than was good for them. Before she had fully come to her senses the small door of the van was wrenched open, waking Alice and Ivy. Three men peered in, grinning foolishly at the older woman.

"What do you want?" she asked calmly, clutching a quilt to her chin, unafraid and feeling in control of the situation, she was used to handling men when they were the worst for drink. The two men in front were suddenly pulled away from the open door by the third figure still barely visible in the darkness, they stood respectfully to one side, obviously used to obeying him.

Ducking low, he stepped into the caravan taking the three wooden steps in a single stride. He was very tall, over six feet, thin but muscular with a large fleshy nose, swollen and mauve with a tracery of broken hair-like veins caused by continual heavy drinking. His deep-set eyes were of a washed-out indeterminate color, small and pig-like with colorless lashes, sunken cheeks and undersized, widely spaced teeth, tobacco stained and diseased, when he spoke they were kept tightly clenched together exposing the pink of this gums, giving the face a drawn, skull like appearance. In stark contrast he possessed a flowing shock of pure white hair, which fell almost to his shoulders. Had he been a woman it could have been described as almost beautiful. He looked strangely comical, bent over in the cramped space, the dull glow of the lamp turning his white hair to gold. But the look in his eyes immediately stifled any thoughts of laughter the woman may have had. She realized the man was no longer looking at her, but was staring open mouthed at young Alice, now sitting up in her cot. Forgetting to cover herself in her fear, her tatty shift laying open, exposing small but well-defined breasts, her nipples like tiny pink shells on a beach of the purest white, framed by the rich walnut color of sun-browned skin.

"What is it you want?" repeated the woman, trying her best to distract him.

"What do you think we want?" called a drunken voice from outside.

"Be quiet!" bellowed the tall man towering about them, startling the women and causing the baby to stir. Turning to the two men he ordered them to go, which they did without uttering a word of complaint.

The man cleared his throat and turning, spat thickly through the open door before addressing the three women. His pale eyes flicking from one to another but tending to linger longest on Alice.

"Please allow me to introduce myself properly, my name is Sir Rupert Balmforth, the Baron Balmforth. You may be interested to learn that I happen to own this field you're camped on, I own the grass your horse is eating and the water you've been drinking and I feel it only proper that you should offer me some token of gratitude for letting you stay here, don't you?" he added with a sneer.

"I must apologize," she responded calmly, "I was informed that this was common land, I had no idea it was in private possession. We will pack up and leave at first light I assure you Sir."

"And I assure you Madam that there is no such thing as common land, all land is owned by somebody and Sorrow Common has belonged to the Balmforth family for generations and only by the benevolence of my Forebears and myself is it allowed to be used by the likes of you."

"'So, am I to take it that I am after all allowed to make use of this ground?" ventured the woman with a hint of triumph in her voice.

It was obvious from the man's expression that he wasn't used to being outmaneuvered, least of all by somebody of her class… and a woman, no less!

"Have I stated that I wish you to leave? I have merely informed you of the legal facts and trust that you have the honesty too offer me redress of some kind."

Guessing his intentions, the gypsy woman turned to Ivy instructing "Take your sisters outside. You can sleep under the van tonight."

Ivy nodded and swinging her legs to the floor she lifted the still sleeping baby. Squeezing past the stooping man she pulled a blanket from the cot and stepped outside, grateful to be free of his gaze.

Alice attempted to join her sisters but found her way blocked by the bulk of the man as his eyes locked on hers.

A pink tongue flicked in an out like a snake, licking his thin lips, "You stay" he said, reaching out and grabbing at the bed clothes Alice held in front of her. He pulled them from her grasp with a jerk. Looking once more at the mother he ordered her to leave, his speech harsh, commanding, used to being obeyed without question.

"But she is only a child" her voice wavered, no longer confident of her position, fearing only for the virtue of her daughter. Too late, she saw the blow coming, before she could react his open palm caught her viciously across the face, her head crashing back painfully into the hard wood paneling of the caravan.

Lifting his hand to strike again, he stopped suddenly, a taught smile stretching across his face, his voice becoming soft, almost pleasant.

"My dear Madam… do please forgive me, I really must learn to control this temper of mine, but you obviously misunderstand my intensions. I promise you faithfully that your daughter has nothing to fear from me, I am, after all, a gentleman… a man of honor."

As he spoke, his ugly eyes once more drifted to Alice, his fingertips stroking the soft skin of her neck, she shivered, hugging herself, his touch felt cold, unnatural, like the flesh of a corpse.

"You must believe me," he continued in the same reasonable tone, "I have no desire to ravish your daughter nor to dishonor her or your family in any way, I truly do apologize for my ungentlemanly behavior."

Taking his hand from the girls neck he sat, perched ridiculously on the edge of Ivy's cot, eyes closed, obviously pondering his next words. Alice and her Mother exchanged anxious glances but remained silent. After what seemed an age the man began to speak once more, almost in a whisper, his voice heavy with sincerity.

"Please do try to understand that although I have all the trappings of wealth and position and all the benefits that it brings, I am still a very lonely man. Lady Emma, my dear wife has only recently passed away."

He paused, looking at the gypsy woman as if for some show of sympathy. Wiping his nose with the back of his hand he continued in the same melancholy tone. "She died in childbirth, there was nothing anybody could do… The child was fine, a son, I named him Oliver, after my own late father. One day he will become the next Baron, but it will be many years before he can share my life. It must be impossible for somebody such as yourself to understand, but the life of a wealthy man is not always as it appears, times are changing, alas my estate is not what it once was. We are currently in the midst of an agricultural depression that threatens to finish us all. The last few years have been very cruel to gentlemen of quality such as myself, I am being forced to sell off much of my farmland, my cottages, my woodland. I am even considering reducing my household staff, yet here I am offering to engage your dear child. You must realize that all over the country fine proud family estates are being broken up. My lands are being ravaged by all and sundry, poachers, people cutting timber, grazing hogs, gypsies making free with my property." He looked pointedly at the woman, her eyes dropping self-consciously. Taking a deep breath, he continued in a calm, reasonable voice. "Did you know that I was once getting fifty-nine shillings a quarter for wheat, now I'm lucky to get fifty. Barley is down from 40 shillings to 35. It's getting worse all the time…"

He stopped suddenly, his pale eyes flicking around in confusion as if unsure of where he was. He looked at the silent uncomprehending women before him realizing that what he had been saying held no meaning to them. He snorted loudly through his nose trying to control his rising frustration.

Turning to Alice, he reached across and took her two tiny hands in his.

"All I wish is to enjoy her company, I have always surrounded myself with beautiful things, with things that give me pleasure. I want merely to have her to gaze upon, and to perhaps bring a little light to my darkness, I promise you she will be given honest work on the estate and have a full and happy life. Sorrow Hall is a splendid place to live, much more comfortable than this." He hesitated, looking at his surroundings with distaste… "Than this cart."

Standing, he looked down at them. "I have made a decision, I will not bargain. You will be given fifty pounds for your daughter. I will arrange for someone to come tomorrow at midday, perhaps later, to collect her. I wish you to ensure that she is bathed and ready to leave. She need not take anything with her. She will be properly clothed and provided for."

Without waiting for a reply, he was gone. The open door of the wagon swayed gently in the night breeze. It was almost as if the whole thing had been a dream, only the faint odor of tobacco and the reek of whisky leaving any evidence of his visit.

Fifty pounds! A fortune!… Fifty pounds!… Enough to live on forever. To never have to take those filthy swine that only wanted to use her body then cast her aside; fifty pounds. Enough money to keep Ivy and baby Mary from a life of misery and sin. And Alice, what a life she would have, to live in a grand house and perhaps to even travel in a carriage, dressed in finery, just like the rich ladies they had seen at the 'Derby' last year when they had been selling their 'lucky white heather.'

Alice needed no explanations; she had taken in every word the man had said. She knew what had to be done. If this was a way she could save her mother and her two sisters from the life that they had been leading since father had died, then so be it.

Her mind drifted back to when, as a young child, she had sat alone with her mother in the darkness of the caravan, eyes closed, their hands joined. Her mother's low voice seeming to penetrate her thoughts, almost as if the words were coming from inside her own head.

"One day child, you shall leave us, you will become someone new, you will change the lives of important people, your children and your children's children will have it in their power to shape the destiny of others."

Alice recalled her mother hesitating, perhaps unsure of her own thoughts, even in her trancelike state her brow could be seen knotting in confusion. Once more she began to speak, her voice slower, halting. Beads of perspiration began to form on her forehead; her breath came in short gasps, almost as if she were afraid of what she was about to relate.

"You… your child… you will…" Her voice rose higher in pitch. Even in the half light Alice could see her mother's face muscles twitching with some inner turmoil; the atmosphere, heavy with tension, grew and grew, the air seemed to become warmer… unable to remain silent as instructed, Alice cried out, half in excitement, half in dread…

"What… what will happen to me?"

The sound of her voice seemed to break the spell that had held her mother, who, shaking her head, leaned forward, pushing open the caravan door, allowing the afternoon light to spill in, dazzling the young girl.

"Well?" asked the exhausted woman, "what did I say…?"

Living in a real house would seem strange at first. Her whole life had been one of constant travel, rarely staying in one place for longer than a month or two, her home had been the confines of the family caravan and the surrounding countryside and she now realized with a pang of sadness that she had never needed anything more.

She would miss her family dreadfully, but as her mother had always said, "The path of life has many turnings and you must follow it for good or evil."

At a little after twelve o'clock a small, gayly painted tumbrel cart turned onto the common pulled by a shaggy looking, skewbald pony, hot and tired under the now blazing midday sun, walked purposefully to the running stream near the gypsy caravan and drank deeply, its long mane hanging over its face, forelock fanning gently in the cool water. On the cart, eyes screwed up against the sun, sat a small, almost dwarf-like character, prematurely balding with sparse black hair clinging to the back and sides of his large head, a thick walrus mustache drooping over his top lip still smeared with the remnants of his last meal, much of which had found its way down the front of his yellow felt waistcoat, buttoned tightly and topped with a smart green cravat despite the heat of the day. His size combined with his baldness gave him the appearance of middle-age. Alice was to learn later that he was in fact barely thirty years old and was excessively proud to be the man-servant of Sir Rupert Balmforth… His single aim in life, to one day become butler of Sorrow Hall, as his father was at the present and his grandfather before that.

Tugging at the reins he jerked the pony's head from the water and turned the cart towards the gypsy family, looking down at them with ill-concealed distaste. Nobody spoke; there was nothing to say. With a sudden flick of the wrist he threw a buff colored canvas package to the gypsy woman who caught it clumsily against her bosom without taking her eyes off the strange little man.

"I'm sure you'll find that everything is as you have agreed with His Lordship."

The man's voice came as a surprise, deep and resonant, completely out of character with his appearance.

Pulling the contents from the package she counted ten, newly minted crisp, white, five-pound notes.

"Say goodbye to your mother and sisters," he ordered Alice with a touch of impatience.

She kissed her sisters lightly on the cheeks and hugged her mother dry-eyed, behaving as if she would only be gone for a short time and would soon be seeing them again, but everyone present knew that her life had taken an irrevocable step forward and that the small group would never again come together as a family.

The journey back to the Hall was a short one, the strange man speaking only once, informing her that her duties would be decided presently by Sir Rupert and that she would be required to do exactly as instructed. She was to refer to Sir Rupert as 'His Lordship,' and to himself as 'Mister Owen' or simply as 'Sir'. She nodded in agreement willing herself to remember his instructions but said nothing.

Her first sight of Sorrow Hall filled her with a feeling of dread, it appeared so big, it seemed to threaten her, its windows like shining eyes glaring at her accusingly. It was approached up a long tree-lined driveway, a young man was raking the gravel as they passed, he stood to one side, touching his cap to Mister Owen. She wondered if the other members of staff would accept her. How did she address them? Did she have to curtsy to the Baron? Her mind was a whirl of questions.

Sorrow Hall was a square block of wisteria clad, mellow red brick, unadorned save for its ornate stone entrance and its elaborately detailed chimneys. She had imagined in her young mind a towering mansion with turrets and ornate fountains and statues. She hoped that the disappointment didn't show on her face.

Owen drove the tumbrel past the main entrance of the Hall, stopping outside a large stable block surrounded by a wide graveled area, where a scholarly looking, middle-aged man was waiting to unhitch the pony. Alice climbed easily from the seat, nodding a greeting to the groom who returned her look with an expression of disinterest.

"This is Alice," said Owen to the man by way of an introduction. "His Lordship has engaged her as a companion of sorts." The two men exchanged glances.

"And your name is?" asked Alice.

"My name is Charlie Burdett, but you can call me Mister Burdett."

Owen interrupted impatiently, "Don't worry about all that, I doubt you will be seeing much of each other, now let's get on, I've better things to do than stand and chatter to you two." He strode off across the gravel bridle path, Alice hurrying to keep up.

After being lead down a bewildering succession of passageways and up various stairways both wide and narrow, Owen had installed her in a small bedroom in the attic area of the huge old house. It appeared that most of the household staff had their rooms up there and she had been informed somewhat grudgingly that she was very lucky to have a room, and indeed a bed to herself, as all the other young staff had to share.

When she had inquired as to the whereabouts of the Baron, Owen had merely looked at her contemptuously, leaving the room without bothering to answer.

She sat miserably on the sagging horse-hair mattress of the high iron bed, gazing ponderously about the small, dismal space. To one side of the bed the entire wall sloped at an acute angle where the room was built tightly under the eaves of the roof. In the center of the wall was a tiny dormer window, the glass yellow with grime, in front of which stood a rickety washstand holding a cracked china wash bowl and jug, its once white surface yellow and crazed with age. Above the tarnished brass bed head hung a large, fly spattered crucifix hanging lopsidedly from a rusty nail. Alice reached out to straighten it, noticing that the faded fabric on the wall behind still carried the outline of the cross where it had hung for so long and where it was determined to stay.

She hadn't eaten since a meager breakfast of dry bread, honey and hard cheese. She had toyed with the idea of going in search of the kitchen, but remembering the walk through the passageways to her room, she decided it would be more prudent to wait until she was called. His Lordship must be attending to some important business or he would surely have come to greet her.

After what seemed an eternity, Alice realized it was now beginning to grow dark outside, closing her mind to her hunger she decided that she should retire for the night. She undressed carefully, laying her linen dress over the back of the only chair and climbed between the cold sheets, clad only in her petticoat. The bed seemed immense and incredibly soft after sleeping on a wooden cot all her life. She lay, wondering what tomorrow would bring, soon drifting into a deep, dreamless sleep.

Her slumber was shattered by the door of her room being thrown open and the sight of the Baron standing in the square of light, naked save for long white, woolen underwear covering him from his neck to his ankles, but open down the length of his body, exposing his freckled, hairless chest and white plumed genitals, his penis erect and pointing obscenely from the folds of his underwear.

"Now my little gypsy virgin, I am going to show you what your duties are, and I expect you to perform them with enthusiasm. Now let's see what tricks your whore of a mother has taught you." His voice sounded slurred, drunken.

Alice stared in terror, unable to speak as he pulled off the bedclothes and fell upon her. She felt his rough hands come up under her petticoat, finding her voice she screamed, pleading with him to stop. In desperation she fought back, raking her fingernails across his face, hesitating for a moment upon seeing the lines of blood well up and run darkly down the Barons cheek. With a bellowing roar of pain and outrage he grabbed her savagely by the throat, his hard fingers feeling like iron on her fragile neck, her body jerking and struggling beneath his crushing weight as she fought frantically for air. She could feel his member trying to enter her, her small vulva unresponsive and dry. Cursing, he spat on his hand and thrust it down between her legs, releasing his hold on her throat.

Her eyes grew misty as she desperately gulped air into her starved lungs. Suddenly, her wrists were clasped by a vice-like grip and forced through the brass bars of the bed head. His face was now inches from hers, his porcine eyes wide with lust, mouth hanging open, panting noisily with exertion, dribbling whisky smelling saliva into her disheveled hair. She felt the pressure of his knees force her legs apart, his rough hand between her legs guiding his penis to allow him to thrust it deep inside her. She screamed in despair and pain as she felt her maidenhead rupture.

After an age she sensed his hardness break and felt the flood of his semen mix with her blood as it ran from her violated body.

A little under one year later…

Once more Alice lay in the same bed, her eyes tightly closed, the woman's encouraging voice seeming to come from far away.

"Push down my lovey, just one more big push," urged Mrs. Heathcoat, "Push down hard. Come on now my lovey, you're doing fine."

Alice bore down as the midwife instructed, squeezing with her pelvic muscles, desperate to be rid of this thing inside her. She screwed her eyes even tighter, almost as if the darkness was capable of blocking out the pain. She had been present when Mary had been born, her mother could never have suffered like this. Is this what being a woman meant? Pain, always pain; the pain and horror of conception; the pain of the beatings and degradation she had endured over the last year and ultimately the pain of childbirth.

If this was to be her life, she was glad it was coming to a close, glad this was going to be an end to the hurt. She knew, as surely as night follows day, that the agony she was experiencing was not the normal horror of giving birth, she had felt her insides rupture, felt her body tearing itself apart. She knew instinctively that no living tissue could withstand such an onslaught and she was glad. Glad to be finally escaping this nightmare that she had been living.

Was it so wrong for a mother to hate, to despise the child that had grown inside her, implanted by a monster, by a fiend who seemed to spend his life in a perpetual drunken haze.

Amid the sweat, the tears, the moans of agony, Alice drifted into the release that was unconsciousness, finally free of the pain, unaware of Mrs. Heathcoat's reassuring voice informing her that she had given birth to a son, oblivious to the outrage of the Baron as he looked for the first time upon his offspring and saw the withered right arm and tiny claw-like hand, the hunched back and slack jaw.

"A freak!" he screamed, terrifying the midwife. "The little gypsy whore has given me a freak. I am Sir Rupert Balmforth. The Baron Balmforth…Nothing of that kind could be fathered by me. God only knows what this foul little whore has lurking in her past family line to produce such an abomination." He turned on Mrs. Heathcoat, shaking the midwife violently by her shoulders as if the whole thing were her doing. "Take it away. Get that vile creature away from me." He bellowed into her face. "Destroy it at once. Get it out of my sight."

The horrified midwife swept up the uncomprehending infant from beside its unconscious mother and crushing it to her chest, she ran from the room; the expression on the Baron's face stamped forever on her mind.

Alice awoke in the depths of the night; the house was silent, the lamp beside her bed had burned low, filling the room with shadows. Nobody needed to tell her that her child had been born, the pain was now a dull ache throbbing deep inside her, the relief of being free of her burden vied with the maternal instinct of a new mother.

Her breasts felt heavy, full, needing the infant to suck, she looked urgently about the room, the wicker crib that had been prepared lay cold and empty beside her bed, had her baby died? With a sigh she pushed her head back into the warmth of the feather filled pillows.

She lay thinking for the thousandth time about her family, her mother, her sisters…

It was almost a whole year now since she had seen them, a wave of panic flowed through her as for one dreadful moment she could not conjure up her mother's face… feeling that she may be trying too hard, she forced herself to relax. Gradually, a look of contentment lightened her traumatized expression as the familiar image came once more to her minds-eye. Once again, she could see her mother's smile, hear the voice of her elder sister Ivy, calling to her… *Where were they now? What were they doing? If only she could see them just one more time before…?*

The image of her lost family slowly faded as the recollection of Sir Rupert fought its way into her consciousness. If only he had not come to her that summer's evening… if only…

Her thoughts drifted back to a happier time. *was it only a year ago? It seemed like a lifetime. Things had looked so very different then, she had been filled with all the hope and excitement of a sixteen-year-old girl embarking on a whole new experience… a whole new life.*

Without warning a spasm of agony unlike anything she had ever known tore through her body, causing her to leap forward, clutching her stomach in terror.

Pulling back the counterpane she let out an involuntary gasp of shock as she saw the blood sodden sheets. Moving her legs in the dark red mass she could feel the sticky wetness running over her thighs… clinging to her buttocks.

With an expression of resignation, she slumped back heavily onto her damp pillows, conscious of the fact that the life force was slowly draining from her body; trying to accept the fact that she was going to die without ever getting the chance to hold her child. Despite everything, she could never hate her baby. With a pang of sadness, she realized she didn't even know if her baby had been a boy or a girl, she hadn't even considered a name… Walter, after her late father perhaps? What if it had been a little girl… ?

The door of the room opened, and the Baron's voice exploded in her skull.

"So, you're awake, you lazy slut!"

Her pained eyes opened to see him standing before her, a small, ivory handled riding crop in his hand. The hatred she felt for him brought a sudden rush of strength to her pain racked body. Without conscious thought she threw herself from the bed, her blood sodden nightgown clinging to her body.

"Where is my baby?" she shrieked, no longer afraid of the man before her.

The Baron smiled, "Gone… Gone where all rubbish should go," he retorted.

He hesitated briefly upon seeing the blood-soaked girl and grasped the seriousness of her condition. The look of uncertainty on his face giving Alice the final surge of strength she needed; her eyes grew wide, aflame with loathing, lips drawn back from her shiny white teeth. Her mind was now unconsciously reaching out to her mother, to her grandmother, calling up all the powers of her family to bring retribution to this evil man standing over her.

As she spoke her voice seemed to change, to grow old, ancient, it was no longer the voice of a young girl, but that of someone who had experienced pain and even death, a voice of someone who had lived long and learned from everything life had thrown at her. Her croaking voice was wielded like a weapon.

"May you and all yours be forever damned for what you have done here this day."

She spoke with a deadly calm.

Sir Rupert hesitated, unsure for the first time, and watched as the carmine covered girl slowly started to circle him, hands held like claws, the drying blood outlining the nails on her fingers giving her an evil quality, like a witch in a child's nightmare. Despite the obvious weakness of her body, the girl's voice seemed to grow in power, no longer afraid but strong and proud.

"You and your entire household, the whole estate that you hold so dear will be a place of horror, whosoever has any association with the name of Balmforth will curse you to hell!"

She knew her short life was coming to an end, here in this tiny bedroom that had become her prison, yet somehow, she knew deep inside that her newborn child was still alive… She moved towards him, wanting this monster to look into her eyes as she died, she wanted him to remember her final words.

He could feel the hackles begin to rise on the back of his neck, he moved slowly, trying to keep some distance between them in the confines of the small room. She came close, her eyes staring directly into his face, for the first time he saw no fear, only strength, only anger. He raised the riding crop above his head, her loss of blood making her slow to avoid the impending blow. She felt the sharp pain across her face, felt herself falling, falling into darkness.

As she lay sprawled on the threadbare carpet, sticky with the gore from her body, she looked up at him, silently mouthing the last words she was ever to utter on this earth.

"May my child live to avenge me…"

With that thought in her mind she slid away from pain, and into the peace that she had been so longing for.

The Baron stared down at the dead girl at his feet. He felt a shiver run up his spine as he looked at her face, which even in death held a proud beauty.

"Oh, my dear God," he breathed aloud, "Why would she smile like that?"

Chapter 1
1904

Sir Oliver Balmforth lowered himself into the dining chair, Owen the butler dutifully sliding it into place in the prescribed manner that had become part of their daily morning ritual.

"Your usual, m'Lord?" he inquired needlessly.

Sir Oliver didn't reply, it was not necessary. In the time it had taken him to remove the linen napkin from its silver ring and spread it over his knees, Owen was placing the huge breakfast in front of him. Home cured ham, sausage, kidneys, mushrooms piled high and topped with two newly laid eggs, their yolks flowing golden over the meats as Oliver sliced them though almost before the butler had removed his hand.

Positioning the toast rack and pouring tea from a Georgian sliver teapot, Owen inquired "Will her Ladyship be joining you this morning m'Lord?"

Sir Oliver, his mouth still full of half eaten sausage shrugged his shoulders. "Hell if I know. She was stuck in front of the mirror when I last saw her this morning. If she's not down by the time I've finished, you may clear the breakfast things away… she barely eats these days anyway," he added, shoveling more food into his mouth.

Owen gave a sympathetic look of understanding to his master and turned away. It was common knowledge among the staff that things were not as they should be between his Lordship and the Lady Felicity. For some time now she had been sleeping in an adjoining bedroom, and it was only on increasingly rare occasions that the bed was found unused.

Baroness Felicity Balmforth sat in front of the large dressing table mirror brushing her blond, shoulder length hair. The ebony hairbrush, a wedding gift from her husband, was inlaid with an ivory and mother-of-pearl design forming an exotic oriental pheasant, sporting an impossibly long tail which curled around the carved handle ending in a single pearl the size of her smallest fingernail.

Its value would be enough to keep a large family for a year.

She studied her reflection ponderously. She was wealthy; she was beautiful; she possessed more clothes and jewelry than a woman could possibly need. Upon marrying the Baron, she felt that her happiness was assured, but now, after five years of ordering servants about, lazing her days away and putting up with her husband's demanding sexual penchants, she had come to the conclusion that her life was unfulfilling, pointless and utterly boring…

Her musings were interrupted by a soft knock on the door. Margaret the housekeeper entered without waiting for permission.

"May I change the bed linen m'Lady?" she asked politely.

"If you must," snapped back her mistress, turning to glare coldly at her.

She watched as the young house-maid entered the room. Placing a basket of clean linen on the floor, Margaret began to strip the sheets from the bed with practiced efficiency. Felicity watched the housekeeper move lightly on her feet. Margaret had the kind of figure Felicity had always envied, a woman's figure, not a girl's like her own, she was adorned with flowing, honey-blond hair and deep blue eyes set in a pale, unblemished complexion which seemed to hold a 'china doll' beauty that appeared to glow with perfect health.

God, why did Oliver insist on having her around? It was well known he had made numerous advances towards her, all of which had been spurned. In a perverse way the rejection seemed to make the whole thing worse. They had had many arguments over it, but yet, he still maintained that just like his horrid father before him, he needed to be surrounded by desirable things. Even young Meg the ladies' maid, although only sixteen years old, had a rare beauty and a body well on its way to becoming voluptuous, just how much longer she would hold onto her virginity was already a matter of some debate among the household staff.

Dropping the hairbrush noisily onto the walnut dressing table, she rose majestically and swept from the room, her nose in the air, and without a backward glance at the knowing house-maid.

Entering the dining room, she smiled politely to her husband. The Baron responded with a nod but said nothing.

"Just tea and toast please, Owen," she informed the butler, equally politely.

She sat at the opposite end of the long mahogany dining table, the expanse of bare polished wood between herself and Oliver seemed to her to somehow symbolize something.

"What plans have you today dear?" he asked conversationally not bothering to look at her, at the same time signaling Owen for more kidneys with an almost imperceptible lift of an eyebrow.

Felicity shrugged her shoulders. “I’ll probably go and see Katerina. She’s promised to help me organize your precious Hunt Ball.”

The Baron gave her a look that did little to hide his displeasure. He did not altogether approve of Katerina Christopher, her wild, staring eyes somehow made him feel uneasy… exposed, as if they could see into his very soul; she seemed to know just what he was thinking, almost before he did himself. Felicity put his dislike down to his innate mistrust of foreigners, but he knew it went far, far deeper than that.

He looked down the length of the table, aware from his wife’s expression that Felicity knew just what he was thinking, rather in the same way as Katerina would. He found the thought vaguely disquieting.

“You seem to be seeing rather a lot of her lately.” He said, “you’ve barely known her six months, do you really think she is the best person to help you? I would have thought Margaret was more qualified to assist with that sort of thing.”

Felicity glared angrily at him. “We can manage perfectly well without the aid of one of your…” She paused, searching for the right words.

“Without one of your ornamental servants,” she lowered her voice slightly, conscious of the butler’s presence.

“Just because you seem to find her so indispensable, I’m afraid I don’t happen to share your high opinion of her, and as for Katerina, she is just about the only real friend I have and if you don’t like her… well, that’s just too bad.”

Standing up, she threw her napkin onto the table and stormed from the room, tea and toast untouched, her voice echoing in the hallways as she called for Meg, her lady’s maid.

Owen began hurriedly clearing away the breakfast things, his face red with embarrassment at witnessing the domestic spat.

Oliver slid his chair away from the table and leaned back, one leg crossed over the other, his left hand grasping his right ankle, he stared up at the ceiling and thought about his wife’s outburst, about her dislike for Margaret, but mostly he thought about Katerina Christopher…

He had often had long, drunken conversations with Katerina’s husband, his longtime friend Gregory. The two of them had grown up together, sharing each other’s confidences, placing their friendship above all, but of course that was before Katerina. Recently, in the comfort of Oliver’s library, over a bottle of twelve-year-old malt, Gregory had confided in his closest and oldest friend, revealing some rather strange and disturbing things about his new wife. Sitting in the deep buttoned luxury of the library’s green leather chesterfield, he told how Katerina and been behaving strangely for some time and had recently taken to shutting herself away in the old tower at the top of their sprawling gothic house. He had challenged her and she had explained that she simply liked to be alone and that she found the seclusion relaxing, when he had suggested having the servants clean the filthy room she had insisted that on no account was it to be disturbed, proclaiming that it was never to be entered by anyone but herself. He had laughingly offered to keep her company one evening and she had turned on him with such ferocity and with such a look of malice in their eyes, it had made him reel, reacting almost as though he had received a physical blow.

Since that evening she had been behaving progressively worse, their love-making becoming more violent, with her often breaking into obscene language, or screaming at the top of her voice, much to the horror, and later the amusement of the servants.

Of late she had begun spending whole nights shut away in the dank, filthy room, '*her*' room as she now liked to refer to it.

Eventually he had decided to investigate further, waiting until she was out riding with Felicity. He had crept up to the small room, furtively walking up the creaking spiral staircase, feeling like a thief in his own home. Entering the room, he found it in complete darkness. Groping his way forward, he discovered that the dust-shrouded windows had been covered by heavy black velvet drapes which shut out the light entirely. Pulling the curtains aside the sunlight spilt into the room, illuminating the dust motes dancing in the air at the sudden disturbance. He looked around; there was no furniture at all. In the exact center of the floor was a small area swept clean and circled by many large candles; candles made of a thick black wax, just where she had obtained them he had no idea, some looked like they were floating in a pool of tar, where they had burnt down and been repeatedly replaced, the dark viscous looking wax spreading across the oak boards of the floor. Thrown carelessly into a corner of the room were the remains of what looked like some obscure pack of playing cards, torn into hundreds of tiny pieces. He tried to piece some of the fragments together, like some impossible jigsaw, but with no success. Examining them closely, he was amazed at the thickness and strength of the card used in their manufacture, a heavy coarse paper reinforced with a stiff linen backing, the strength required to have torn them must have been phenomenal.

That evening he had confronted Katerina with his discoveries. She had merely fixed him with a piercing stare, a stare which had filled him with such dread, with such horror, he had to turn his back and walk trembling to his study, where he sat in a daze, huddled in a chair, hands clasped together, gripped tightly between his knees to prevent them from shaking.

He was in a state of utter, uncontrollable terror that he could not comprehend.

Oliver could recall clearly the expression of desolation on his friends face as he had explained how he had felt that evening, Gregory had always been both physically and mentally the stronger of the two. Oliver had found it distressing to witness the influence Katerina's behavior was having, not only on Gregory but also on Felicity, and conversely on himself.

At a similar dining table less than a mile away Gregory too was finishing his breakfast alone, his mind yet again pondering the change in his young wife.

What had happened to the woman he had married, his '*Russian Princess*,' as he liked to think of her?

He would never forget their first meeting, less than two years ago. He, a young officer in the British army at the end of the Boer War, serving bravely under Lord Kitchener. The peace treaty had been signed. The war in Southern Africa was finally over.

A huge reception was held in honor of the regiment; a telegram of congratulations from his Majesty King Edward VII was read out to all the officers present, filling Gregory with a feeling of pride he had never before known. As he stood listening to the words of praise being spoken loudly for all to hear he had seen her, standing alone on the far side of the room, looking demurely at him, a shy smile creasing her round face, her jewelry and fine clothes testament to her obvious wealth.

Over the next weeks they had become inseparable, dining together almost daily, a handsome couple, attending all the best social gatherings. His slight, muscular frame and dark hair complimenting perfectly, her voluptuous body, cherubic beauty, and bubbly fair curls.

Sitting together on the porch of her father's impressive home she had told him the story of how, half a century earlier, her family had left Russia at the start of the Crimean War, how her grandfather had been a Russian representative of Tsar Nicholas the First, stationed at the naval base of Sebastopol and how the family had finally settled in Dutch South Africa, prospering in the Transvaal, making a modest fortune in diamond mining and later, gold.

He found the story of her life both enchanting and romantic. He told her tales of his much different upbringing in England, of the green fields surrounding his fine home in Norfolk, of a life of leisure, garden parties and hunt balls, a life with no wars, no danger of being murdered in your sleep, no deadly insects or snakes. It had sounded to her like paradise, to walk alone without fear, to not need protection whenever she ventured outside the high walls of her father's estate, with its locked gates and ferocious dogs, to be free of the primitive beliefs and strange customs of the servants that surrounded her.

Her mother had always been a distant figure in her life. Reveling in the responsibilities of a rich landowner's wife, she was a firm believer in children being 'seen and not heard,' keeping her daughter at arm's length, never cruel...but never loving. Preferring to assign the duty of childcare to a native nurse who had all but raised the young Katerina single handily, filling the susceptible child's mind with many of her own fears and superstitions, explaining how all life was controlled by powerful beings that were born at the start of time and who watched over the children on earth. Katerina struggled to relate these tales to her own bible studies preached by the visiting tutor who worked his way around all the prosperous families in town.

She had known instinctively never to mention her nanny's teachings to her parents for fear of the punishment that would surely follow; she had often witnessed her father whip recalcitrant servants until they bled.

Mr. Sibson the pastor would bellow his warnings of redemption and damnation from his pulpit, his thin face burnt almost as black as the tribesmen by the searing African sun, his rheumy eyes standing out terrifyingly. What young child wouldn't find her nanny's stories so much more appealing?

Six months later, Katerina and Gregory were married in a small ceremony officiated over by the young Chaplain of the regiment.

Over the months that followed a casual friendship developed between Gregory and the Chaplain, a handsome, impressionable man by the name of James Underwood, who confided in him that now that the war was over he was desperate to return to England and find a nice quiet parish far away from the horror and bloodshed that had dominated his life for so long.

In a moment of inspiration Gregory had contacted his old friend, Sir Oliver Balmforth, who had in turn approached his friend the bishop.

As the recently wed Mr. and Mrs. Christopher prepared to sail for their new life together in England, Gregory handed a sealed envelope to James containing an official document offering him 'The patron of the living' to the benefice of the Norfolk hamlet known as Sorrow, to include an annual remuneration of three hundred and eighty-two pounds, seventeen shillings' and fourpence. Also, a great tithe in the form of rent for glebe lands totaling eighty-eight acres paid annually by Thomas James Morton, tenant farmer.

A further eight months was to see James Underwood thanking Sir Oliver Balmforth in person for his intercession on his behalf, when he was officially made Rector of Saint Michael's, the home church of the estate of the Balmforth family in the tiny Norfolk village named Sorrow.

Chapter 2

Noblet Swallow was a third-generation blacksmith, his grandfather, also called Noblet as was his father before him. The unusual name originally being the maiden name of his great-grandmother. Noblet's grandfather had built the smithy with his own hands, converting the existing barn that was built onto his small cottage. He had added a wide lean-to along the entire length of the building to allow him to work outside of the stifling interior. A massive brick forge dominated the barn, the fire-back and iron hood made by the blacksmith himself, as was the majority of the tools, the dozens of various tongs used to hold the red-hot metal, the long racks that housed the tools of his trade, even the long water-bath, the size of a horse trough, that was used to cool the annealed iron horseshoes and the many implements that were so relied upon, anything from an ornate garden gate to a bag of nails. To one side of the furnace stood the immensely heavy anvil on its stand, the sister to another housed outside for summer use. Suspended from a stout beam above was the pulley system that helped manhandle the heavier sections of ironwork. Adjoining the building were two small loose-boxes, one of which that was used to house any riding ponies or cart horses waiting to be shod. In his grandfather's time, the other had housed the huge old mare that pulled the cart with its small anvil and mobile forge used to travel to neighboring farms to shoe the many plough horses. Noblet as a child would often accompany his grandfather on these trips, sitting on the horse's back which seemed as wide as a table top to the small boy. He was fascinated by the ease with which his grandfather would handle the huge creatures, coaxing them to lift a massive hoof for him to work on the shoe. He loved the smell of the leather harnesses and the acrid stench of the burning hoof as the red-hot shoes would be pushed home for their final adjustment before being plunged into the tin bath of water. The hiss and the sudden cloud of steam seemed like magic to the small boy perched high atop the old mare. Noblet Junior knew, even at that young age that what he wanted most in life was to one day work alongside his grandfather and father.

The adult Noblet often looked in on the now empty loose-boxes, fondly remembering his childhood and his grandfather and father, both alas no more. He rarely bothered with the farrier side of the business anymore, instead letting

Peter Wright in the next village handle all the horse trade. In return, Peter would send many of his customers Noblet's way for their new pitchforks, shears, latches, hinges and the thousand and one other items that the villagers could not manage without.

The cottage itself was very small but fine for he and his wife, having yet to be blessed with any children, the blacksmith accepting that that day may never come, he being an only child as was his father before him. His wife Rachael always said that it was in the hands of God but Noblet was well aware of how difficult it was for her to accept, after spending her days teaching the many children of Sorrow and the surrounding farms and hamlets and watching them run off at the end of their school-day to their waiting parents.

He stood outside the entrance to his blacksmith's shop, feeling hot and uncomfortable in his best Sunday church going clothes, the stiff, white collar chafing his neck and the starched cuffs feeling like manacles on his wrists.

"Will you please hurry?" he called irritably to his wife.

"I'm just coming," she replied brightly, tying the ribbon of her best bonnet firmly below her chin as she skipped childlike along the front path of the small cottage.

"I have to look my best to welcome the new Rector," she said, standing in front of her husband. "How do I look?" she asked, turning slowly for his inspection.

He glanced sulkily at her, but as always, was completely disarmed by her pretty smile. "You look beautiful and you know it," he grinned back at her, feeling an enormous pride swelling inside him as he invariably did when walking with Rachael at his side. Even after five years of marriage it still filled him with wonder that a woman as handsome and as intelligent as she, should actually consent to become his wife. He was, after all, just the village blacksmith, and if it wasn't for his profitable sideline they would barely make ends meet…

Noblet Swallow was arguably one of the most successful poachers in the county.

Rachael was of course well aware of her husband's illicit nocturnal activities, but she chose to shut it from her mind. The subject was never discussed, never even mentioned in passing, she accepted the food provided for their table as one of the necessities of survival in a harsh and difficult world, but as the teacher of Sorrow's tiny one room school and a respected member of the church committee she could never openly condone such criminal behavior.

They walked arm in arm through the center of the village towards Saint Michael's church, nodding a polite greeting to all that they met, everyone remarking on what a fine couple they made, she in her pretty summer frock and straw bonnet tied with a bright red ribbon, hiding her rich brown hair which was cut short, contrary to fashion, exposing prominent cheek bones, small mouth framed by a mass of freckles and huge blue-grey eyes the color of the sky in winter, which gave her an attractiveness all of her own. He, by comparison, tall, muscular, and as dark-skinned as she was fair, thick black hair protruding from his collar and even growing over the backs of his hands, looking incongruous in his smart black suit and crisp white shirt.

They certainly made an odd pair when he, working at his anvil, stripped to the waist save for a stout leather apron, perspiration running down through the matted hair of his chest, swinging a huge hammer, the light from the furnace reflected on the glistening sweat of his enormous forearms, stopped work to kiss his petite wife goodbye as she set off to the tiny corrugated iron school-house on the other side of the village, her pretty clothes and freckled 'little girl' face in such stark contrast to her husband's rugged, almost brutal countenance, but they loved each other with a passion of such intensity as to at times almost frightened them.

Soon reaching the church, they were quickly engulfed in the familiar gathering of villagers resplendent in their Sunday best, parents calling to the children more interested in chasing each other around the gravestones then joining the adults as they filed slowly in through the high, arched entrance of Saint Michael's, the sudden coolness of the interior a pleasant surprise after the humid heat outside.

Everyone eagerly found their places in the ancient oak pews, the close-grained timber worn to a satin smoothness by the thousands of worshippers that had slid in and out of them over the past hundreds of years. The mumbled greetings and conversations slowly died, the congregation unable to conceal their anticipation of gaining their first glimpse of the new rector. Some had heard that the Reverend Underwood was a decorated war hero, recently returned from fighting the Boers. Others had been told that he had fled Africa in terror. Yet more believed that he was a young man more interested in sport and his own pleasures rather than performing God's work...... Such was the gossip of a small community where a spoken word of opinion or an overheard comment could be repeated as fact to a near neighbor.

The silent congregation were taken completely unawares by the sudden appearance of the Reverend, who had apparently entered quietly through a small door at the back of the church and all but leapt up the four steps into the ornately carved pulpit.

"Welcome, one and all," he called loudly in his clear voice. "I am gratified by this impressive turnout. I trust this is usual and not merely out of curiosity."

It was due in no small measure to his disarming smile that he managed to avoid offending the more diehard parishioners, although it must be said that not all were so easily mollified.

By the time his sermon was over most people present had made up their minds about him. His mischievous smile and sparkling green eyes gave him the look of a naughty schoolboy rather than a man of the cloth; a fact which made the young girls present be immediately smitten by him. The boys take an instant liking to him and many of the older members of the congregation mistrust him as matter of course.

"He's very young." Rachael Swallow whispered to Margaret, seated at the very end of the pew reserved for the household of Sorrow Hall.

"Yes, and very handsome," replied the housemaid coyly.

The villagers were relieved that the new rector's sermon was kept relatively short and to the point. All they really wanted was to get outside the church and discuss this strange new entity that had entered the midst of their close-knit community.

The Reverend James Underwood stood in the shade of the carved portals of the church porch bidding all good day and thanking them for their welcome with a pleasant smile or a firm handshake, fending off countless invitations to tea. He was relieved to see the friendly faces of Gregory and Katerina Christopher heading towards him across the graveled pathway and was more than happy to accept their offer of lunch.

Last to leave were the Baron and Baroness Balmforth and their staff. James had only met them on two previous occasions, once when introduced by their mutual friend Gregory and secondly at an official introduction by the bishop sometime later, and although he found Lady Felicity as disturbingly attractive as any man would, he also sensed a brooding danger in her which he didn't quite understand and decided against all logic to keep her at arm's length.

As the last member of the estate staff stepped from the darkness of the church into the bright sunshine, the Rector could only stand and stare open-mouthed at a beauty that almost took his breath away; she was the answer to every fantasy his mind had ever conjured up as he had lain under canvas on the other side of the world listening to the sounds of distant fighting and wondering if the woman in his dreams could really exist. Here she stood before him, perfect in every detail. As he took her small hand to shake it, the shock of her cool skin gave him a sensation that was to keep him awake deep into the night.

"My name is Margaret. I'm the housekeeper at the Hall," she said, bobbing down politely, extracting her hand with some difficulty from his.

"I liked your sermon very much."

He barely heard a word. He was completely captivated by her voice. He watched her moist lips move as she spoke, they seemed to softly caress every word she uttered, the sound of which was like sweet music ringing in his ears.

God, what on earth is the matter with me? he thought, his mind reeling in a state of confusion.

"Are you feeling all right? You look very pale."

Her words snapped him back to his senses.

"Yes, yes." he stammered, "please do forgive me, it's been a very tiring morning."

He realized with alarm that he was talking too quickly trying to hide his embarrassment. He was starting to panic, searching desperately for something to say.

"Is your husband not with you?" he asked as casually as he could, dreading what her answer may be.

"Oh, I'm not married," she laughed, her blue eyes watching him mockingly. His heart leapt into his throat with relief.

"I hope to see you next Sunday in church, Miss?" He gave her what he hoped was a look of polite interest.

"Please call me Margaret," she replied, "and I'm sure we'll meet before then."

With a sparkle of those china blue eyes, she was gone…He watched her retreating back as she turned the corner by the old yew tree where some of the other Hall staff were waiting for her, his eyes still on the spot even after she had disappeared. His legs felt weak, he had to lean against the fluted stone pillars of the church entrance for fear of stumbling. He was in a daze and for one moment actually feared he might faint.

This is ridiculous he thought to himself. He had seen battle-worn infantrymen in Africa in a similar condition; he shook his head trying to lose the thought of the absurd comparison.

"Is anything wrong old man?" Gregory's voice broke in on James's thoughts.

"Pardon? No, of course not. I'm fine," he replied, his face red with embarrassment.

"You don't have to look so worried," smiled Gregory, putting a hand on the Reverend's shoulder, "You're only human after all, and there's no doubt she's a fine-looking filly. I have a feeling that you're going to find an excuse to visit the Hall in the very near future." He grinned knowingly and with a coarse glint in his eye.

“Don’t be so absurd.” protested James, feeling ridiculous at how easily his thoughts were read. He was almost glad of the distraction when the sound of raised voices brought their attention to a commotion by the churchyard gate.

Noblet Swallow and P.C. Edwin Townsend, the village constable, ran past him towards the barn at the rear of the church where the parish fire pump was housed.

“There’s a fire at the Hall,” shouted the policeman as he rushed past.

From behind the round flint church tower, dense grey smoke could be seen rising slowly into the cloudless midday sky.

Chapter 3

Mrs. Black, as cook of Sorrow Hall, took her duties seriously but felt confident enough in the abilities of the kitchen staff to manage without her for an hour or two. She had a final look around the cavernous, green tiled kitchen full of steam and the smell of cooking. Lizzy, the kitchen maid, was standing in front of the massive black cast iron cooking range built into the wall, stirring the contents of a gleaming copper pan, the mutton was roasting nicely, and young Bridget was busily preparing vegetables, picked fresh that morning from the walled garden and delivered by the basketful by Jock, the gardener.

Satisfied with what she saw, the elderly cook marched quickly along the narrow passageway towards the tradesman's entrance at the rear of the hall. Pausing to grab a worn, brown felt hat, she crammed it down over her coarse grey hair, before viciously stabbing it through with a long hatpin, narrowly missing her scalp. Her reflection in the hall-stand mirror looked back at her grimly; the watery grey eyes under drooping eyelids hidden deep among the myriad wrinkles of her puffy, mottled flesh, a large square mouth housing discolored, uneven teeth framed by thin cracked lips, the color of raw meat. Fleshy jowls met her puckered neck, which protruded, tortoise like, from the loose collar of a thick cotton blouse. Pulling a black crocheted shawl across her heavy breasts, she stamped off through the open door and across the courtyard towards the stable block, scattering gravel with her large feet as she crossed the bridle path and entered through the high arched door of the building, waving her arms above her head to clear a path through the cloud of small flies attracted by the growing heap of soiled straw being forked energetically from the nearest loose box by Lucy.

"Haven't you finished your chores yet?" scolded Mrs. Black. 'You know well enough that I have to be back in the kitchen before his Lordship returns from church.'

Lucy Burdett gave the old woman a look of apology as she leaned the muck-fork against the open half-door; her small bosom heaving gently with the exertion of her labors, beads of perspiration clinging to her finely sculptured face. Her long black hair was pulled severely back and tied with a thin yellow ribbon, she wore a man's work shirt, stuffed into baggy, brown corduroy trousers tied with a stout leather belt, so long it went around her slim waist twice. The loose-fitting male clothing did nothing to conceal the lissome nineteen-year-old body beneath, her small muscles firm and wiry, from her daily work as stable girl and now groom to the Balmforth's; an unheard-of position for a young woman.

The Burdett family had been grooms to the Balmforth estate for three generations and it had always been her father's one regret in life that he and his wife had only been blessed with a daughter. Somehow, he had managed to raise her, even after the death of his wife when Lucy was still a child.

Charlie Burdett had been a good friend of Harry Black the late gamekeeper and had relied heavily on the grudging assistance of Harry's wife the cook.

Living in two small rooms above the stable, Lucy had been brought up among the smell and sounds of horses. Charlie had always said that it had been the proudest day of his life when young Oliver came into his inheritance and boldly announced that Lucy was to be officially made 'stable girl' and would be paid the same wage as her male counterparts, and would one day take over her father's position as groom, upon his retirement or demise.

The act of putting a woman into a man's job raised many eyebrows, word soon got about, actually being reported in the local newspaper in an article written about the recent growth of women's rights and the actions of Mrs. Emiline Pankhurst and her stirring speeches about female emancipation. Sir Oliver even being made a presentation at a large rally held by the Norwich branch of the newly formed 'Women's Social and Political Union.' They had heartily applauded his brave decision and had no idea whatsoever about his ulterior motive of filling his household with desirable young women. It had even been rumored among the Sorrow Hall staff that he would have replaced his butler, Owen, with a woman, if he had dared.

Mrs. Black led the way up the steep, open tread stairway to the small loft area above, her heavy footfalls causing the ancient wood floor to creak alarmingly; so different to the nimble delicacy of the agile girl who followed close behind.

Upon entering the small room, Lucy struck a match, putting it to a battered brass oil lamp, whilst Mrs. Black approached a large oak table completely covered by a thick maroon colored velvet cloth hanging to the floor where it ended in a fringe of dirty gold tassels.

From a range of stone jars set upon the table she selected two and moved across the room to a small copper and pewter brazier, which she proceeded to light.

Hanging the lamp from an overhead beam, Lucy opened a long pine cupboard and removed two loose fitting, brown calico robes which reached down to their feet and were topped with large hoods. The women removed their shoes and donned the garments knotting the thick rope sashes about their waists, Lucy completely swamped by the outfit that had once belonged to the long dead gamekeeper, Harry Black.

Mrs. Black searched among the folds of her shawl, which she hung from a convenient nail and produced a sheet of stiff card, both women looked at it apprehensively. The untidy, spidery handwriting of the cook covered both sides with a multitude of corrections and misspellings.

It had taken Mrs. Black many years to arrive at the present text, a text that had been started by her late husband. Many of the words she didn't truly understand but had been copied from her collection of books and writings, added to, and refined by her limited knowledge of the occult, almost all of which she had learned from the late Harry Black.

Her lips moved as she silently reread the recent additions to the script that she already knew so well. The amateurish phrases, disjointed sentences, and poor grammar of which she had grown so proud filled her with a familiar feeling of power, a power which she felt had increased to new heights now that she had recruited Lucy into her own obscure beliefs that she had kept such a closely guarded secret for most of her adult life.

The small fire now glowed brightly in the brazier, Mrs. Black sprinkled powder from one of the stone jars onto the hot charcoal, filling the air with an acrid, eye watering smell as the mixture of camphor, sulphur, salt, and laurel juice purified the room in preparation of the summoning.

After the atmosphere had cleared, she poured some of the contents of the second jar into the glowing embers, a thick sickly smelling paste made from hemlock, cedar ash, rams semen, calves blood and grave dirt, replacing the stone jar on the table. The strangely attired pair stood facing each other without speaking for several minutes, eyes closed, mentally preparing themselves for their weekly search for the spiritual leader that Mrs. Black believed to be so close and whom she had been trying to locate unsuccessfully for so many years. Now, with the added help of Lucy's occult beliefs she hoped to have the power to enlist the aid of one of the minor gods they both worshipped so ardently.

As if by some predetermined signal, both women opened their eyes at precisely the same moment, lean towards each other and kissed chastely on the mouth. Stepping forward the cook reached up to a threadbare horse blanket that was stretched between two rusty nails in the loft wall. With a flick she let it drop to the floor revealing a richly embroidered tapestry of mystic symbols and pictures woven entirely out of goat's hair and stretched over a grotesque framework of horn, bone and teeth. In the center was a large bordered circle depicting a naked man with long flowing hair and beard, in his right hand was held an open book, in his left a golden scepter, upon his head was a crown of two spiral horns. He stood legs apart upon a yellow sun with a red-eyed face. Beneath the circle were runes of ancient script in a continuous line with no spaces between the words, around the border of the tapestry was a series of framed scenes showing various act of depravity and torture.

For the thousandth time she couldn't help but wonder at its origins. Who had originally made the tapestry? and how many years ago? Mrs. Black could not imagine. Her late husband had once told her that he had obtained it from a fellow believer he had met as a young man, but when she had tried to discuss it further he had refused to talk about it and had ordered her never to again question him on the subject, the look in his eyes sufficient for her to obey the command, but still she suspected that nobody could willingly part with such a powerful talisman, to do so could only involve an act of great treachery or extreme violence.

Returning to Lucy, the two women stood hand in hand in a roughly drawn pentagon chalked onto the straw strewn floorboards.

Looking down at the dog-eared card held in her open palm in the manner of a book of prayer the older woman began to address the hideous image, pleading and chanting,

"O Lucifage, we two Daughters of man search for the magus hidden in our midst. By the power of our beliefs we command you to bring him to us, that he can instruct us in life and that we may willingly and happily succumb to his dominion; we enjoin you to now do our bidding. By the abstruse power of these sacred vestments we have donned the armor of salvation and redemption, thus claiming the strength and vehemence of the most high, Amides, Amicar, Ancor, Anitor and Theodonias, hence our desire be thus accomplished.

O Adonai, through thy mighty dominance to whom we extol and esteem for evermore."

Lucy, eyes closed, moved her lips in time with the older woman's words as Mrs. Black turned the card in her hand, continuing her recitation without hesitation.

"If so ever thou do not obey our words without tarrying we are empowered by the unknown Magus of our quest to commit thee to further torment for one thousand years in the abyss.

"We impel thee therefore to come forth before us in comely human form by the most empowered name of God, Hilay, Hain, Sabaoth, Redusha, Adonay,

Jehovah, Emmanuel, Tetragrammation and Jesus who is Alpa and Omega, the beginning and the end, that thee be rightly established in the eternal flame being powerless to abide in this place henceforth, thus we crave thy doom by the virtue of the said names that Saint Michael drive you to the utmost edge of the eternal inferno of Hell.

"If thee do not appear before us may thee be driven into the lake of flame contrived for the damned and accursed spirits to dwell there until the day of wrath, no longer recalled to affront the face of our Gods whom shall judge the dead of this earth by fire."

As Mrs. Black's voice filled the loft, Lucy, her eyes still closed, listened to the power in her mentor's words, determined to use all her satanic faith to lend the extra strength required for the summoning.

As the medieval sounding phrases droned on, Lucy sensed a sudden drop in the temperature of the stifling room. Within moments the air about her grew perceptively colder, so cold that Mrs. Black's breath turned to vapor as she spoke. Drawing to a conclusion, the cook too became aware of the coldness. The two women looked uneasily at each other, but before either could say a word, there came from within the archaic tapestry a deafening scream of such a high pitch as to force the women to cover their ears with their hands.

As they stared transfixed at the grotesque woven image before them, it appeared to swell and buckle as though being blown from behind by a strong gale. The ear-splitting shriek stopped as suddenly as it had begun, a heartbeat later the tapestry erupted in a sheet of white flame, the grisly framework bursting asunder, the burning fragments flying across the room, igniting the dry straw which lay strewn about the floor. As the small fires sprang up around them, the women came out of their shocked trance, Lucy, running into her tiny living quarters to grab the wash jug of water in a desperate attempt to douse the spreading flames. Mrs. Black tried to smother them with her shawl, which was totally inadequate for the job and soon started to singe and smoulder until it too burst into flames. Both women realized instinctively that the fire was out of control and as one they made a dive for the steep stairs leading to safety. Lucy, the younger and more agile of the two, took the steps three at a time, jumping from half way to land lightly in the soft straw below. Mrs. Black, hampered by her long robe, tripped in her haste and fell heavily on her outstretched arm, the bone snapping like a dry twig with a sickening crack that even Lucy heard from down below. Clumsily, the elderly cook threw herself to one side in an attempt to get her weight off of her shattered arm, too late, she knew she was falling. With a shriek she tumbled headlong down the stairway, her head striking the bottom tread with enormous force. Instantly her left eye and the whole side of her face ballooned hideously, as the soft tissue was torn open like the flesh of a rotten apple.

Lucy, her wits about her, grabbed the semi-conscious woman under the arms and dragged her awkwardly from the burning stables, leaving two lines in the gravel outside, as the skin was torn from elderly cooks heels.

Looking back through the open door, Lucy watched what had once been her home become an inferno as flames engulfed the tinder dry straw, thankful that the stalls were empty. She stood in a daze, still supporting Mrs. Black, oblivious to the heat singeing her face, turning, she saw old Jock the gardener lumbering towards her across the courtyard, a pail of water in each hand.

"I've raised the alarm," he puffed in his thick Arbroath accent, throwing water uselessly into the flames.

Chapter 4

"Not a very auspicious start" declared the new Rector, folding a slice of roast beef onto his fork and coating it with horseradish sauce.

"What on earth do you mean, James?" responded Gregory, "everyone seemed to enjoy your sermon, I know I did."

"Maybe" mused James, "but it certainly looks a bad omen when my first Sunday service ends with a valuable block of stables burning down and the Balmforth's cook almost getting killed in the process. Did you see that poor woman's face? I do hope that she will be all right. I promised the Doctor that I would drop by the Hall later this evening to see if there was anything I could do for her."

Katerina stood up suddenly, startling the two men, her heavy dining chair scraping loudly on the polished wood floor. Her eyes stabbed into the Rector's.

"There's nothing you can do, I assure you, and I suspect your presence would not bring Mrs. Black any comfort whatsoever."

Without another word, she stalked from the room, leaving her plate of food half-finished. Gregory, red faced with embarrassment, apologized to the stunned Rector for his wife's outburst, explaining that she had been working too hard helping to organize the Hunt Ball and what have you, and was probably feeling over-tired. James graciously waved away the obvious excuse in his understanding way, but could not help wondering about Katerina's strange manner and her inexplicable comment about Mrs. Black.

He had first noticed her odd behavior earlier that day, when they had all hurried to the Hall and the burning stables. The whole village seemed to be there, doing their best to douse the flames, Noblet Swallow and constable Townsend, their white shirts filthy, were pumping the parish fire appliance, while Edward, the Balmforth's footman directed the fitful spurts of water into the burning building.

James could vividly recall the ashen look on Katerina's face as she saw, first the stable girl, and then the cook, both clad in those outlandish monastic habits. He could remember her going wordlessly up to Lucy, and gently, almost affectionately, running her hands down the flowing sleeve of the robe, Lucy giving her a curious look before hurrying away.

Katerina had barely spoken a polite word since, responding to their attempts at conversation with monosyllabic indifference… until her little outburst over the dining table.

The Reverend Underwood wasn't the only person wondering about the two women and their strange outfits…

Back at Sorrow Hall, Doctor Ellis sat in the richly furnished splendor of the Baron's library, a large snifter of brandy warming in his hand.

"Have you discovered how the fire started?" he asked Sir Oliver, who was resting comfortably on the edge of a huge walnut desk, his long legs outstretched and crossed at the ankles, his thin pale hands toying with a pair of horn-rimmed spectacles.

"Some absurd story about Lucy dropping the oil lamp in the hay loft and the fire getting out of control," he replied, obviously not believing a word of it.

"What I would like to know," he continued, "is exactly what Mrs. Black was doing there in the first place? She should have been in the kitchen getting our lunch ready, and what on earth were those outlandish costumes they had on. Lucy waffled on about wearing them to keep her clothes clean when she mucked out, but that's absolute piffle and why, in God's name did Mrs. Black have to wear one? I assure you Doctor Ellis, I will get to the bottom of this, one way or another. We can only be thankful that the wind wasn't in the other direction or the whole Hall could have been burnt to the ground." He looked up as the door opened and Felicity entered, nodding a greeting to the Doctor.

"I've just spoken to young Bridget, the kitchen maid," she said, "And it seems that Mrs. Black has been visiting Lucy in the stable every Sunday whilst we are all at Church. Apparently it's been going on for some months… they are both resting at the moment but tomorrow I intend to have a word with the pair of them and I'll find out exactly what they have been getting up to behind our backs."

"Well, given a bit of time Mrs. Black should be fine," declared the Doctor rising from his chair and placing his empty glass onto the silver tray beside him. "It looks a lot worse than it really is, but she's had a very bad fall and her injuries are quite severe. I'm afraid she will be out of action for some weeks."

When it was obvious that he wasn't going to be offered another brandy, he bade the Balmforths good day and departed. Descending the steps of Sorrow Hall he looked across at the still smoking remains of the stable block and couldn't help pondering on the mystery of the two women in the strange clothes and wondering what exactly they were doing on a warm Sunday morning, in a dark and airless hayloft. It was certainly food for thought…

Indeed the whole episode was a subject of some speculation throughout the entire village. Most people coming up with their own theory as to what actually took place on that bright Sunday morning.

That evening 'The Wheatsheaf Tavern' had its busiest Sunday since the celebrations for the relief of Mafeking three years earlier, everybody present wanted to hear if there was any more information about the Balmforth's cook and the stable girl. Every corner of the small bar was full of groups of men animatedly speculating on possible explanations as to what may have transpired that morning. All had something to say on the subject, all that is except one.

He sat alone, at the end of the counter, a pint of local cider untouched in front of him, neither speaking nor being spoken to, by any of the customers. He had always been looked on as 'odd' by the villagers, treated with suspicion and mistrust and on the rare occasions that he visited the local tavern, nobody had much interest in engaging him in conversation.

He was known simply as 'Michael,' or sometimes 'Mike,' apparently named after the parish Church of Saint Michael's. He was aged about twenty-five, but looked younger. He lived in a small, tumbledown cottage in the center of Yarrow Woods, reached only by a muddy, overgrown track. He had been raised by old Mrs. Heathcoat, the local nurse and midwife, nobody even suspecting his existence until, at the age of nine, she had tried unsuccessfully to get him accepted into the village school.

Many thought at first, he was the illegitimate result of some past indiscretion on the midwives part and that she had kept him a secret to protect her reputation, but this idea was soon dismissed as people realized that an unwanted pregnancy could never be kept hidden in a community the size of Sorrow.

Upon seeing the boy for the first time, people understood why he had been kept concealed for so long. His right arm was shriveled and infantile, permanently curved back against the joint, the hand skeletal, with fingers held like the talons of some emaciated bird of prey. He had very small teeth, showing large areas of pink gums, his mouth hung open constantly, often dribbling saliva down his chin. He walked with a stiff, loping gait caused by his curved, almost hunched back, making him seem shorter than he really was. Hanging across his face was a curtain of filthy grayish hair, which he constantly pushed out of his eyes; long straight hair, which on the rare occasion it was washed, shone the purest White.

Mrs. Heathcoat had finally decided to educate the boy herself, moving them both into the tiny cottage hidden in the woods, far from the prying eyes and wagging tongues of the villagers. She announced publicly that she was going into semi-retirement declaring that her remaining days were to be devoted to the upbringing of her strange adopted child.

Over the next few years people almost forgot about Michael and his odd appearance, only rarely catching glimpses of him in the remotest part of Yarrow Woods, or skulking about after dark around the village and the surrounding fields.

And so life went on, no one giving a thought to Michael, some even questioning his existence, his name forgotten by most, but recalled suddenly on the night of Mrs. Heathcoat's 'accident' some years previously.

Police constable Edwin Townsend had stepped out of the side door of the Wheatsheaf Tavern where he had enjoyed perhaps a little too much ale with his best friend and archenemy, Noblet Swallow, the most consistent law breaker on his beat. Lifting his huge frame onto his bicycle, he was approached from out of the shadows by young Michael, who hesitantly asked if he might have a word.

Dismounting, the constable leaned his cycle back against the pub wall and looked the strange boy up and down, wondering, not for the first time, what the real story was behind the birth of this misshapen oddity standing before him.

"Well, what seems to be the trouble son?" he asked, his deep stentorian voice shattering the evening silence.

"I…I can't find my…mother… Mrs. Heathcoat," replied the nervous young man in his quiet, stuttering voice. "She's been missing since yesterday evening, I've looked all over but there's no sign of her anywhere."

P.C. Townsend, never one to shirk his duties flipped open his pocket book and quickly jotted down the meager details supplied by the hesitant Michael, then proceeded to organize an immediate search enlisting the help of most of the men still drinking in the Wheatsheaf, much to the annoyance of Tom Baldwin, the business-minded landlord.

Old Mrs. Heathcoat was found early the next morning in a crumpled heap at the bottom of the disused well behind the church, her neck broken, presumably by the fall. Michael had stood by and watched unemotionally as the frail body of his surrogate mother was dragged from the dark recesses of the moss-encrusted chasm. A stout rope tied unceremoniously about her chest, cutting grotesquely into her flesh and causing her soiled clothes to ruck up under her splayed arms, her head hanging at an impossible angle, eyes still open gazing unseeing through an opaque cataract-like film.

The constable had asked Michael some cursory questions, namely what reason Mrs. Heathcoat could possibly have had for visiting a well that was known to have dried up long ago, but the boy's answers revealed nothing. After some days of investigation by the ill-equipped policeman, the whole episode was slowly forgotten. There was no apparent evidence of foul play and nobody wanted a fuss, least of all P.C. Townsend who, after all, was only the village 'bobby'. He just wanted a quiet life and could well do without the thought of foul play in his easygoing existence.

From that time on, Michael started to be seen much more frequently about the village, occasionally drinking in the tavern or browsing around the stalls on market days. People often wondered where he obtained any money from, as he was never known to do any work and it was unlikely that the retired midwife would have left him much of an inheritance.

It was often commented on that the one place where he was never seen was the church that was assumed to be his namesake. This was often put down to the fact that it was in the church grounds where the one person that had ever loved him had met her untimely end.

Chapter 5

Felicity had barely finished her breakfast when Owen announced that Mrs. Christopher had called and was waiting for her in the withdrawing room. The Baron looked up at his wife suspiciously over the top of his newspaper.

"Don't forget that you are to have a word with Lucy and Mrs. Black today, will you dear?"

He received no reply as Felicity hurried from the room, obviously intrigued to learn what had brought Katerina out to see her so early in the day. The two friends kissed cheeks, after the French fashion, and linking arms, strolled by some unspoken agreement through the open French windows and out onto the paved terrace.

"I'm sorry to disturb you at breakfast Felicity, but there is something so very important that I have to talk to you about." Katerina spoke quickly, a note of suppressed excitement in her voice. "I presume you are going to question Mrs. Black and young Lucy about yesterday's fire?"

Felicity nodded, her forehead wrinkled with a frown of interest, but she said nothing.

"I wanted to speak to you first, that's why I called so early," continued Katerina. They wandered across the dew-covered grass, leaving two sets of pale footprints on the immaculately manicured lawn with its miniature box hedges and ornamental herb garden. The pungent smell of the herbs mixing with the scent of roses filled the morning air with a heavy fragrance that almost, but not quite, shut out the acid tang of smoke and burnt wood that reached out from the ruined stables.

They sat together on the carved wooden seat next to the summerhouse, the climbing sun already making the damp bench warm to the touch. In the short time Felicity and Katerina had known each other they had become increasingly close, perhaps disturbingly so; they often sat together on this seat in the shade of the old timber and glass summer-house, far enough into the garden to speak without being overheard by Oliver or one of the servants. Somehow, the seat was like an old friend, sharing in their confidences, knowing of their plans. Felicity had purposely steered her friend towards it, knowing instinctively that whatever it was that was bothering Katerina would be easier for her to explain seated together in this place that had become, in some strange way special to them both.

Taking Felicity's hand in both her own, Katerina looked deeply, searchingly, into her friend's eyes, her voice heavy with emotion as she spoke.

"The things that we have discussed. The things I have been trying to instruct you in, the powers of the universe, the wonders of Prospopine, of Pluto, you say you believe, you say that you trust me to lead you to our Savior, but do you? Do you really? Do you truly believe in what we are attempting? In his ability to make our lives whole, to bring us the fulfillment that is our right? Or is it all just a game to you, just a bit of fun to take some of the boredom out of your life?"

She looked pleadingly at the frowning face before her, the worried expression causing wrinkles to form in the corners of Felicity's eyes, making her seem older.

Katerina gripped her friend's hands even tighter, lowering her eyes she continued "Please, think carefully and answer me truthfully. This is more important than you can possibly know."

Felicity cast her eyes down into her lap, her hands still linked with Katerina's. She thought of the things they had discussed, here in this very spot… the secrets they had shared. She recalled clearly Katerina first broaching the subject of religion, of God, as she knew him perhaps not being the one and only supreme power. Of the possibility of the existence of other, more potent forces, far older, far stronger, wielding powers untold, powers that the Church, in its wisdom dismissed through ignorance and fear. She had listened. Her life was boring. The things that she was hearing sounded exciting, they sounded different. The things they had done together, the time they had taken their clothes off and lain naked on the wet grass in Yarrow Woods, caressing each other and themselves in a form of prayer to some obscure 'God' with an outlandish name, and the time that they had stolen a new born lamb from Tom Morton's barn. Felicity had watched fascinated as Katerina had killed it, smearing the warm blood up their arms and over each other's faces. She could still taste the sickly-sweet stickiness of the blood on her lips, and the power that seemed to flow through her body as she swallowed the thick, red, life-giving fluid, full of the adrenalin released in a surge by the terrified animal at the moment of its violent death at the hands of the wild-eyed Katerina. Once again she could feel the tiny heart in her hand, the muscles still twitching a faint, irregular pulse. True, it had all started as a way to break out of the rut that she found herself in, but as the time went by, she found she was turning more and more to these strange Gods when she was alone, closing her mind to everything except the unspoken words to the Lord Pluto, to Prospopine, finding unexpected comfort in their medieval sounding names. Gradually, but surely, she began to grasp the power that could be achieved from them. She slowly began to accept that her future may lay in serving these Gods and in turn having them serve her, that she could never be truly whole without their help. Felicity finally looked up at Katerina's worried face, and spoke with a voice full of strength and assurance.

"I honestly and truly believe that what we are doing is our only way of becoming real people in our own right, instead of just chattels owned by wealthy men. I believe that the power around us is there for us to take and use to our own advantage. The Lord Pluto is the only true master and through him, and Prospopine, we, and others like us, can become complete, and to wield power over others to dominate and not be dominated."

After her short speech, she felt strangely weak, her hands shook. She watched as Katerina's face broke into a relived smile, eyes filling with moisture as a heavy tear rolled down her cheek. Felicity, reaching out, gently put a fingertip to it, and placed the wet finger on her tongue, tasting the salty warmth of the teardrop.

"Now," she asked, "what has all this got to do with yesterday's fire?"

Katerina stood and paced uncertainly to and fro, looking first at Felicity, and then down at her hands, which she wrung together anxiously.

"Yesterday, in church, just before the end of the sermon," she hesitated, unsure of herself, her eyes still flicking from her hands to her friends face and back again, "I felt something… something deep inside of me." She struck her chest with the flat of her palm, "He was close… the one that we have been searching for all this time… he was close to me, he was so near. I always felt that there was some connection between Him and that church, and now I am certain of it. My mind was reaching out to him. It almost felt that I could stretch out my hand and touch him. He was so close to me… so close." Her voice fell to a whisper as she repeated the words.

Sitting once more beside her friend, she looked intently into Felicity's eyes, her voice could not control a note of excitement as she continued . . .

"Then it happened. I felt another presence. There was somebody else, a second person interrupting my thoughts, another believer close at hand, reaching out to the Magus, the High Priest, and our spiritual leader. He was out there somewhere close and I wasn't the only one trying to communicate with him. I'm convinced without any doubt whatsoever that right here in Sorrow there is another with the same purpose as ourselves."

Felicity gaped with astonishment at Katerina's revelations. It had never occurred to her for a single moment that others shared their beliefs, least of all somebody so close to home.

Katerina continued, her eyes wide with the recollection. "I sensed a massive disturbance, almost as though a part of my brain had burst into flames. I could physically feel the heat burning inside my head."

She stared directly at Felicity.

"Don't you see? That must have been the precise moment that your stables caught fire?" Felicity's mouth dropped open in amazement. She stared incredulously at Katerina, a surge of understanding seemed to flow through her. "Of course, it all makes sense… those strange clothes that Lucy and Mrs. Black were wearing. Katerina, you're right, you are absolutely right, it makes complete sense."

Katerina nodded her head excitedly, but said nothing as Felicity stood and began pacing in small circles, her forehead lined with concentration as she spoke.

"I found out yesterday that Mrs. Black has been going to see Lucy every Sunday whilst we are all at church. Now it's all beginning to make sense, the strange outfits, the fire, everything."

She stopped walking and faced her friend. "What are we going to do?" she asked.

Katerina took her hands once more – they trembled slightly. "Don't you understand what I've told you Felicity? This is just what we need… we know that we haven't the power to reach him, not just the two of us. Obviously they must be in the same situation." Her face broke into a beaming smile.

Felicity, a look of comprehension in her eyes, picked up the conversation where Katerina had left it, "But the four of us together…"

Chapter 6

Mrs. Black finished her thick chicken broth, the shiny globules of fat clinging to the sides of the white china bowl reflecting a rainbow of light from the small mullioned window near her bed. Her head ached mightily and the left side of her face throbbed with a continuous stab of pain. Doctor Ellis had strapped her shattered arm onto a pine splint, and swathed her left eye and jaw in cotton wool and bandages, the smell of iodine flooding her sinuses and mixing unpleasantly with the taste of the hot soup. He had told her that she was to stay in bed and rest and that she had been very lucky indeed not to have lost the sight of one eye.

She didn't feel very *lucky.*

Wiping her grease smeared lips on her pillowslip she slid the empty soup bowl onto the bedside table, '*get some rest*' she had been instructed, 'how can I rest?' she thought, picking a morsel of meat from between her teeth. 'I must find out who it was who broke into my thoughts, who it was that was so close, somebody's intrusion had the strength to destroy the summoning spell, I have to speak to Lucy and tell her to start searching immediately.'

Her thoughts were interrupted by a gently knocking on her bedroom door, "Lucy… at last. Come in," she snapped irritably, wincing at the sudden stab of pain in her swollen jaw as she spoke. Lady Felicity entered and quietly closed the door behind her, a look of alarm showed on what could be seen of the cooks bandaged face.

Mrs. Black realized with a jolt of fear the position she now found herself in. Having been so preoccupied with her thoughts of the previous day's events, she had given no consideration whatsoever as to what the household would say about the circumstances of the fire, she had no excuse prepared, no believable explanation and even if she had, there was no way of knowing if it would tally with Lucy's account.

Felicity sat on the foot of the bed, a sympathetic half-smile on her face, "Good morning Mrs. Black, I do hope you are feeling better, you gave us all quite a scare but Doctor Ellis tells me you'll soon be on the mend and that all you need is a complete rest, so I don't want you to worry about anything except getting well again."

The confused cook, taken aback by her Mistress's unexpected kindness answered hesitantly, 'I'm sure I will be fully recovered very soon, your Ladyship and I'm dreadfully sorry for any inconvenience caused by my…" she paused, unsure of herself, "caused by our accident." Her mind was racing, trying desperately to think of some plausible explanation for the fire and for her strange robe which now lay, begging an explanation, over the back of a wooden chair in the corner of the sparsely furnished room.

Felicity, deciding to come straight to the point, silenced Mrs. Black with a knowing look, her voice became stern, almost brusque. "I'm sure we will have plenty of opportunity to discuss things when you are feeling better, but I think you should know that I am fully aware of what Lucy and yourself were trying to do… I too have been reaching out to him, it seems we have both been searching for the one thing." The astonished cook suddenly broke into a violent coughing fit, the pain throbbing at her temples increasing with every wracking cough. This can't be true, she thought through the pain, how could her Ladyship share her beliefs? Felicity leaned across and patted the still coughing woman tenderly on the back and fluffed up the massive feather pillow in a gesture of matronly concern. "Are you all right Mrs. Black? Can I fetch you anything, a drink of water perhaps?"

"No… no, I'm fine now, thank you m'Lady," the elderly woman's voice came through thick and distorted by her injuries and the constricting bandages. She continued, her eyes averted from those of the Baroness,

"It's just that you've given me quite a shock to say the least. I would never have dreamed that… "

Felicity gave her a smile of encouragement "Please continue, you can speak quite freely."

After a long pause the cook cleared her throat and turned to face Felicity. "I could feel you, I could feel your presence, your thoughts, I would never have imagined, not in my wildest dreams that you… that it would turn out to be yourself… oh! m'Lady." Her rheumy eyes filled with tears as Felicity put a comforting arm around her shoulders.

"Actually it was not I that you sensed," she replied. "There are two of us, as there are two of you, perhaps with each other's help the four of us together will be capable of achieving what two alone could not."

Mrs. Black, wiping her nose on the cuff of her nightgown looked at her mistress joyously but was still too taken aback by the revelations to think of anything to say. Felicity carried on, pleased with the reaction that her news had brought. "Doctor Ellis will be paying you a visit later today to see how you are getting along so I want you to get some rest, I'm off now to speak to Lucy, I will send her to you after we have spoken and you can discuss with her all that you have been told." With a final pat on the hand, Lady Felicity rose and left the bewildered cook alone with her thoughts.

Mrs. Black stared at the closed door long after her Mistress had left, pondering on this unexpected ally.

Outside the door Katerina had stood waiting, the two friends nodded to each other and arm-in-arm headed along the narrow corridor to where Lucy was now sharing a room with Bridget and Lizzy, the two kitchen maids.

Chapter 7

The female wood pigeon flew low over the straggly quickthorn hedge that ran the length of the small field of barley to the west of Sorrow Hall, the stolen corn of her last meal resting comfortably in her full crop. Too late, out of the corner of her eye she caught sight of the alien color against the greens and browns of the countryside, instinctively veering off to one side as she registered the sudden movement from among the foliage. She heard the deadly explosion… flying in terror, desperately trying to win the race for survival. She felt the red-hot stabs of agony as the lead shot drove into her body, snuffing out her life as surely as one extinguishes a candle. The dead bird plummeted earthwards, crashing into the barley in a flurry of feathers torn loose by the power of the blast.

Sir Oliver Balmforth strode purposefully to the corpse of the pigeon and picking it up, looked at it appraisingly before stuffing it into his leather shoulder bag.

Reloading the Holland and Holland twelve bore he stalked off along the perimeter of the field, the shotgun broken over his right forearm. The last thing he needed was yet another pigeon, the game larder of Sorrow Hall was already full to overflowing but to be out early on a bright, cloudless morning, pitting his wits against nature, his stealth against the instinctive caution of his quarry was his only way of truly relaxing. It enabled him to think, to take stock of his life, to try and work through his anxieties.

He had set off that morning, not to bag game but to give himself a chance to ponder on what was going on around him. Felicity's behavior of late had begun to hedge in the direction of Katerina Christopher's, or was it just his imagination, brought about by their new found friendship, of which he did not approve one bit.

And the strange incident of Mrs. Black and Lucy, with their outlandish costumes and the unexplained fire in the stables? Yesterday, Felicity had supposedly questioned the two of them about it, but when he had asked her what they had to say for themselves she had fobbed him off with some waffle about letting her handle the situation and for him not to get involved.

Suddenly, from almost under his feet, a hare broke cover, zigzagging from left to right as it sped through the hedge and across the neighboring field. Oliver watched the escaping meal without interest, not even bothering to cock his gun.

Reaching the five-bar gate at the corner of the barley field, he swung his gangly body over the top rail, his large feet landing heavily in the soft earth, his free hand holding his horn-rimmed spectacles in place to prevent them from sliding down his prominent nose and falling to the ground as they had done on countless previous occasions.

Last night things certainly seemed to be changing with Felicity's attitude towards him. Retiring early, he had laid out her things. Her outfit that he had sheepishly presented her with on their wedding night. The straw boater with the blue band, short grey pleated skirt and white cotton blouse, and the thick woolen black stockings. They lay on the huge feather bed ready to greet her when she entered the room.

He lay naked beneath the over-starched sheets, his erection aching in expectation as he studied the small pile of schoolgirls clothing, his hand absentmindedly fondling the smooth contours of the bamboo cane lying concealed under the covers beside his thin, pale body. Eyes staring straight up at the ornate plasterwork of the ceiling, he pondered on his wife's unusual behavior of late. She had seemed preoccupied all day long, ever since Katerina's early morning visit.

"I'll give her something to think about when she comes up to bed," he whispered lewdly to himself. Too often lately she had slept alone in her own adjoining bedroom, tonight would be different, he had been more than patient with her but enough was enough, was she his wife or not?

He lay listening for her approach in frustrated anger for another thirty-five minutes before she finally entered the room. The Barons flagging erection returning to life the moment he saw her. Closing the door behind her she saw the familiar clothing lying at the foot of the bed and recognized the expectant glint in her husband's eyes.

With a sigh of resignation she began to undress… slowly, acutely aware of his eyes upon her, watching every movement she made, caressing himself below the sheets with one hand whilst fondling the cane with his other. Felicity was aware that once again she was going to be expected to debase herself to satisfy the perversions of her prurient husband. To have to act out the ridiculous role that he demanded… that he had to have to achieve his orgasm.

Throwing her discarded clothing into a corner she looked with revulsion at the man she had married. Without his spectacles he would screw his weak eyes up unattractively, the action causing wrinkles and frown lines. She had always hated that look, it reminded her of his horrid father. She recalled some of the more unsavory stories she had heard about the late Baron and feared that Oliver may be heading the same way. She squirmed under Oliver's gaze as he openly studied her nakedness, in the back of her mind she could hear Katerina's voice telling her that she was strong, stronger than her husband, while he was weak, weak as all men were. The whispering in her subconscious grew louder. The words were no longer Katerina's but her own, the time was coming when she herself would wield the cane and he will lay prostrate across the bed whimpering, pleading for the beating to stop. The time was coming when she would throw away that ludicrous school uniform and refuse to act out his warped fantasies.

"Hurry darling, I don't think I can wait much longer," breathed Oliver, a note of urgency in his voice. Felicity looked down at him with open disgust. Snatching a green velvet dressing gown from the back of a chair she wrapped it tightly about her shoulders. From the top of a chest of drawers she lifted a folded flannelette nightgown. Turning to her husband she informed him that she intended to sleep once more in the adjoining bedroom. She spat the words at him with distaste, adding that the door would be locked, as she closed it loudly.

Oliver looked stupidly at the heavily paneled door. The loud tick of the clock seemed to fill the room. The hollow ache was still there in the pit of his stomach. The urgent desire could not be put off. Grabbing the coarse black stockings from the pile of clothes he thrust them between his legs, bringing himself to an immediate but unfulfilling climax.

"Who needs her?" he said quietly to himself, throwing the soiled stockings across the room. "I do," he answered himself, "I do."

Chapter 8

The young rabbit lay exhausted among the lush grass. The white roots of torn vegetation standing out starkly against the rich, black earth, scratched bare by the frantic struggling of the dying creature helplessly caught in the cruel snare made from fine brass wire, which had cut so deeply into its neck as to completely disappear into the denseness of its thick coat. The paler fur of its chest, now dark and matted with congealed blood from a vicious gash in its throat caused by the bare end of the wire left protruding during the making of the crudely fashioned snare.

The rabbit, its face against the dry soil, felt the vibrations of approaching footsteps. The sound of a human, the instinctive alarm signal going unheeded by the half-conscious animal. It had nothing left. It's will for survival being choked off, as surely as the breath was being choked from his tortured body. The tongue turning mauve and hanging grotesquely from its mouth, partially bitten through by the rabbit's sharp incisors in its futile struggle for release from this terror that was holding him, slowly bringing an end to his short life. Mist shrouded eyes focused on the man leaning towards him, the restraint was lifted from its neck. The stick went back, raised high into the air and then back down. The blow mercifully bringing an end to the torment that he had been suffering since dawn when the rabbit had hopped through the space in the long grass. A path it had taken so many times before.

Michael tucked the rabbit into a shabby hessian sack slung carelessly over his shoulder. Returning to his tiny cottage, he emptied the contents of the bag onto the long pine table dominating the filth encrusted kitchen. The elm beams of the low ceiling black and greasy from the years of cooking. The ancient cast iron range built into the fireplace was soot blackened and rusty with neglect.

Three small rabbits and a good haul of wild mushrooms "Enough for a good stew," he said out loud, stepping through the door into the garden. He eyed the vegetable plot with disappointment. Straggly lines of wilting green leaves sprang half-heartedly from the dry soil. Stooping, he pulled a handful of half-grown carrots from among the scant selection of vegetables he had attempted to grow. He looked at the small, misshapen roots with frustration. "Fuck!" He exclaimed loudly. How his mother had managed to produce such fine vegetables and herbs for so many years he just could not imagine, he was starting to regret not paying more attention to her when she had tried to teach him the secrets of gardening. But, he thought on reflection, it was to be her love for the garden that was to bring about her untimely death. If only she had not tried to enlarge the area of the vegetable plot, if she had not begun digging among the weeds and nettles at the edge of the track she would never had found the grave and he would never of had to shut her up. At the memory of her and the events of that fateful day he felt a twinge of regret, even remorse at what happened but somehow he knew, deep inside that what he did had been necessary.

She had tearfully confronted him with her discovery before storming off in the direction of the village, threatening to inform the constable. Whether it was an idle threat he never found out. Unsure of what he should do, he followed her at a distance as she headed along the track and across the common, finally catching up with her as she cut through the church grounds of Saint Michael's.

He often played back in his mind the ensuing argument and his loss of control. But even then he felt he had some destiny, some task that he alone was fated to perform and perhaps the death of his adopted mother was part of a task appointed him, a compulsion he could not understand. Something was driving him… to do what? He didn't yet know, he only knew that for good or evil nothing nor nobody would be permitted to stand in his way, nothing was going to prevent him doing what he had to do. If only he knew what it was…

That night he lay in his bed staring up at the cracked and flaking ceiling, the sepia patches of dampness reminding him of some ancient map. He imagined himself exploring the coasts and inlets of this mythical land, searching… searching for what?

The rain outside beat a steady rhythm against the small window next to his bed, the draught from the ill-fitting casement causing the scrap of soiled curtain to sway eerily in the shadows and the cold night air to wash over his face.

As was usual of late he searched fruitlessly for sleep, recently it seemed, no matter how tired, he would lay awake for much of the night, often not until the first light of dawn reddened the sky and the morning call of song birds broke the silence did he finally drift into a fitful sleep only to wake shortly after, sweating and frightened, as though being woken suddenly from a nightmare… a nightmare of which he had no recollection.

He lay on his back, eyes open, pondering the cause of his insomnia . . .

It had started on the day that he had heard the scream. For the hundredth time his mind had searched hopelessly for an answer to the mystery of that scream. *The scream…* The scream that had made his body tremble as if in the grip of a seizure. The scream that had burned itself into his sub-conscious, into his very soul, like a maggot eating into a pear.

He would never forget that day, two months ago. It was a warm Sunday morning, the air was alive with the small flying insects that seemed to appear from nowhere as the heat of the day grows, Dandelion seeds floated, fairylike on the slight breeze, the drone of bees was everywhere, from the surrounding woodland came the different songs of cock birds, chests puffed out competing with each other in their ritual search for a mate.

It was the sort of day to bring joy to the heart of most people, but Michael failed to appreciate the splendor of his surroundings. After being buried for so long in the confines of Yarrow woods it had long since ceased to hold any fascination with him. Since first light he had been plagued with the familiar feeling of being watched, being spied upon, a feeling he had experienced repeatedly over the last several weeks or even months? An inexplicable desire to meet someone, someone important, someone he didn't yet know.

That day the sensation was stronger than at any time before. He paced heavily along the overgrown beaten-earth path, to and fro from the forest edge, across the garden to his cottage door, now standing wedged open to allow the summer breeze to enter and cleanse the interior of the ramshackle hovel.

In the distance he could hear the sound of the bells of Saint Michael's ringing forlornly, summoning the villagers of Sorrow to church. The sound had always given him an uneasy feeling in the pit of his stomach, even as a child. As he had gown older the dislike for those bells and what they represented had become an obsessive hatred, a hatred that at times could send him into an uncontrollable rage in which he was capable of almost anything. Few people had witnessed these rages and those that had, were no longer living.

Today the steady, repetitive peal of the bells seemed to him no more than a mild irritation. He felt sure in his own mind that he would one day silence those accursed bells for good, and somehow, he had the strangest feeling that the time would soon be at hand.

Sitting hunched on the threshold of the cottage door, his shoulder leaning against the rotted wood of the loose door jamb, he picked his teeth with a filthy fingernail of his deformed hand, his long white mane hanging over his face, eyes staring unseeing through the curtain of fine hair. His thoughts were elsewhere, paying no heed to the hordes of flies alighting and crawling on his freckled face and arms. The sun, riding high in the sky, sent stabbing rays of light through his swaying fringe of hair that would make anyone else screw up their eyes with pain but it caused barely a twitch from this strange young man.

He could feel the pressure growing inside him, like water coming slowly to the boil. Unable to stand it any longer he leapt to his feet.

"Who's out there?" he screamed at the top of his voice, "who are you? What do you want of me?" His vision clouded over as his eyes filled with tears, he stumbled drunkenly into the garden, dropping to his knees in the dirt, hands clutching fistfuls of dust dry earth. He pressed his forehead to the ground.

"Tell me where you are," he moaned into the dirt, the soil sticking to his face and lips.

Slowly raising his head he looked around himself, becoming aware of a strange intense silence, a silence so total, so complete as to make him fear that he had lost all sense of hearing. There was no bird song, no insects, nothing. He looked about, eyes wide with fearful anticipation, his tear stained face streaked black with grime and perspiration.

As though from some immense distance, he heard a faint but piercing scream. It seemed to grow, to come closer, the high-pitched screech turning to a blood curdling shriek of pure horror, louder and louder until the very air seemed to throb with the intensity of the sound, the world was now full of nothing but this cry from the very hubs of hell.

Feeling like his head would burst with the pressure of the noise he rolled in the dirt, hands clasped over his ears, head buried between his knees, his mouth suddenly filling with the metallic taste of blood as he realized that in his terror he had impossibly bitten through his bottom lip, the loose piece of flesh hanging like some uneaten morsel of meat in his mouth.

As suddenly as it had started the scream grew fainter and seemed to recede quickly back whence it came, in a matter of moments all was once again silent, save for the humming of insects and the twitter of birds.

Michael remained huddled in the same fetal position for some time, slowly trying to regain control of his senses. Pale and shaken he staggered upright and dragging his feet in the dirt, he stumbled towards the sanctuary of the open cottage door, his mind thinking of nothing other than to shut out the horror he had experienced. Reaching the threshold he turned and looked into the direction he fancied the sound had come from. Above the trees he could see a pale cloud of smoke hanging over the distant outline of Sorrow Hall.

"Do you think that we will find him? After all this time, do you really think that today could be the day?" Felicity asked conversationally as she sat beside Katerina in her familiar spot, on the remains of a long-felled beech that lie beside the main bridle path running through Yarrow woods.

"I honestly don't know," admitted Katerina, "but I have the strangest feeling deep inside me," she stuck her breast with the inside of a clenched fist to emphasize her words. "Somehow I know that these woods hold the secret, even Mrs. Black and Lucy had come to the same conclusion, let's hope that today we may at last get some answers."

Seemingly at the mention of their names the other two women appeared from behind the trees, having taken the short cut from the Hall by following the brook and crossing the village common. Mrs. Black panted loudly, red faced with the unaccustomed exertion of walking so far. Lucy, however, looked as fresh as a spring flower as she strode lightly up to Felicity and Katerina, greeting them with a respectful nod of the head and a "m'Lady" and "Good morning Mrs. Christopher."

Felicity, never at her best when faced with another attractive woman, snapped accusingly at them, "Your late!"

"I'm afraid I'm not as fit as I once was m'Lady" answered the still puffing cook, nervously touching the partially healed scars on the side of her face, which for the rest of her days would give her a permanent grimace caused by the corner of her mouth being pulled up to meet the turned down flesh of her left eye where the scar tissue had puckered up the loose skin.

"Never mind, we are all here now." broke in Katerina, in an attempt to diffuse the nervous tension that seemed to envelop them all. "Do you still think we are on the right track?" she asked Mrs. Black, who responded with a slow nod but said nothing.

Over the last two months the four women had met often, repeatedly going over their accumulated knowledge and were utterly astounded by the similarity of the conclusions that the two pairs had independently reached. They had decided to jointly focus the total of the combined power of their beliefs on various sections of the district of Sorrow and its surrounding areas. Through a process of elimination they had finally agreed that they were being drawn towards the region of Yarrow woods.

They walked slowly along the bridle path, barely saying a word, each preoccupied with their own thoughts, none really sure what to expect, the alarm call of Jay and Magpie sounding loudly in the still of the woodland.

The going was slow and arduous, despite the warm weather, a brief but torrential shower the previous night had turned the heavy clay of the track into thick clinging mud full of water filled hoof prints, many of which had been caused by Felicity's and Katerina's very own mounts, this being a regular path for them when out riding. Indeed, even Lucy knew the path well from exercising both Lady Felicity and the Baron's horses. Mrs. Black, on the other hand, had rarely ventured into the woods and continuously looked about her nervously, her senses pricked for anything out of the ordinary.

After some time the bridle path was joined by an overgrown dirt track cutting off at a tangent of about eighty degrees and disappearing into the ferns and undergrowth of the woodland. Over the years people had walked or ridden past the unused pathway so often that now it was barely noticed by anyone, few people even considering that it may actually lead anywhere… It was only used very rarely… By one particular person.

As the women came to the junction, inexplicably, Mrs. Black fell sprawling in the mud, the pain in her still weak wrist shooting agonizingly up her arm. Her companions rushing to pull her clumsily to her feet, thinking that she had stumbled on the loose clods of earth. She shook them away impatiently, and with eyes staring wildly, she slowly turned her head to look along the tiny overgrown path plunging into the depths of the woods.

Katerina felt the pull immediately, Lucy let out a quiet gasp and looked at Felicity, who too, felt a clutching at the heart, like the cold hand of death reaching inside her body. Inexplicably a feeling of dread welled up inside her, the air about her seemed to lose its warmth, the sounds of the woodland receding until all she was aware of was the thud of her own heart, a dull throb in her ears. She gave an involuntary start as the warning chatter of a cock pheasant came from close by. Glancing at her three friends she saw that they were all grinning foolishly. Why did they look so pleased, yet she felt so afraid?

Katerina, noticing the paleness of her friend, looked deeply into Felicity's eyes. "Are you feeling unwell… is there anything wrong?"

"No! No, of course there's nothing wrong," she replied, a little too quickly, "you just caught me a bit unawares."

"You mean you didn't feel anything?" asked the cook, a note of accusation in her voice.

Feeling the color rush to her cheeks, Felicity gave the cook a withering look. "I'll thank you not to take that tone with me Mrs. Black, I fear you may be forgetting your place… come, we need to be getting on."

Mrs. Black and Lucy glanced furtively at each other as Katerina stepped into the lead and strode purposefully along the barely discernible path, followed by her companions. The hesitant Baroness dragging to the rear, her mind in a turmoil of uncertainty.

Michael sat in his usual spot, on the threshold of the cottage door, trying unsuccessfully not to look in the direction of the clearing of the footpath. Since first light he had been outside, pacing the damp grass, keeping his eyes averted from the small space between the trees that lead to the outside world, the world that he was sure would one day provide the answers to the questions eating away at his brain. Somehow he knew, with no doubt in his mind whatsoever that in the next few hours someone or something was going to use the tiny pathway leading to his door. As much as he tried to ignore the path his eyes and thoughts were repeatedly drawn inexorably to the same spot, ears straining for any alien sound of footstep or voice.

"Not much further now," Katerina looked back over her shoulder excitedly, "Felicity, do keep up."

Mrs. Black and Lucy glanced at each other as they ducked under an overhanging branch, both turning furtively to watch the hesitant movements of the young Baroness as she slowly caught up with them,

"Is everything alright m'Lady? You seem rather uneasy," ventured Lucy. Felicity ignored the question and strode past to catch up with Katerina, now disappearing into the greenery ahead.

Waiting until their mistress was out of earshot, Mrs. Black turned to Lucy. "I think we're going to have to be a bit careful with her Ladyship." She used the term like an insult, "She claims to be a true believer but take it from me, it's all one big act, I've suspected it for some time. I've no idea what she thinks she's playing at, I doubt she knows herself, but mark my words, sooner or later she's going to make a mistake and show her true colors, mark my words," she repeated once more.

Lucy nodded in agreement, "I think you may be right, I wonder if Mrs. Christopher suspects anything?"

They quickened their pace, eager to catch up with Felicity and Katerina who were now completely out of view among the dense growth of the woodland.

He looked up with alarm. Yes, there it was again, somebody was walking along the footpath. The sound of a dry twig breaking underfoot echoed distinctly from among the trees, the alarm call of a blackbird confirming his conclusion. Who was it? A poacher? Children from the village? What were they doing coming here?

Leaping to his feet he stared wide-eyed at the exit from the path, a thin strand of saliva hanging like a silver thread from his lower lip as his mouth opened and closed wordlessly. The varied expressions of fear, pleasure and curiosity vying with each other for prominence on his face.

Suddenly before him stood the Lady Balmforth and her friend. He had often watched them riding through the woods and listened to their lovely voices as they chatted and laughed less than a stone's throw from his hiding place among the trees. What were they doing here? Had they lost their mounts? Surely they couldn't possibly be here to see him.

Two more women entered the clearing, one young and vaguely familiar, yes; it was the girl who exercised the Baron's horses, but the other? Old… ugly," he didn't know her.

Mrs. Black pushed her way to the front and studied him appraisingly, looking him up and down, nodding her head and smiling as though he filled some specifications she had planned in advance.

"You have been expecting us, have you not?" she asked the still dumbstruck young man, "We four have been searching for you for a very long time, but then I'm sure you were already aware of that."

Michael backed slowly towards the cottage door "What… what do you want with me? Why are you here? I've done nothing… what is it you want?" he repeated, his voice on the edge of breaking.

Katerina walked confidently up to him, her face inches from his, she looked deeply into his grey, watery eyes. Nobody spoke. He felt overwhelmed by the smell of her perfume, by the nearness of such beauty, he could feel her warm, sweet smelling breath on his skin, sense the heat of her body, his eyes were held by hers, incapable of looking away.

"We four have sought you out only to do your bidding, say that you wish us to leave and we will do so," Katerina's voice sounded clearly in his ears, yet it seemed her lips had not moved, she was speaking but she was not. The words were loud but he suspected that only he could hear them.

As her voice echoed in his head he became aware of a strange sensation growing deeply within him, an exquisite pain coursing through his misshapen body, filling him with strength, with power. The weakness that had formed so much of his existence seemed to fade to nothing, being replaced with an inner strength that possessed him utterly.

Smiling, Katerina took both his hands in hers, the touch of her soft, cool flesh seeming to cleanse his mind and give him a feeling of purpose he had never before known. Still looking down at his hands in hers, he realized that they had been joined by the three other women. Putting a hand on his shoulder Lucy leaned forward and kissed him lightly on the mouth, followed by Katerina, who letting go his hands after the kiss was shoved brusquely aside as Mrs. Black took his face in her two gnarled hands and crushed her wet lips viciously against his, their teeth scraping painfully together as she tried to force her probing tongue into his mouth. Coming to his senses he pulled himself from her grasp, his tanned face still showing white finger marks from her grip. Taking a step back, he breathlessly looked at the four women. His body seemed to throb with the force building inside of him. He could feel his own pulse circulating its potency around his body. Feeding his mind. His heart…

Mrs. Black turned to Felicity. "Well, m'Lady, surely you are going to greet our savior?"

The words hung in the air, all eyes were on the Baroness as she reluctantly stepped forward and kissed Michael chastely on his filthy, unshaven jaw.

Turning red faced to Katerina she asked, "Are you sure this is the right person?"

With those words her companions knew immediately that she was not truly one of them, that she was not a believer. Lucy accepted it with a shrug of resignation, Katerina with a sigh of disappointment and hurt, and Mrs. Black with a malicious grin of pleasure.

"I… I think I would like us to leave now," Felicity's voice shook as she felt an inexplicable wave of fear wash over her.

"You cannot leave."

The deep, resonate voice startled the women, "Any who come to me, come to me for life."

The booming voice, though coming from Michael's lips, was not the sound of a nervous and overawed young man but a voice of authority, a voice of power, used to commanding and to being obeyed. It seemed to echo around the enclosed garden, his mouth formed the words but the sound did not seem to come directly from him, rather it just appeared to surround them with sound, to be present in the very air more an audible thought than a spoken word.

Gripped by a feeling of terror of its most basic kind, Felicity turned on her heels and ran towards the footpath expecting at any moment to feel hands grasping her from behind. Attempting to leap through the undergrowth, her foot caught on a thorny brier. She fell heavily into a patch of docks and nettles. Ignoring the pain of the stings and the vicious scratches across her ankles she lurched to her feet drunk with fear and ran headlong back along the path, headless of the whipping branches and clutching thorns tearing at her clothes and body as she hurled herself through the damp leaves and knee-high ferns as though pursued by the very hounds of the Devil, her brain screaming at her to get away from this place, to run… *run.* But she knew not what she was running from, nor where indeed she was running to.

"Here drink this," Lucy handed Michael a tin mug of water, which he accepted gratefully, gulping it down in one huge swallow. He sat at the pine table still littered with the remnants of his previous days meal, flies circling and alighting among the small gristly bones and greasy stains on a chipped enamel plate that was probably older than Michael himself.

Mrs. Black and Lucy stood watching him with interest, their composure regained now that he had returned once more to being the shy, ungainly man they had discovered. His voice was once again the hesitant whisper of someone unsure of what was happening around him. Katerina sat opposite on the only other chair, looking intently at this strange person whom they had been seeking for so long. Perspiration beaded on his face, a thin trickle running from his temple down the line of his jaw to loose itself among the stubble of his unshaven chin. His dirty white hair hung over his eyes as he sat in silence, head bowed as if in prayer, peering into the empty mug still held in his two mismatched hands.

At the revelation of this unknown and undreamed-of force that seemed to be capable of taking control of his body at will and the effect it had on Lady Felicity, even as the rumble of the booming voice had died away, he had sagged as if with exhaustion and if not supported by Katerina, would surely have fallen where he stood.

Now seated in his small kitchen surrounded by the clutter of familiar possessions he was once more 'Mike' the strange deformed young recluse of Yarrow woods.

He lifted his head and self-consciously looked at each woman in turn. What did these women want of him? What was the strange feeling of power that had welled up inside of him when the Baroness had kissed him? Was that really him, had that been the real Michael, the inner being that had lain dormant for so many years, buried deep in his subconscious, waiting to be awoken by the coming of these women? Or was it the kiss of the Baroness that had been the stimulus? Could this finally be the answer to his question, the solution to the puzzle of who he really was and why he was here.

Mrs. Black broke the silence, speaking from behind Katerina, "what are we going to do about her Ladyship? If she mentions any of this to the Baron it could cause us no end of problems."

The question lay on the air unanswered. Michael looked up at the women once more, an incongruous grin twitching at the side of his deformed mouth. His eyes seemed to film over, the whites darkening to a watery shade of pink… once again the deep, evil voice rolled out, like the roar of a lion coming from the family tabby.

"You must fetch her to me, she, of the four of you is the most important to me. You say that you have been searching for me, that you sought me all this time." He looked again at each in turn, a half smile on his face. "You are mistaken, it is I who have been seeking. It is I who have found you. There are forces at work far more powerful than you can possibly conceive."

He turned to Katerina, seated across the table from him, "you are her friend, she trusts you. Make her see the error of her ways and bring her to me, she has a service to perform for me that she alone can fulfill." Katerina nodded her head obediently, completely overawed by the force emanating from him.

Turning his head slowly, he addressed Mrs. Black, "you will be informed of what is required of you when next we meet. Go now and return when I send you word."

"How… how are you going to get in touch with us?" she replied in a whisper.

Michael stood suddenly, his chair tipping and falling noisily to the flagstone floor. Stepping across the room he faced the silent figure of Lucy, her eyes slid from his uneasily, this was not what she had expected, not one bit as Mrs. Black had told her it would be.

Reaching out he began to stroke her long black hair with the back of his claw-like hand. All was silent in the room, the women seeming to shrink in his presence. His hand slid down behind Lucy's neck, bending his already curved back to bring his face close to hers. She could feel the warmth of this foul breath, her senses were filled with the overpowering stench of sweat and unwashed clothing.

The deep voice was gentle, caressing the words as he spoke. "How am I going to get in touch?" he repeated Mrs. Blacks question, "How am I going to get in touch? Why! This lovely young lady here will carry my messages. I have chosen her to stay with me tonight. We will be as one." He spoke directly to the wide-eyed stable girl, "Tonight you shall grow, my power will enter you, you will ride me as you ride those horses of which you are so fond, you will cleanse my body as I will cleanse your spirit."

A look of alarm spread across her face, she looked pleadingly at her two companions who returned her gaze helplessly.

Mrs. Black took Katerina firmly by the arm. "It's time we were leaving, Mrs. Christopher," she said, leading her from the cottage. As she exited she turned and gave a final sickening glance back at the stricken stable girl, a look almost of envy. Michael's fist was now knotted viciously in Lucy's long hair. He was not about to let a second woman run from him this day.

Chapter 9

Owen stood stiffly to attention, his back held ramrod straight in an unsuccessful bid to add more height to his stunted figure. He paced, hands clasped behind his back, along the line of household staff gathered together in the sprawling kitchen of Sorrow Hall, rather as a general might inspect his troops before the final confrontation that would turn the tide of the battle.

"As you are all no doubt aware," he began, "We are fast approaching the time of the annual hunt ball. Needless to say his Lordship looks on it as something of an honor to be chosen to host it this year, here at Sorrow Hall. Now, I realize that it's still some time away but the ballroom hasn't been used for a formal function since his Lordship's marriage to Lady Felicity and I'm sure it will be in need of some urgent attention." He stopped his pacing and spoke directly to Margaret, "The hunt ball has not been held in Sorrow Hall since the time of the late Baron… may he rest in peace." Owen glanced heavenward as he crossed himself before returning his gaze level with the housekeeper's bosom, he wavered momentarily as he studied the outline of her fine breasts pressing against the starched fabric of her uniform. Looking up into her knowing face he continued. "Margaret, I expect you to see that the ballroom is spotless, everything must be at its best." He turned to the elderly gardener, "Jock, we are going to require flowers to decorate the Hall, also a large variety of soft fruits and of course vegetables for the hot buffet, please discuss the requirements with Mrs. Black."

The gardener and cook exchanged glances, there was little love lost between the two oldest members of staff.

Mrs. Black cleared her throat to attract the butlers attention, "Pardon me for mentioning it Mr. Owen Sir, but I am still waiting to discuss the menu with her Ladyship, I was under the impression that she was supposed to be organizing everything but she seems to have more important things on her mind, if you don't mind me saying so."

Owen looked at the sneering cook with contempt. "But I do mind you saying so, I mind very much indeed and I'll thank you not to speak of your mistress in that tone, it is not for the likes of you to question the actions of your betters. I'm sure her Ladyship has everything in hand." It was obvious from his expression that he didn't believe his own words. Mrs. Black shrugged her broad shoulders, a lopsided grin of defiance making her scarred face look even more unattractive.

The butler spoke once more to the housekeeper, "Margaret, you had better make a start on it today, Meg can help you, if her Ladyship can spare her." He looked inquiringly at the young lady's maid who nodded assent, "if you need any more assistance the staff is at your disposal," he added as he turned to leave.

As the assembled servants made moves to disperse, Owen turned once more to face them, "Just one more thing before you go, I take it nobody has heard any news of Lucy?" All faces looked blankly back at him.

"This really isn't good enough, it's been four days now, Jock's been having to do her work as well as his own, if she doesn't turn up by the end of the week I have been instructed by his Lordship to inform the police… Right, you may return to your duties." He turned his back as a dismissal and headed for the butler's pantry.

The staff slowly made their way from the kitchen, discussing in hushed tones the strange disappearance of the stable girl, eye's furtively glancing in the direction of the elderly cook as she returned to a boiling pan, tasting its contents from a wooden spoon.

As they walked towards the ballroom Meg asked her older namesake, not for the first time, if she had any ideas about Lucy's whereabouts.

"Well," answered Margaret, "she certainly seemed to be acting strangely ever since the fire, and I'd bet anything that Mrs. Black knows a lot more than she's saying…"

"Yes, the pair of them have been spending an awful lot of time together," pointed out Meg, "and Lady Felicity has certainly had something on her mind since Lucy went missing, why! She's barely left her room, she just sits and stares at herself in the mirror, you don't think she has any idea where Lucy may be, do you?"

"I honestly don't know what to think," replied Margaret with a sigh, "Mrs. Christopher hasn't been near or by and she was supposed to be helping her Ladyship organize the ball. I wouldn't be a bit surprised if she could tell us a thing or two about what's going on."

And so the speculation increased. The staff of Sorrow hall conjuring up many weird and wonderful explanations for the mysterious disappearance of Lucy and whether it was linked in any way to the recent stable fire.

Even the Baron was concerned enough to try to speak to Felicity about it but she had just shrugged her shoulders and changed the subject. He had decided it would be better not to push the point, but was convinced in his own mind that his wife was to some extent involved. Perhaps it would be a good idea to have a quiet word with Gregory. Katerina had been conspicuous by her absence for four days now, which in itself was unusual, rarely did a day pass when she and Felicity did not meet… It would certainly be interesting to find out what her opinion was about Lucy's unexplained absence. Yes that's what he would do, he would discuss the whole matter with Gregory.

Tom Morton clicked his tongue at the two horses, the heavy chains rattling as they lifted under the tension against the pull of the immensely muscled shoulders of the matched pair of Suffolk punches, almost identical, with light sorrel colored hides and white blazed faces. Magnificent descendants of the great war horses that carried the armored knights into battle, ever willing to do his bidding, a quiet 'Gid up ol gal' or 'Dupwhee' to go right, 'Waarrdee' to go left, little more was needed.

Old Tom had won many a rosette at the county show with these two and he loved them as much, if not more than his wife.

The heavy, spiked harrows cut into the dry Norfolk soil with ease, most of the field was already completed. Tomorrow he would return and begin to plough, he was proud of his skill with the plough, when he was done, the newly turned soil, dark and fertile, would resemble a corduroy cloth, the furrows perfectly straight, perfectly spaced.

The old farmer followed the squat power of the horses rumps along the outside edge of the field, the stumps of their docked tails twitching uselessly against the flies that flittered around their hindquarters. The only sound, the gently rattle and strain of harness and the squabbling of the rooks that followed at Tom's heels fighting over the exposed grubs and leather-jackets.

The early morning sun was already hot and sweat was starting to form on Tom's leathery face. How many miles he had travelled with his two companions he could not imagine. He looked on them as the best of friends, unlike his human acquaintances they never argued with him, never questioned him, they were always there when needed. Tom thought absentmindedly to himself that they indeed possessed a lot more honor and dignity than most people he knew.

Tom Morton was never more content than when he worked his horses.

Noblet Swallow glanced up at the sound of the slow jingle of the team, he could smell the newly exposed earth as the farmer's harrows were dragged across the field. He looked through the branches at Tom and saw the old, silver whiskered farmer bent over with concentration, his red face shaded by a battered hat. The blacksmith's eye was drawn with professional interest to the engineering simplicity that was the tined harrow, that primitive but marvelously efficient invention.

Never known anyone get so much pleasure out of staring at a horse's arse all day, he thought to himself with a smile as he carefully hid his nets in the hollow trunk of an ancient willow, still alive despite the massive hole eaten into its heart. Covering them with dead leaves he set off back towards the village.

Tonight he would come and retrieve his long nets and after some hours in the moonlight he would return home with a sizable haul of rabbits, rabbits that were already sold to Rex Matchet, the butcher in Stanbridge, some five miles away.

As the poacher walked silently though the sparse woodland his practiced ear pricked up at the sound of heavy footsteps. Someone was running through the dead leaves of the forest floor. He stopped, senses straining… two people, both moving fast. He could hear the panicked calling of a blackbird clearly in the distance. As the sound faded out of earshot his attention was caught by the raised voice of Tom Morton and the angry cawing of rooks.

Rushing back once more to the forest edge, he saw the disturbed rooks circling high. On the far side of the field the old farmer was struggling to calm his horses as they reared and bucked, completely oblivious to the shouted commands of their master. The frail figure of Tom Morton looked painfully inadequate matched against the huge bulk of the two powerful animals as he hung on to the leather reins, fighting desperately to calm the struggling horses. The three linked sections of the steel harrows bounced and twisted on the end of the thick chains, at one point jerking forward to entangle themselves under the wooden whipple-tree forming a mass of knotted steel spikes and chain, crashing and twisting behind the frenzied animals. Tom clung on desperately, trying his best to quieten them but he had never seen horses act this way before, even a lifetime of experience giving him no idea what was wrong with them.

Noblet forced his way through the hedgerow and set off at a run across the field to assist the old man. As he drew close the horses took off, galloping across the newly turned soil, Tom running as best he could behind, still holding tightly to the leather harness until stumbling into the dirt and being dragged some twenty yards into the field before finally surrendering his grip. He looked up in bewilderment at the retreating horses, the tangled mass of harrows and chains bouncing and tearing their way through the ground. He felt Noblet at his side,

"What the hell…" he began, but he could see Noblet's attention was elsewhere. From the far corner of the field a young woman was running towards them, one hand holding the tattered remains of her clothing across her breasts. Her long dark hair streaming behind her. As the two men watched helplessly the horses, almost as if being driven by some unknown force, turned as one, to bare down on the running figure. Too late, she saw the huge creatures almost upon her, with a last despairing look at Noblet she was engulfed by the rage of the once docile animals. She bounced between their massive bodies to emerge, still standing as they passed her, the fleeting moment of relief left her as the bucking whipple-tree crashed into her legs, knocking her to the ground, the eight inch steel spikes of the harrow crushing and tearing her young body beneath it, rolling her along into an unrecognizable, bloody heap of flesh and splintered bone.

Old Tom, still lying where he fell, stared transfixed with disbelief. Noblet was already rushing towards the mutilated remains of what had once been a beautiful young woman.

In the few seconds it took him to reach her the pair of horses had settled, almost as if nothing had happened, apart from their heaving chests and foam flecked muzzles. They stood at ease waiting for their master to come to them… that they may resume their labor.

Noblet looked down at the bloodied mass at his feet, soil clinging to the exposed organs hanging grotesquely from the rusty harrows. The sun glinting on the stark whiteness of the shattered skull, eyes open, wide with terror, seeming to still be looking pleadingly into his own…

"My God, Lucy." He tore his gaze from her shredded remains as his stomach started to heave, falling to his knees beside her, he felt the gorge rising in his throat. Clamping his hands over his mouth as the hot vomit forced itself between his fingers, spraying over the remains of the dead girl.

Lifting his head, a distant movement caught the corner of his eye. He looked up quickly. At the far end of the field a flash of white, somebody was watching from among the trees. His mind flew back to the sound of people running through the woods. Two people running… or somebody being chased?

Noblet started as Tom Morton rested a hand on his shoulder. He looked back across the field, if somebody had been hiding there, he was gone now.

Constable Edwin Townsend licked the end of his pencil stub, jotting the time and date in his pocket book, the pages were filled with Noblet Swallows statement concerning Lucy's death.

"Would you care for another cup of tea, Edwin?" offered Rachael Swallow, taking the empty teacup from the low table beside the seated policeman.

"No thank you kindly, Mrs. Swallow, I'm just about done here." He stood and shook Noblet's hand, "Well, I appreciate your assistance in this dreadful matter, you agree pretty much with what old Tom Morton told me, apart from the bit about seeing someone hiding in the bushes."

"I said, I *think* I saw someone. I can't be sure," interrupted the blacksmith.

After showing the policeman out, Rachael returned to find Noblet pouring himself a large whisky, one of the few times he had drunk strong drink in his own home.

"Are you feeling alright?" she asked him, pouring herself another cup of tea, "I noticed you didn't mention about her being chased, you just said you thought you saw someone."

With a sigh he put a huge arm around her shoulders, leaning forward to kiss the top of her head, "I'm not sure what I saw, but I'm convinced somebody was chasing that girl, I'll never forget the look of fear on her face as she ran towards us, and I tell you… something terrified those horses!"

Chapter 10

Reverend James Underwood sat in the shade of an immense beech tree, his back against the smooth bark, the sunlight through the small leaves throwing a dappled pastiche of shadow onto Margaret's face and arms as she lay on her back in the long grass, eyes closed against the glare of the midday sun, the remainder of their picnic lunch spread on the tartan table cloth between them.

"James, you know the Christopher's quite well, don't you?" she asked.

He considered the question for a moment, "I wouldn't say I knew them particularly well, but yes, I'm probably more friendly with them than with anybody else in the village. Except you, of course." he added with a smile, "why do you ask?"

Margaret tried to keep her voice casual. "Oh, I was just wondering what you thought of Mrs. Christopher?"

"Katerina? Ah! Now that is a very interesting lady"'

"In what way, *interesting*?" Margaret sat up on her haunches, in expectation of his reply, surprised and delighted to find him so communicative. It was very unlike him, normally he was so closed mouthed about his parishioners, even to her.

"Well, perhaps intriguing may be a better description."

"Ok then. In what way *intriguing*." she urged.

James felt pleased at having the opportunity to tell somebody his concerns over the events on that fateful Sunday and went on to relate Katerina's strange actions over lunch following the stable fire. For the next two hours they discussed every aspect of the strange events surrounding Lucy, from the fire in the Balmforth's stables, to her tragic death. Margaret told him of Lucy's involvement with Mrs. Black and now the unusual behavior of Lady Felicity and the obvious rift between her and Katerina Christopher.

As they cleared away the picnic things, arranging them neatly in the wickerwork hamper, James was strangely silent, deep in thought, going over what he had learned.

"Why the long face?" asked Margaret, shaking crumbs from the tablecloth.

He immediately replaced the frown with his familiar grin. "Sorry, it's just this business with Lucy and the others; after all, Katerina is the wife of a good friend of mine. Why! I even married them and I can't help feeling a certain responsibility towards them, surely it's my duty to attempt to get to the bottom of all this. If she is getting involved in anything dangerous I feel I have a moral obligation to find out exactly what it is."

Smiling to herself she studied his worried expression. Over the weeks, as their friendship had grown, she had come to understand just how seriously James took his responsibility towards his parishioners, she had thought it such an endearing trait but somehow his concern over this matter seemed in her mind to bode ill for all concerned.

Margaret came close and put a hand on his arm, "Oh! James, do you really think it's something as serious as that? Lucy's death… you do believe it was an accident, don't you?"

He kissed her lightly on the forehead, "I wished I knew, I just have an uncomfortable feeling about the whole dreadful episode. I feel I should have a quiet word with Gregory, and perhaps it may be a good idea if I paid a discreet call on Mister Swallow and perhaps Tom Morton and try and find out firsthand what happened with those horses. I'm sure Constable Townsend is an admirable policeman but I can't help feeling… ?"

His words hung in the air.

Margaret parted with James at the gate of St. Michael's rectory. Upon returning to the Hall she was mildly surprised to learn from Meg that Gregory Christopher was in the library with his Lordship, and judging by the raised voices coming through the door it didn't sound the friendliest of meetings.

Owen, turning the corner of the sweeping staircase, spotted Margaret and Meg loitering around the library entrance.

"If you can't find anything better to do, I can soon find you something," he bellowed, startling the two friends, who both bobbed their heads respectfully to the butler and hurried away.

Owen, glancing around to ensure he was alone, furtively took their place by the library door, where he made a show of examining a tiny crack in the jardinière holding a huge aspidistra that stood conveniently close by.

"Now see here, Oliver, what exactly are you inferring?" Gregory asked angrily, his voice shaking slightly as he faced his friend. "If I understand you correctly, you're accusing my wife of coming between you and Felicity, and if that's not enough, you have the damn audacity to infer that she's somehow connected with the death of that stable girl of yours?"

Oliver banged his heavy glass down onto the mantelpiece, slopping whisky onto the polished surface.

"I'm not accusing her of anything," he retorted in a rage. "It's just that Felicity has changed completely since she started spending time with that damn wife of yours… Hell! Don't look so indignant. You even told me yourself that Katerina's been acting strangely for months… "

Gregory opened his mouth to interrupt, but Oliver would not be put off. The angry flow of words continued unabated.

"Felicity has shut herself away in her room and refuses to discuss what's bothering her and by your own admission Katerina has done the self-same thing. Does she still lock herself in that shabby little room of hers?"

Gregory lowered himself slowly into the high-backed, leather armchair, head bowed, peering into the untouched tumbler of whisky held lightly between his fingers. The trembling of his hand causing tiny ripples on the golden surface of the twelve-year-old malt.

His voice no longer held the tone of outrage he had summoned earlier…

"Yes," he conceded, "it's true, things haven't been right for some time now. She's changed so much… and this last week she's barely spoken at all." He looked at his friend pleadingly, "God, what do you think's happening to them, Oliver? She just sits and stares out of the window. It's almost as though she's waiting for someone to arrive."

Oliver, relieved to find Gregory calmer, sat on the edge of his desk, looking sadly at his boyhood friend. "Look, I think the time has come when we both have to admit that our wives are definitely trying to hide something from us. There's no sense in us denying it or being secretive with each other. I'm afraid we have no choice but to swallow our pride and accept that we may have a big problem."

Gregory nodded in agreement, "Well, I'm at my wits end. What do you suggest we do?"

"First and foremost, we need to put our cards on the table. Whether you admit it to yourself or not, I'm convinced that there's some link between our wives and Lucy's accident… If it was an accident."

"What on Earth do you mean, if it was an accident?" Gregory rose from his seat. "What do you know?" he added, a look of fear on his face.

The two long-time friends discussed all that had happened over the past few months; Gregory disclosing for the first time Katerina's strange reaction to the stable fire. He described the things he had discovered in her filthy room at the top of the house, finally coming around to the fact that these two close friends had not seen each other since Lucy first went missing.

"I think it may be a good idea if we enlisted some impartial advice," Gregory suggested. "How do you feel about mentioning all this to James? After all, he saw how Katerina reacted on the Sunday of the fire."

Oliver seemed to consider the idea for an eternity before replying.

"Well, I suppose it wouldn't be a bad thing. Who better to have on your side than God almighty?"

Pleased that they were finally taking some action, Gregory drained his glass, "I'll invite the Reverend around for drinks this very evening," he said.

"I'll be there" responded Oliver.

James arrived punctually at the Christopher's' sprawling monstrosity of a home. The warm yellow brick of the walls all but obscured by a rampant growth of wisteria crawling over the exterior and trying to engulf the high pointed windows. The imposing oak double door was opened before he had a chance to knock. Strangely, he wasn't surprised to see Gregory himself holding open the door.

"Do come in James, it's good of you to come at such short notice, we have been waiting for you to arrive."

The Rector followed him into the withdrawing room, over furnished with an eclectic clutter of furniture of vastly differing styles and taste giving the room the feeling of an auction house more than a home.

The Reverend had not expected to see the Baron Balmforth in attendance. They greeted each other cordially, Oliver rising to shake James's outstretched hand, his grip was dry and firm.

"No Katerina?" asked James innocently.

Oliver and Gregory exchanged uneasy glances, "Er… No, she's upstairs," answered Gregory hesitantly. "Would you care for a drink, old man?" he offered, trying to change the subject, waving a cut-crystal ship's decanter at the rector who smiled and nodded, hoping it contained a good brandy.

After some minutes discussing everyday trivia Oliver broached the subject of Lucy. James, thinking at first that it was merely the Baron enquiring as to the proposed funeral arrangements, started to explain the procedure before realizing he was being listened to politely but with little interest. Stopping in mid-sentence he turned to Gregory, "This isn't why you asked me here, is it?"

The three men sat and discussed the recent events, James relating the various facts and suppositions that Margaret had shared with him at their picnic earlier that day. Oliver listened in silence, his head nodding as if what he was being told seemed to agree with his own suspicions.

James revealed to them that after leaving Margaret he had paid a visit to the blacksmith, who had related the whole episode of Lucy's horrific death, going on to explain that Rachael Swallow had remarked that her husband had been even more open with his thoughts than he had been to Constable Townsend. Noblet had justified this by explaining to her that the police were only interested in the facts and not his opinions.

James repeated the blacksmith's version of events word for word, finally sitting back in his chair to allow his audience time to consider what they had been told.

"If Noblet Swallow says he saw someone, I'd be inclined to believe him." said Gregory, refilling their glasses.

Oliver nodded agreement but said nothing for a while, obviously pondering something. "Did he say if the person he thinks he saw was a man or a woman?"

Both men looked at him, realizing what he was worrying about. James considered his reply before speaking. "He didn't say for definite, but I got the impression he was talking about a man. I'm sure he said that when he looked back, *He* was gone."

Oliver and Gregory both let out audible sighs of relief.

As the level in the crystal decanter dropped, so too did Oliver and Gregory's reticence. They found themselves discussing the intimate details of their lives, everything concerning their wives, much of which had seemed so trivial at the time, but now appeared to be small but important parts of the whole jigsaw that they were trying to construct.

By midnight it was agreed, the three of them working together would find out what they could about Lucy, Felicity, Katerina and the Baron's cook, Mrs. Black, whom according to Margaret, was involved in everything up to her scrawny neck.

Arrangements were made to meet at the rectory in one week's time. James was to enlist Margaret's help in keeping an eye on the cook, whilst Gregory and Oliver were to find out what they could from their wives. Although both admitted it was not going to be easy confronting their respective spouses.

Chapter 11

Meg stood behind Lady Felicity, brushing her Ladyship's hair in front of the dressing table. There was no small talk, none of the idle pleasantries that Meg had come to enjoy so much of late.

The small muscles at the base of Felicity's slim neck, which had been knotted with stress, were slowly relaxing under the gentle motion of the maid's hands.

"Meg? May I ask a small favor of you?" Felicity's voice sounded loudly in the room, after the long silence.

"But of course, m'Lady," replied Meg, speaking to the reflection in the mirror. She stopped her grooming and placed the hairbrush onto the dressing table.

Felicity turned her body on the padded stool beneath her. She faced the maid, but kept her eyes averted. "Now, Meg, you are to tell no one of this, no one at all, do you understand?"

"Yes, of course, m'Lady," repeated Meg.

"I would very much like you to take a message to Mrs.. Christopher. I want you to tell her it is of the utmost importance that I speak to her urgently. Explain to her that if she is willing, I will meet her today at precisely four o'clock by the fallen beech tree outside the woods. We have met there before. She will know where I mean. Oh, and tell her to come on horseback."

She asked Meg to repeat the message back to her, twice, before she was satisfied that the maid had it word perfect.

"Remember, this is to be our secret. You must tell no one but Mrs. Christopher. If Mister Owen tries to question you as you leave, you are to refer him to me."

"I shall go right away, m'Lady." Meg couldn't help feeling strangely honored to be sharing such an obviously important secret with her mistress. She was determined not to let Lady Felicity down.

Hurrying to the small loft room that she shared with Margaret, Meg opened a cheap deal cabinet and removed a green velvet cloak, which she hurriedly tied about her shoulders. Opening the door of the room, she hesitated, her lips clamped together with concentration as she considered her actions. Coming to a decision, she crossed the room to a small pine dresser, from a drawer she took paper and a stub of pencil and hastily scribbled a short note to Margaret, telling her where she was going and why. Whatever reason she had to do such a thing she could not imagine. Margaret would not return to the room until later that evening and Meg was only going to be away for a short time. Considering this, she crumpled the note into a ball and drew back her hand to throw it into the enamel pail that served as a waste paper basket. Something seemed to stop her… a twinge of indecision. Feeling rather foolish she opened up the ball of paper, flattening out the creases as best she could. Folding it once, she slipped it under the corner of Margaret's trinket box, an ugly, seashell covered monstrosity full of cheap pinchbeck jewelry. Meg then left in a hurry, trotting noisily down the back staircase and out through the servants entrance.

After fifteen minutes of brisk walking she found herself on the steps of the Christopher's home, she knocked hesitantly. The Christopher's maid listened without interest as Meg explained her reason for calling. Left standing in the large tiled hallway she stepped from one foot to the other, nervously looking around her. After some minutes the maid reappeared and lead Meg to an upstairs room.

Katerina was seated at an ornately carved dressing table. Meg was immediately struck by the similarity of the pose to the one that she had left Lady Felicity in a short time earlier.

"That will be all. Thank you, Becky." Said Katerina pleasantly to the maid, who bobbed her head respectfully and left, closing the door gently behind her.

Meg went to speak, but was silenced by Katerina as she held a finger to her lips and stepped quietly to a door obviously leading to an adjoining room. She put an ear close to the wooden paneling and after a moment, pulled the door open and peered in. Meg caught a glimpse of a large four-poster bed heavily draped with thick brocade; it appeared to be the master bedroom. Katerina closed the door and turned smiling at the anxious girl, "We don't want anybody overhearing us, do we?"

Meg shook her head, but said nothing.

"Don't look so worried, come and sit down, here by me."

Katerina sat on the edge of an ugly over stuffed chaise lounge, patting the space beside her. Meg sat down obediently.

"Now Meg. It is Meg, isn't it? Now what is this message you have for me?"

Michael sat on the Norwich Milestone, his chin resting in his hands; back hunched, elbows on knees, watching a colony of red ants swarming over a dead shrew in the dirt at his feet. To his left the high gates and graveled entrance of Sorrow hall.

He pondered all that had happened in the last week. His life was finally starting to have purpose. At long last he felt that his time was coming. He was slowly beginning to feel at one with the inner being that seemed to be able to control his voice, his thoughts and his actions. Just let anybody point and laugh at his disfigurement. Just let them try to mock him. He would show them the meaning of real power. He laughed quietly to himself; then, they would show him respect. He would drive the fools before him like sheep.

His thoughts drifted back once again to the power he had exercised as he had watched the stable girl running from him, he had found it so easy, controlling the minds of those horses, compelling them against their will to do his bidding. The memory of that moment filled him with a feeling of supreme contentment. One day he would control people with equal ease. If Lucy had done as he had wished, she would still be alive today. She had sealed her own fate when she had been foolish enough to defy him.

Looking up at the sound of approaching footsteps, he saw, walking hurriedly in his direction, the figure of a young girl clad in a green velvet cloak. Grinding his heel into the feasting ants, he stood and strolled over to one of the lichens covered stone pillars flanking the gateway of the Hall.

Meg noticed Michael for the first time, leaning at ease against the carved column, his bent shape and hideous hand stirring no feelings of pity in the usually soft-hearted girl. She knew who he was; she had seen him about the village at various times. The sight of him had always filled her with loathing. At first she had felt ashamed of herself for thinking ill of someone less fortunate than herself, but she soon realized it was nothing to do with how he looked, or for any other obvious reason that she could name. Somehow, it seemed to her that his disfigurement was like some form of divine punishment. His whole being seemed to radiate an aura of menace. The mere thought of him was enough to send a shiver of fear through her body.

She nodded shyly at him as she passed, trying not to catch his eye. The only thing on her mind was to give Lady Felicity Mrs. Christopher's reply.

"Excuse me, young miss. Might I have a quick word with you?"

Michael's deep, laconic voice made Meg's blood run cold. She stopped in her tracks. Turning against her will to face the strange young man.

"Would I be correct in thinking you work at the Hall?" he asked, pointing with his eyebrows in the direction of the huge house at the end of the gravel drive.

Meg nodded. For some inexplicable reason she felt afraid. Michael had done nothing more than speak to her, yet already she was struggling with an inner fear that seemed to be creeping through her. She looked into his pale eyes, convinced that he knew exactly what she was thinking; his simple question seemed to ask much more than the words alone.

Taking her silence as affirmation he continued in the same officious tone, "I would like you to deliver a message for me."

"A message?" answered the bewildered girl, "Another message?"

Michael's extraordinary senses pounced on her hesitation, telling him that luck was on his side, inexplicably he knew immediately that he had stumbled upon something of importance. Seizing the opportunity, he held her eyes with his own.

"Really? And what might that message have been?"

Meg's mind reeled with Lady Felicity's words echoing in her head: 'This is our secret. You must tell no one.' Trying unsuccessfully to tear her gaze from his, she clamped her jaws tightly shut, willing herself not to answer his question. Michael smiled inwardly at the futile resistance of this simple girl. His voice grew heavy with malice.

"I will not ask you again," he insisted.

Meg, her resolve somehow hardening, started to speak, her voice filtering and hesitant.

"I… I… cannot say."

Michael's eyes grew wide with rage, his pupils seeming to shrink to small orbs of fire.

Meg felt the inner strength and resistance drain from her body. Her legs grew weak and started to buckle. She sagged, falling forward, cutting her knees painfully on the sharp gravel of the drive. She looked up at the leering young man, towering above her.

"You will answer," he informed her, with certainty.

Meg heard herself speaking quite clearly and fluently, almost as if her vocal cords had a will of their own.

"Mrs. Gregory has agreed to meet Lady Felicity by the dead beech next to the bridal way on the edge of Yarrow Woods today at four o'clock."

"Has she now." his voice quieter. "You will inform your cook, Mrs. Black, that she is to come to my home before nightfall this evening."

Meg nodded understanding and looked up obediently into his eyes, her legs, still feeling weak, were beginning to tremble violently.

Though subdued, Michael's voice held a menacing tone in its calmness as he continued to give Meg further instructions.

"You will mention our meeting to no other."

Without warning, Michaels arm flew out and a fist grabbed Meg by the stout ribbon fastening her cloak. He pulled her to her feet, his bony knuckles forcing themselves painfully into her throat, choking the petrified girl.

"Do you understand?"

His voice grew louder once more, "you will tell no one...No one. Be warned, for I will surely know."

"Yes...Yes," she sobbed, the ineffable spell having broken at last.

With terror in her eyes she twisted from his grasp and ran towards the Hall, her only thought to deliver the message to Mrs. Black. She must do it immediately or else... or else? The consequences were to her young mind inconceivable.

After hastily giving Mrs. Black Michael's instructions, Meg took off at a run towards the Baroness's room, the cook desperately bellowing at her to come back, there were things she wished to ask her.

The terrified lady's maid ran on, ignoring Mrs. Black's shouting. Owen, attracted by the commotion, hurried from the butler's pantry all but colliding with the fleeing girl. He called after her to stop immediately but with no effect. He looked back at the cook in bewilderment before hurrying up the stairs in pursuit of Meg.

Owen eventually caught up with her outside Lady Felicity's room just as Lady Felicity was opening her bedroom door in response to Meg's frantic knocking.

Owen, red faced and almost out of breath, grabbed the still sobbing lady's maid by the arm, gasping "I'm dreadfully sorry m'Lady, young Meg here, seems rather upset, I'm sure it's nothing to worry about, I'll soon get to... I'll soon get to the bottom of this." He panted.

Felicity put a comforting arm around Meg's shoulders before the butler had any chance of dragging her away.

"You can leave us now Owen," she instructed. "Leave her with me. I'm sure she will be fine."

Owen looked at his mistress with ill-concealed surprise. "As you wish, m'Lady," he courteously responded, bowing his head respectfully as the door was closed in his face.

Felicity lead the distraught girl into the room, trying her best to calm her as they walked. "Heaven's above Meg. Whatever's happened?" she asked, gripping the maid firmly by the shoulders.

Slowly, Meg began to regain control of herself. She breathed deeply, paused, took another deep breath and informed her mistress "I delivered your message just as you instructed. Mrs. Christopher says that she will meet you just as you asked m'Lady... may I go now please?"

Felicity took her hands from Meg's shoulders. "No, I'm afraid you may not, not until you tell me what's wrong. What in God's name has happened to you? Why are you so upset? Just look at you... Why, your trembling!" Felicity looked down at Meg's torn stockings and bloodied knees, small pieces of gravel still adhering to her grazed flesh.

"Please m'Lady," answered Meg, "I… I cannot tell… he… he would know."

Without waiting for permission, the distraught girl turned and wrenched open the door. Running from the room, Felicity called for her to stop but her only answer was the maid's retreating footsteps echoing loudly down the passage way.

As Felicity watched the door swinging slowly on its hinges, she felt herself grow cold. Her hands shook, as she sat heavily on the edge of her bed. She could still see the look of fear in Meg's eyes.

"God, what have I done," she breathed to herself. Have I caused this terrible thing to reach out and affect an innocent young girl? What had made her ever get involved in all this hocus-pocus? Surely Katerina would listen to her… she would surely see that what they were doing was wrong… so very wrong.

Owen entered the ballroom. Various members of the household staff were busy preparing the room for the fast approaching hunt ball. Margaret, an open tin of 'Harris Metal' polish in her hand, crossed the room towards him in response to the crook of his finger.

Leading her outside, he snatched the tin of polish from her irritably, almost throwing it onto the long sideboard. "Margaret, I would like you to go and have a word with young Meg. Apparently she ran some kind of an errand for Lady Felicity and has returned dreadfully shaken up, then she seems to have had some kind of heart to heart with her Ladyship and has now locked herself in her room and refuses to open the door, even to me. She appears to be in a terrible state, crying and what have you, she has blatantly disobeyed me and far worse has even disobeyed her Ladyship. This cannot be permitted no matter what the cause, obviously something has badly upset her, now go and find out what's wrong, and get her down here without delay. There's work to be done and she's needed."

Margaret rushed immediately up the stairs, leaving Owen still talking.

"I don't know what's happening to everyone in this house, really I don't." The butler muttered to himself as he re-entered the ballroom. "This would never have been permitted in Sir Rupert's day."

Using her own key to let herself into the small room Margaret found Meg huddled fetus like on the soft bed that they shared. Clutched in her hands was the old crucifix that usually hung crookedly on a nail over the bed. It had hung there as long as anybody could remember.

Closing the door behind her, Margaret walked over to the bedside and knelt on the floor in front of her young friend.

"Whatever's wrong, Meg? Come on now. You can tell me."

Meg threw her arms around Margaret's neck.

"I wish I could tell you but I… I just can't." she sobbed.

Margaret gently stroked the crying girl's hair; it seemed to have a soothing effect. Meg's heaving shoulders slowly began to subside, her breathing to grow steadier until she finally pulled away, wiping her red eyes on her sleeve.

Margaret took the girl's hands in her own, "Now tell me what this is all about. Is it anything to do with Lady Felicity?" Meg hesitated, fighting an inner turmoil that she simply didn't comprehend. She wanted so much to confide in her only true friend, but inexplicably felt certain that if she did, that horrid Michael would be sure to know and the idea of angering him filled her with absolute dread… but why, she simply could not imagine.

Meg's eyes involuntarily glanced across the room, Margaret noticing, turned her head and caught a glimpse of white on the dresser. She stood and removed the creased and folded notepaper from beneath her trinket box. Opening it, she read slowly to herself. Sitting once again beside Meg, she refolded the note carefully and placed in the pocket of her apron.

"Now I understand some of it. You obviously intended to tell me about it or you wouldn't have left me the note… now why don't you take your time and tell me exactly what has happened."

Meg remained silent, wringing her hands with indecision.

Margaret gently prompted "So, her Ladyship sent you to see Mrs. Christopher… did you go?"

Meg looked up red eyed.

"Yes… yes, I went. They're going to meet this afternoon, in the woods." she answered in a rush of words.

"And did either of them do anything, or say anything to upset you like this?" continued Margaret.

"No… No… You don't understand," answered Meg, "It has nothing to do with her Ladyship."

Meg then slowly and almost in a whisper told of her chance meeting with Michael, if chance it was, and the message he had given her to deliver to Mrs. Black.

Margaret made her go over the whole experience again, leaving nothing out. She made her repeat her conversation with Michael word for word.

"I promised her Ladyship I'd keep it a secret. But I just had to tell him everything. I know it sounds crazy but I seemed incapable of keeping anything from him."

She looked in bewilderment at her friend, "Does that make any sense?"

Meg suddenly jumped to her feet at the sound of a soft tapping on the door. Margaret opened it to find Lady Felicity standing there, her hand raised to knock once more. She seemed surprised to find the housekeeper with Meg. Ignoring Margaret she spoke directly to the young Lady's maid.

"Are you feeling better now?"

"Yes… Yes. Thank you, M'Lady," she replied, wiping her eyes with the heel of her hand and sitting once more on the bed. "Can you ever excuse my behavior, I'm so dreadfully sorry, I really don't know what came over me… It was…"

Protectively, Margaret interrupted her friend, "She just had a bit of a fright, your Ladyship. That strange fellow, Michael, who lives in the woods, it seems he put a bit of a scare into her."

At the mention of Michael's name, the color seemed to drain from Felicity's face. Stepping further into the room, she closed the door behind her, leaning her back against it as if to steady herself.

"My Lady, is anything wrong?" asked Margaret.

Felicity took a deep breath, slowly regaining her composure. "And what did he say to you, this Michael?" She looked almost fearfully at Meg, seated on the bed, her fingers toying with the crucifix lying beside her on the counterpane.

Margaret quickly interjected, "He asked her to deliver a message to Mrs. Black. Or rather he *ordered* her to deliver the message."

As Margaret had suspected, this revelation caused quite a reaction from the Baroness.

Felicity looked hard at the two maids "Tell me everything that happened. Absolutely everything, please don't be frightened. I promise you we are all on the same side."

Chapter 12

Margaret sat uncomfortably on the hard oak settle in the entrance porch of Saint Michael's church watching James pace back and forth, his hands locked behind his back, head down, a frown of studious concentration making his usually boyish face look far older.

It was now out of her hands. She had told him all she knew and trusted him to make the right decisions.

"And you say Lady Felicity is still going to meet with Katerina?" he asked.

"Yes. She seems determined to try and reason with her, but she said that she would remain on horseback, just in case he should be there. She's convinced that this Michael is the cause of everything that's been happening and that if he gets to Mrs. Christopher first… "

James held up his hand to silence her.

"Calm down Margaret, you're starting to let your imagination run away with you. Lucy's death was a tragic accident, no more. Now, what I would like you to do, is for you to go back to the Hall and repeat to Sir Oliver all that you have told me. Frankly, I'm astounded that Lady Felicity didn't tell him all this nonsense herself before undertaking such a reckless act. She must realize that this fellow Michael is possibly mentally unhinged, I've met soldiers out of their minds with fear or pain, they are capable of anything. This Michael fellow needs being questioned and we need to find out just what his involvement is in everything."

Margaret opened her mouth to protest, but he paid no heed.

"I assure you." he continued, "His Lordship will not be as surprised as you may think, and perhaps he can find out just what Mrs. Black has got to do with all this, she obviously knows far more than she's letting on."

A look of alarm spread across Margaret's face as she rose to her feet.

"James, I couldn't tell his Lordship, I've given my word to Lady Felicity not to speak of it, not to anyone."

"But my dear, you've already told me all about it," responded James. "Be assured there is no sin in breaking your word for the greater good."

She lowered her eyes with embarrassed doubt and considered the premise of his assurances. "I will do as you ask," she replied after a long deliberation.

"I'll speak to his Lordship the moment he returns home.... Now I had better get a move on. Heaven only knows what Mr. Owen will say when I get back?"

He instinctively placed his hands lightly on her shoulders. "Good girl" he said. "I'll do what I can." He bent forward and kissed her gently on the cheek. She retired feeling more assured but still in trepidation of the potential repercussions.

James smiled happily to himself as he watched her hurry away along the gravel path. With a sigh of resignation he checked the time on his gold hunter. *He must hurry…*

Rushing back to the Rectory he quickly changed into a pair of stout walking boots and his old tweed jacket. His activities were accompanied by loud shouts along the hallway to Mrs. Stanton, his housekeeper, telling her not to bother about preparing his usual late lunch.

No sooner changed he set off at a brisk pace along the track leading up behind the church and past the disused well (now securely boarded over) and across the common in the direction of Yarrow woods.

At that precise moment Katerina and Felicity were arriving almost simultaneously at their prearranged meeting place, their horses snorting a greeting of recognition to each other. The two riders sat motionless and looked at each other in silence, both conscious of the rift in their relationship. Katerina then turned in her saddle as if to dismount.

"No! Don't." Felicity almost shouted. In a calmer voice she continued, "I think it might be safer if we remained mounted… perhaps we can ride while we talk like we used to," she added as an afterthought.

Katerina nodded and they set off slowly across the meadow that skirted the woods edge.

"You said safer?' safer from what?" questioned Katerina.

Felicity felt her eyes filling with tears. This was her best friend talking, but they were behaving like two strangers.

"Oh! Katerina. Don't you know what's happening? Because of us Lucy is dead! Surely you can't believe that what you are doing is right?"

Katerina laughed scornfully, "Lucy's death was an accident. You must know that! When I next speak to Michael, I'll ask him exactly what happened."

"When you next… ?" Felicity stared in disbelief. "When you next speak to him? You mean you're actually going to see him again?"

"Why of course I'm going to see him again, surely after all the trouble we had in finding him, you don't expect me to change my plans now? What on earth's wrong with you, Felicity? I thought you were with us, you know that we can never be complete without his leadership. If you turn your back on him now it will have all been for nothing. It was our power that found him and now there is no going back. It's too late to deny your beliefs, we are his… all four of us!"

"Four?" questioned Felicity.

"Oh very well, then… three!" conceded Katerina, "But I told you, Lucy's death had nothing to do with this."

"Maybe two, but certainly not three!" Felicity replied. "I came here today to try and convince you that what you are doing can only lead to more suffering and pain. Is there nothing I can do or say to make you realize how wrong you are and think again?"

Michael moved furtively through the trees that he knew so well; he would soon be coming up on the blind side of the dead beech by the bridle path. Things could not have gone better had he planned it. He would let the women have their little chat just to see what he could pick up and then he would make his entrance. The Christopher woman would help him. At last he'd have the Baroness in his power. Oh, how the Baron would suffer when he finds her gone. The thought of his plans for Felicity filling him with a lust he could almost taste.

Stepping through the undergrowth he could feel his erection chafing painfully against the course flannel of his trousers.

Drawing near the meeting place, he knew somehow that he wasn't alone. His whole body could sense the presence of another.

Peering, through the midst of an overgrown dogwood, he saw the two women riding slowly into the distance.

"Hell!" he exclaimed out loud, "Where are they going?" He took a moment to gain control of his anger. Growing calmer, a wretched smile spread across his face as he realized that they were riding… riding horses! More horses! Those animals seemed to be figuring most prominently in these plans.

"Horses," he sniggered to himself. He had already proved he had control over their simple minds and laughing inwardly, he started to bend his will towards the animals, now almost out of sight behind a small copse in the distance. Concentrating only on them, he would compel their return with his prize, to turn back, regardless of their rider's wishes, or whips!

"What are you doing here?"

The sudden unexpected voice came like a blow. He spun around, his mind still full of horses and women. It took him a moment to come to his senses, almost as if being awoken from a dream.

Torn between fear of discovery and outrage at the interruption, he looked into the stern face of the man without recognition. Although he had shunned the local inhabitants, he knew most of them by sight. His eyes ran quickly over the tweed jacket and trousers and down to the good quality footwear, before coming back to rest on the stark white band of a clerics collar.

"I asked you a question. Now tell me what you think you are doing here?" repeated James.

The realization that this person represented the church, the church he despised, was enough to send him into a fit of uncontrollable rage. His face appeared to physically darken with his pumping blood, even seeming to reach the whites of his eyes, which glowed a dirty pink.

James felt himself go suddenly weak, a wave of nausea began to grip him. His throat seemed to constrict, cutting off the air to his lungs. As he stared into the grotesque face coming closer, he knew instantly that he had badly underestimated the evil power of this strange young man.

Michael smiled, mockingly, revealing his small, unhealthy teeth in an expanse of vivid pink gums; the evil emanating from that smile was enough to cause James to grab instinctively for the crucifix he always wore about his neck.

The Rector's sudden movement seemed to act on Michael like a signal to attack. With a leap, he was upon James, the air filled with a shriek that turned the Reverend's blood to ice. James fell to his knees in fear, hiding his face with his forearms against the onslaught of the scratching, biting fury that was upon him. The strength of his attacker was totally unexpected and James, although physically larger and certainly in normal circumstances, far stronger, was no match for the screaming form that tore at his head and body with fist, feet and teeth.

Cowering even lower James buried his head under his arms trying to ward off the heavy blows that rained down upon him. He felt the backs of his hands being torn open by Michael's claw-like nails, his cheek now running with warm blood as his exposed ear was almost bitten off in the frenzy of Michael's blood lust.

As the agony continued, James felt himself slipping into a red mist of pain, sinking slowly into unconsciousness. As if from far away, he could still hear Michael's unearthly screams ringing in his ears.

Chapter 13

Margaret tapped lightly on lady Felicity's bedroom door. When there was no response, she knocked once more and called out in a loud whisper.

"Your Ladyship, it's Margaret. I was wondering if I might have a quick word with you?"

She waited, biting her bottom lip fretfully, the steady rhythm of the clock on the oak paneled wall sounding far too loud in the silence of the empty passageway.

The dull click of a key turning in the lock brought a flood of relief to the housemaid's overstretched imagination which had already started conjuring up visions of her mistress lying dead, having taken her own life, or having disappeared never to be seen again.

The Baroness looked worn, her long blond, usually perfectly groomed hair, hung untidily across her face.

"Come in, Margaret. I'm afraid I was sleeping." She explained as she ran her slim fingers through the disarrayed tangles of her hair.

"Oh! I am so sorry to disturb you, m'Lady, it's just that we… that is Meg and I were concerned about you."

Felicity looked across at her through tired eyes.

"Close the door behind you, please Margaret, and then tell me what you really came here for. You said you wanted a word with me."

Margaret felt uncomfortable in Felicity's room, talking to her mistress in such an informal way. She knew that her presence in the household was resented by Felicity and although she had always been spoken to with restrained politeness, the Baroness had never been quite able to conceal her contempt, especially in front of the Baron.

"Your Ladyship, I hope you don't think that I am interfering, and I do understand that it may not be my place to speak…" she hesitated in her prepared speech, shuffling her feet nervously.

Felicity sat down on the corner of an antique blanket box at the foot of her bed. She gave the housemaid a look of encouragement as Margaret continued haltingly.

"It's just that we… that is I, have decided to speak to his Lordship about this Michael business… and Lucy, and the fire and everything."

She paused, waiting for Felicity to jump to her feet and start hurling insults and threats of instant dismissal. Instead, the Baroness simply sat quietly, hands in her lap looking resignedly at Margaret, who resumed her speech with far less anxiety.

"I'm aware that I promised to keep it a secret, but with all that's happened recently, with Meg and poor Lucy, I really feel it's my duty to…"

Felicity stood and placed a hand lightly on the housemaid's mouth, silencing her in mid-sentence. Felicity spoke clearly, her voice full of strength, sure of herself at last, relieved to have the burden of deceit lifted from her shoulders.

"Let's both go and see him together, shall we?" We'll tell him all about it.

The two women were amazed at how calmly Oliver took the news. Everything from the fire in the stables, up to the meeting with Michael and the death of Lucy, and on to the events earlier that day. While he seemed somewhat surprised at the obvious fear in his wife's face when she told of Michael's involvement, he didn't appear in any way shocked. He sat and listened in polite silence to the whole tale, his only interruption being, 'I told you so' when he heard about the role played by Katerina Christopher.

At last, Felicity finished her account. She turned to Margaret, asking her if she had anything to add.

Margaret shook her head, still trying to take in what she had just heard and more than a little amazed that she had been allowed to witness such a private moment.

"Well," sighed the Baron, "That's some story. And you say that this Michael chap didn't put in an appearance when you met up with Katerina?"

Felicity shook her head. "No, we talked as we rode but nothing I said seemed to have any effect on her, she seems completely under his sway…"

"Poor old Gregory." muttered Oliver, "I think we'll have to pay this Michael a visit tomorrow and settle his hash once and for all. But first thing's first. I suggest we get Mrs. Black up here and see just what she has to say for herself."

"Yes, that's just what James suggested you do," interrupted Margaret, who had been standing unobtrusively in the background.

Oliver and Felicity exchanged glances.

"It seems our dear housemaid has been discussing our situation with the good Reverend," said Oliver, good-naturedly.

Margaret felt her face flush with embarrassment as the Baron gave her a reassuring grin.

“Don’t look so worried,” he said, “James and I have already discussed the whole matter in some depth.”

At this revelation both Felicity and Margaret gaped, open mouthed at him in disbelief.

Pleased with the ladies reaction, he continued in the same relaxed manner; “After I have spoken to our erstwhile cook, I suggest we all pay the good Reverend Underwood a visit.” Striding over to the fireplace, he gave a tug on the embroidered bell pull summoning Edward his footman. Whom upon arrival, was instructed to fetch the cook. He returned some moments later to inform the Baron that Mrs. Black had left the Hall some hours earlier, and as yet, had not returned.

“The message that Meg had to deliver was for Mrs. Black to go to Michael before nightfall.” said Margaret.

“Yes, I wager that’s where she’s gone,” agreed the Baron. “By God, I’ll make her pay for her actions in this sorry affair, when she returns.” he added.

With no telephone installed at the rectory it was eventually decided that Margaret should go and fetch James, so that Sir Oliver may remain in the Hall, and await the return of Mrs. Black.

The Baron and his wife sat close together on the leather couch in the front parlor, a sliver tray set with tea things on an occasional table drawn up in front of them.

The atmosphere in the room was now heavy with emotion as their conversation slowly drifted towards the reasons why Felicity should have ever entertained the overtures of Katerina and her ungodly teachings and so on to their own feelings for each other, discussing the direction of their marriage and it’s future, if any. Sometimes joyfully, sometimes tearfully, she asking forgiveness for her actions of late, and he promising to be more understanding and to forget his more unusual excesses, explaining that he never appreciated how much he loved her until he felt he may be losing her.

Their intimate mood was suddenly shattered by Margaret bursting into the room without knocking, her cheeks wet with tears.

“Whatever’s happened?” asked Felicity, leaping to her feet and rushing over to the distraught maid.

“He’s missing. James is missing,” sobbed Margaret. “Mrs. Stanton, his housekeeper, says that he never returned from his walk. I told him about your meeting with Mrs. Christopher and he knew that Michael was aware of it. He would have tried to intervene. I just know something dreadful must have happened to him.”

Chapter 14

Rachael Swallow sat in her fireside chair catching up on her mending, the wicker needlework basket lay on the floor beside her. Noblet, his thick leather belt undone, lounged in an upholstered rocking chair on the other side of the fire, his stockinged feet resting on the polished brass fender framing the tiled hearth.

This was the time he liked best, one of his infrequent evenings at home, relaxing after a long day at his forge, his dear wife seated opposite, but still finding something to do, either going over some schoolwork, or continuing with her sampler, (which he secretly suspected she would never finish), or, as tonight, mending some item of worn clothing which was invariably his.

Noblet's eyes flickered open, suddenly alert, his practiced poacher's ear picking up the sound of the front gate opening and footsteps making their way along the brick path towards the cottage.

Opening the door, even before the knock came, he was surprised to see Baron Balmforth standing in the gloom of the front porch, even more surprised to see Lady Felicity and Margaret hovering behind him.

"Ah! Noblet. Might we have a quiet word with you?" asked the embarrassed Baron, not at all happy at having to ask a favor of the scoundrel that made so free with the game on the Balmforth Estate.

The blacksmith stood to one side, inviting the unexpected callers to enter, noticing as they passed that Margaret's eyes were red and swollen.

Rachael, with her instinctive eye for such things, was at Margaret's side in a moment, an arm around the housemaid's shoulder in a gesture of comfort.

"Well! How can I help you?" asked the blacksmith, self-consciously buckling his belt, and buttoning his collarless shirt.

Oliver quickly explained their fears for Reverend Underwood, and that upon Margaret's suggestion had sought his assistance, as he was undoubtedly the best qualified if it came to searching for James in Yarrow woods after dark.

Noblet sensed a sarcastic tone in the Baron's voice, but accepted it as no more than justified. Still listening to the Baron's account he pulled on heavy boots and warm coat.

Against their better judgement, the two men gave in to Margaret's insistence to accompany them; Felicity made no such offer and was happy to return to Sorrow hall as nothing on this earth would make her ever enter Yarrow woods at night.

Armed with oil lamps supplied by the blacksmith, the unlikely party set off, leaving Felicity at the entrance to the Hall and preceding with all haste towards the distant woodland and the fallen beech.

A little over an hour later they were hammering loudly on the front door of Doctor Ellis's home, only stopping when they saw a glow of light come from an upstairs window.

The doctor was completely unperturbed at being roused from his bed at such an unearthly hour. It seemed that babies invariably chose this quiet time to enter the world and if people were ill or in pain, many would often wait until the last possible moment before calling for his aid; but he was not at all prepared for the shock of finding Sir Oliver Balmforth and Noblet Swallow on his doorstep supporting the semi-conscious form of a battered and bleeding Reverend Underwood.

The two men half carried, half dragged James into the doctor's house and laid him carefully on the couch in the examination room, Margaret fussing in the background, a tear sodden handkerchief knotted in her small fist. They stood obediently to one side as the doctor proceeded to rush about, grabbing various instruments and swabs, as he simultaneously filled a kidney shaped, enamel bowl with warm water from the kettle, which was constantly kept warming on the range for just such a situation. He bent low over the unmoving Rector, keeping up a continual muttering as he gently cleaned away the filth and congealed blood from around James's partially severed ear. Easing away the dark crust, the blood began to flow brightly and clean, causing Margaret to turn away with a sob of anguish.

Upon hearing this unexpected female sound Doctor Ellis looked up, seemingly surprised to find he had additional company.

A sympathetic smile spread across his face as he tactfully assured Margaret that James was in good hands. He then turned back to his work and once again resumed his muttering.

"He has taken some vicious blows to the head." the doctor advised as his commentary on his examination continued unabated.

"There are some quite serious lesions, particularly around the area of his ear. See, look here." Doctor Ellis moved his hands away to show his audience the state of James's injury, and then puffed clouds of white antiseptic powder into the wounds from a rubber bottle before applying a dressing of thick layers of cotton wool, bound securely into place with what seemed like yards of bandages.

As Doctor Ellis continued his ministrations, he calmly explained that over the next few days, James's face, hands and shoulder would turn all kinds of colors, and that the blows he had received had caused contusions of the skin with a resulting rupturing of the blood vessels in the deeper layers of the tissue. The blood escaping the damaged vessels into the surrounding tissue would certainly bring about discoloration of the skin.

"How can you be so casual about it all?" burst out Margaret, "look at him! His face, his hands!"

The sound of her voice seemed to stir something in James. Opening his eyes, he looked at her and smiled painfully.

"I do believe the good reverend is back with us," declared Sir Oliver, grinning foolishly at Noblet.

James looked about him, his expression of bewilderment quickly hidden by Margaret's embrace.

After agreeing to leave James in the care of the doctor, the unlikely trio set off once more into the night, hurrying through the silent village, they soon reached the blacksmiths cottage.

"Thank you again for your help tonight, Noblet. I just don't know how we would ever have found him without you," repeated Margaret for the fourth time.

"Yes, I quite agree," admitted the Baron somewhat grudgingly, "We indeed owe you a debt of gratitude."

Noblet acknowledged the appreciation with a smile and a nod.

Entering his home he was surprised to find Rachael still waiting up for him. Experience had taught him that his wife was quite used to him returning home in the small hours and he would normally find her, soft and warm, buried beneath the bedclothes.

Hanging his hat and coat on the wooden peg behind the door, he leaned his weight against the wall whilst he removed his muddied boots.

His wife gave him a smile as she bustled past from the kitchen, on her way to his fireside chair, carrying a wooden tray containing a bowl of steaming broth and a whole fresh loaf, the bread knife sticking out of it. The food had obviously been prepared in advance and was just awaiting his return.

Noblet slumped heavily into his chair, Rachael placing the tray on his knees.

"This is something I could get used to," he told her with a grin, "But I've a feeling it has less to do with my well-being and more to do with female curiosity."

Rachael sat in her usual chair facing him as he unfolded his strange account of that night.

The Baron and the housemaid bade each other goodnight and went to their respective rooms, Margaret creeping quietly into bed so as not to disturb Meg. The Baron, not having that particular worry, walked wearily past Felicity's room, wondering for a fleeting moment if he dare knock and enter, but recently, that door had been closed to him in more ways than one. As he entered his room, he was somewhat surprised to find the heavy brocade curtains drawn wide, the first moments of dawn casting a soft glow in the half-light of the huge room. With eyes closing with fatigue he sat on the edge of the bed to remove his soiled, high leg boots. Sensing a movement behind him he leapt to his feet and spun around, his moment of fear turning to one of joy as he saw the familiar mound of his wife's body sleeping soundly in his bed, her naked shoulders showing above the single cotton sheet.

Chapter 15

Oliver and Felicity were awakened early the next morning by the persistent knocking of Owen, who informed them that Mrs. Black was nowhere to be found; apparently she had left the Hall the previous evening and had yet to return, going on to explain that young Lizzie had taken the cook her morning tea as usual and had found her bed unslept in.

The butler looked mortified at the shortcomings of his staff. "I really don't know how to apologize, my Lord, I have instructed Bridget to prepare your breakfast as usual, and I assure you that you will not be inconvenienced in any way by this unforgivable occurrence."

Owen bowed his way hurriedly from the presence of the Baron and his wife.

"Well, what do you make of all that?" asked Oliver, turning to Felicity as she climbed from the bed, wrapping a sheet around her nakedness.

She nodded thoughtfully, before answering, "Mrs. Black knew that we were sure to question her today. Do you think she's hiding? Or do you think that perhaps something may have happened to her?"

The question hung in the air, neither of them wishing to contemplate the idea of a second violent death.

At last Oliver broke the silence, "I think the first thing we should do is get in touch with the police and pay a visit to this madman living in the woods. I'll send Edward to find Constable Townsend, he can get on touch with somebody with seniority from Norwich who can accompany us." He stopped speaking suddenly and began to chew on a thumbnail as he tended to do when worrying about something. "On second thoughts, it may be better if we let Townsend handle this himself, after all, it is only a local matter. Best to keep the big-guns out of it. We better let Gregory know what's happening, he will want to come with us, he's got his own score to settle with this Michael character."

As Felicity turned to walk towards him she suddenly stopped in her tracks. Walking over to the window she peered out over the distant woodland, from the midst of which rose a dense cloud of grey smoke, drifting lazily into the morning sky.

Oliver, sensing something amiss, came to her side.

"Where exactly did you say this Michael lives?" he asked pointlessly, making a mental note of the location of the fire.

The air was thick with the heat and smoke of the almost spent fire. The light breeze disturbed the still glowing embers sending little clouds of grey cinders into the air. The circle of black ash was edged by a border of brown, scorched grass and undergrowth before giving way to the lush green of the untouched foliage of Yarrow woods. One or two of the closer trees had been scorched and now stood, smoke blackened and forlorn, shriveled leaves clinging to discolored branches, a stark contrast to their cousins around them.

P.C. Edwin Townsend kicked the still smoking remains of what had once been somebody's home, the billow of grey dust coating his boots and the bottoms of his blue serge trousers. "It's a miracle the whole forest wasn't set ablaze. Young Michael's going to be in plenty of trouble if he's behind this."

Oliver looked at the elderly policeman with ill-concealed dismay, "Good God man, haven't you understood a single word I've been telling you? This damn fire should be the least of your concerns. What about my stable girl, young Lucy and perhaps my cook? This madman seems to have developed an obsession with my staff and my family. Have you seen the condition he left the reverend in yesterday? Why, if we hadn't found him so quickly last night, Lord alone knows what would have become of him, it's only by the grace of God that he was left alive."

The Baron turned his back angrily on the cringing policeman and stamped off through the smoldering remains to join Gregory, who seemed to be gingerly pulling away hot stones from the base of the surviving stone chimney stack that stood incongruously upright among the mound of still hot and smoking rubble and charred timber surrounding the small kitchen range.

"What on earth are you doing?" asked Oliver sharply, still enraged by the ineptitude of what he considered an impotent, plodding village bobby.

Gregory didn't answer, but grabbing what appeared to be a blackened toasting fork started to probe into a squared off space between the old cast iron stove and the rough flint wall.

Oliver could see by his friend's expression that he had found something of interest.

With his free hand, Gregory gingerly reached into the gap and triumphantly brought forth a small tin box, distorted and discolored by the heat of the fire but never-the-less intact, the legend '*OXO*' still discernible against its familiar red background.

He moved quickly out of the circle of ashes to drop the still hot prize onto the singed grass surrounding the clearing.

“Hello, what’s that you’ve found, Sir,” asked the constable, trying to re-establish his authority, whilst still smarting from the onslaught of the Baron.

The heat had caused the box to buckle badly, but after some effort they managed to pry its lid open. Inside they found what appeared to be a small diary, obviously very old, the leather-bound cover cracked and broken by the intensity of the fire. The pages were dry and brittle, most by now curled and brown, but many in a surprisingly readable condition.

Gregory threw the box to one side and carefully turned the pages of his find, some, falling loose as the dry glue cracked in its spine.

“A diary,” he whispered, „it’s old Mrs. Heathcoat’s diary. She must have kept it hidden in that old niche behind the stove.”

“I’d better have that if you don’t mind, Sir,” bustled the constable, reaching out to take the evidence but it was snatched quickly away by Sir Oliver.

“Why would she want to keep it hidden from her own son?” he asked.

“I suggest we make ourselves comfortable and settle back for a good read,” suggested Gregory.

P.C. Townsend cleared his throat noisily. “Very good, Sir. I don’t see how that can do any harm, but I must insist that you hand the book over to me, after all, it may be vital evidence.”

He stood nose to nose with Oliver, not at all happy at defying his Lordship, but confident in the authority of his uniform.

“I really think you should,” agreed Gregory, unexpectedly coming to the constable’s aid.

With a shrug of his shoulders Oliver thrust the book angrily towards the policeman.

Sitting in the shade of the trees, the diary resting on his knees, P.C. Townsend flicked through the pages, skipping most of the first part which seemed mainly full of accounts of births that the midwife had attended, in and around Sorrow; many of the names familiar to him. He continued leafing through the diary, despairing of finding any mention of Michael. Slowly as he read, he felt a cold chill climb up inside his body. Gregory, seeing the color drain from the policeman’s face, took the diary from his loose grip. He proceeded to read out aloud from the pages that were still legible.

May 12th 1877. Called upon by Baron Balmforth’s footman.
It seems that one of the servant girls was in the final stages of a difficult labor.
On arrival I found a young girl of about sixteen or seventeen years of age in terrible pain. I knew it was going to be a bad birth.

After a protracted and very difficult labor she delivered of a male, slipping into a coma before holding the child.
The baby was severely disfigured. Having a malformed hand and arm. The jaw also seemed distorted, so to, his back. Upon seeing the child, Sir Rupert, (whom it transpired was the father), flew into a fearful rage, cursing both the unconscious mother and myself. To my total disbelief, he actually commanded me to take the child away and destroy it.
I have never seen such a look of hatred in a man's eyes. In fear for the child's life I picked it up and left the Hall, bringing the child to my home.

May 15th 1877. Have found out from one of the servants at the Hall that the young mother had died without regaining consciousness. It appears she was not just a servant, but more an unwilling plaything for Sir Rupert Balmforth, having been purchased like an animal from a passing gypsy family some time last year. May God forgive the likes of people who could treat a young girl in such a fashion.

May 21st 1877. What am I to do with this poor child? I could never return him to the Baron. Indeed, I don't think I could ever look on that evil man again without showing my revulsion. I was present at the birth of his son and heir, young Oliver, and at the death of his dear wife, Lady Emma. Perhaps it was this tragedy that drove the Baron to madness when history seemed to repeat itself with the birth of a second son? Nonetheless, I can never entrust the life of this dear infant to such an obvious madman.

May 29th 1877. I have no hope of finding a family to care for this poor disfigured child, not yet. Would it be possible to raise him in secret? I have managed to give him adequate nourishment and have taken delivery of a milking goat to that end but without his mother's milk, I fear for his health, no child seems to fare well without its beestings and he is sure to suffer for lack of it. I pray to God for guidance.

June 5th 1877. I have named this poor child Michael, after my church. I have spent much time searching for an answer. It seems I have become responsible for this young life.
It was the final readable entry in the battered diary.

Gregory and Oliver walked slowly back to Sorrow hall. Gregory some paces behind, following his old friend in silence, not knowing what to say. As they entered through the front door the Baron turned and faced him.

"He's my brother. He's actually my brother… that mad bastard! That freak is actually my brother!"

"Half-brother," corrected Gregory, surprised at just how well Oliver had taken the news. He wondered how he himself would have reacted in similar circumstances.

The moment was interrupted as Margaret came rushing across the hallway, Owen following in the rear.

"Your Lordship. Thank God you're back!" she exclaimed, "Mrs. Black returned soon after you left this morning…"

"Ah good," exclaimed Oliver.

"No. No! You don't understand," continued Margaret, "She's left again, and she's taken Lady Felicity with her."

Chapter 16

Felicity and Mrs. Black slipped furtively through the red brick archway leading from the grounds of Sorrow hall to the graveled pathway that curved its way between the ancient leaning headstones surrounding Saint Michael's church.

Felicity followed the elderly cook in silence, eyes glazed and staring straight ahead, her lips tenuously moving, forming soundless words, speaking to the man that possessed her, the man who, even now, was waiting for her.

The single thought focused in Felicity's mind was to be by his side, her consciousness aware only of the overwhelming desire to reach him. It seemed barely minutes earlier she had been in her room, a note pad in her hand trying to compose a shopping list for the coming Hunt Ball; trying to throw herself into the tedious business of organizing the party as was expected of the Baroness Balmforth, but try as she might to take her mind off the recent events, it kept wandering back to Michael and Lucy and Meg… and Michael… and Mrs. Black, and Michael… and her husband, out searching with the police. Looking for Michael… Michael! The thought of him seemed to engulf her, driving everything else from her mind. Dropping her note-pad and pen she had called his name, her voice rasping in her own ears. *"Felicity"* He was calling for her; waiting for her; she had to go to him. She *would* go to him.

Walking to the door she stood, hands at her sides, aware of nothing but the need to wait, to wait for someone to fetch her. Seconds passed, or was it hours? A single tap on the door was followed by Mrs. Black letting herself into the room. Walking straight past the entranced Baroness, she searched quickly in the dressing room and returned with a light lace shawl which she carefully draped over the shoulders of her mistress. Grinning into the Baroness's eyes she crooked a finger, bidding her to follow and lead Felicity through the hall past a horrified Meg on her way to the ballroom. Sensing her Ladyship's danger, she ran to find Margaret. Mrs. Black grabbed Felicity by the hand and pulled her stumbling along the passageway and quickly out through a side door.

He sat on the dusty wooden floor of the high belfry of Saint Michael's, his back against the wall, the sharp flints digging uncomfortably into his shoulder-blades. His eyes were closed, secure in the belief that nobody would think of looking for him here, of all places. Even to his simple mind it seemed ironic that the very place he most loathed was to become his sanctuary. He opened his eyes and looked around the small circular room.

A foot or so above his head, in two rows, hung the six bells of Saint Michael's, the very bells whose sounds had tormented him all his life, and now they were so close he could reach up with his hand and touch them, but in some strange way he feared the feel of the cold metal. Its dark patina of age giving them the appearance of stone, unadorned, save the legend; 'Mears of London, 1805.' The pulley wheels gave the supporting framework the impression of some radical new design for a hay wagon; the thought amused him, turning his mouth up at one side in the semblance of a grin.

He heard the church door open and the echo of footsteps on the stone floor far below, his smile grew even wider.

Time passed. The room grew darker and colder. Michael sat, arms around his knees, looking at the sleeping forms of Mrs. Black and Felicity. His mind full of plans for the future… their future. Contemplating the two women, his thoughts came back to the present, they were his to command, their minds were his to use as he would, their bodies too, were his to do with as he pleased. His thoughts drifted back to that momentous night with Lucy; the things he had done to her, the things he had made her do to him. The memory began to arouse him, he looked across at the sleeping women opposite him, the grey-haired hag, arms folded across her huge bosom, head back, mouth hanging open, snoring noisily. At her feet, curled in a ball, like a kitten in front of the fire, lay the tiny form of Lady Felicity Balmforth. Even asleep, her petite prettiness lit up the interior of the dim, cold, space.

Shuffling on his knees, Michael edged towards her until his thighs framed her face. Kneeling there he watched the gentle heaving of her small breasts and listened to the soft whisper of her rhythmic breathing. He had willed these women to come to him, it was his will alone that induced their slumber. He could will them to do anything… anything!

Unbuttoning the front of his trousers, he pulled his swelling erection from the knot of yellowing, woolen underwear. Cradling Felicity's head in his disfigured hand, he slowly stroked her soft face with his penis, his exposed gland leaving a moist trail across her cheek as it came to rest against her pink lips. Felicity's mouth involuntarily opened, allowing Michael's blood engorged penis to brush against her white teeth. The sexual pressure building up inside of him was too much, his body broke into a wracking orgasm, his hips thrusting with the spasm of his ejaculation, the flood of semen pouring into the sleeping woman's mouth.

Unaware of what was happening to her, she instinctively licked her lips and swallowed, moaning contentedly in her innocent sleep, the mere sight of Felicity's pink tongue cleaning the residue of his sperm from her mouth causing him to instantly regain his flagging erection. Leaning across her he started to remove her clothing.

Mrs. Black awoke with a start, her eyes taking in the grey outline of the great church bells suspended above her by the stout wooden framework. She closed her eyes again, trying to clear the cobwebs from her head. She had gone to Michael. He had sent her to fetch Lady Balmforth. They came to him at the church… *the church…* the ladder, high and steep. Opening her eyes she became aware for the first time of the two bodies locked together in front of her.

She watched enthralled as Michael's filth-encrusted buttocks rose and fell between her mistresses outstretched legs, his breath heavy with exertion, Felicity's frail body lying spread-eagled in the dust, head back. The moonlight dancing through the stone slits in the tower walls illuminated her face, her mouth was cast in a grimace of pleasure, but her eyes… Her eyes were filled with loathing, with terror.

Felicity knew what this madman was subjecting her to again and again, she hated and despised this disgusting creature on top of her. Yet, against all reason, she could feel her body reacting to his touch. Why couldn't she scream, bite, scratch? Her body refused to obey her. She felt her spine lift from the wooden floor, her back arching with physical ecstasy, …yet mental agony. She was now aware of the cook, finally awake, watching them. Felicity looked at her pleadingly, wanting to cry out to the old woman to help her.

Mrs. Black rose clumsily to her feet, stepping to one side to avoid the bells. Without taking her gaze off of the naked couple, she let her black, crocheted shawl fall to the floor, and then, in frenzy, began tearing at her garments, throwing them behind her in her haste to undress.

The sagging, aged body of the old woman looked grotesque in the moonlight, the thick-corded veins on her legs standing out obscenely against the patchy white of her flesh. A huge mat of iron-grey pubic hair covered the inside of her thighs and stretched almost to her navel.

She moved towards them, her breath coming short, huge breasts heaving with a lust that hadn't been satiated for so many years.

At her movement, Michael now became aware of Mrs. Black's presence, his mind, so full of the pleasure of the soft body of Felicity's beneath him, had momentarily drifted away from the control of the old woman, releasing her from her enforced slumber. Enraged by this interruption as he struggled to reach his third climax, he turned all his corrupt power to the mind of the old cook, now hovering expectantly over them. In that instant, as all his thoughts were concentrated elsewhere, Felicity felt her body react, at last she felt her muscles responding to the urgings of her brain.

Twisting with a grunt under his crushing weight she flung herself from beneath him. Michael's mind tried frantically to focus on the two conflicting emotions of the women; oblivious to her nakedness, Felicity made a desperate lunge towards the square of darkness in the floor leading to freedom.

As she sprang across the small room she felt his long nails bite painfully into her ankle. She plummeted forward, hands outstretched in the darkness, eyes still focused on the open trap door. Bracing herself for the impact, her head struck one of the bells a glancing blow, the force of which caused it to emit a slight hum, as she plunged into unconsciousness.

Michael stood, looking down at the prone form at his feet. Stepping over her he looked questioningly at Mrs. Black; the rising moon outside filling the bell tower with an eerie half-light, flickering with the shadows of bats crossing and re-crossing his line of vision.

He ran his eyes over the naked woman standing before him, proud, despite the obvious ravages time had made to her aging body. His feelings of revulsion started to dissipate, as he became aware of his erection, once more turgid and strong. Placing his hand on the cook's shoulders, he exerted the little pressure necessary to make her drop willingly to her knees in front of him.

Chapter 17

It had been many years since the library of Sorrow hall had been used for such a gathering. Not since the still unexplained disappearance of Sir Rupert Balmforth some years earlier had so many villagers, staff and police sat around the oak-paneled room.

By the unlit fireplace stood two police constables and a sergeant, hands inimitably held behind backs, ramrod straight and unspeaking, models of police efficiency; the pride of the Norfolk Constabulary.

Above them, in an ornate gilt frame hung the portrait of a handsome, if not quite beautiful woman, seated in a classic pose, long black hair draped over one shoulder, hands holding an open bible. Oliver looked up from behind his desk at the painting of his late mother and thought to himself, if Felicity is returned safely to him, he would have her done in oils and hung in the same place, his mother could be moved to join Sir Rupert's portrait in the ballroom.

In front of the high window stood Owen at the head of his staff who were seated on high-backed chairs brought in from the dining room. Next to him stood an empty seat awaiting Edward, who was busy at that moment pouring drinks for some of the company.

Facing the fireplace, on the green leather Chesterfield couch, feeling uncomfortable and thoroughly ill at ease sat Noblet Swallow and old Tom Morton, both somewhat overawed by the luxurious surroundings. The thick pile, Turkish-red carpet, the works of art in heavy gilt frames and walls lined with hand stitched leather-bound books, the intricately tooled calf-skin volumes probably worth far more then both men would earn in their entire lives.

"Do you think anybody ever reads 'em?" whispered the farmer to Noblet with a smirk.

Perched on the arm of the couch sat Gregory Christopher, legs crossed, brandy in hand, appearing perfectly relaxed in this familiar room, but inside he felt very uneasy, conscious of his wife's involvement and her steadfast refusal to attend this gathering despite a definite summons from a police Inspector.

Next to the desk, in Oliver's favorite winged armchair, slumped the heavily sedated body of the Reverend James Underwood, a huge pad of gauze covering his ravaged ear, much of his face and both hands swathed in bandages. At his side stood the motherly presence of Doctor Ellis, fussing over his patient who had insisted on attending this meeting against the doctor's better judgement.

By the open door, along with Constable Townsend, stood the man who had initiated this gathering.

Inspector Basil Talbot watched the assembled group through gold-rimmed spectacles, his clean-shaven, rather gaunt face very pale, even lifeless, but his dark eyes were alert behind the lenses; ever moving, ever searching, missing nothing. Talbot was a painfully thin man, standing six foot two inches in his stockinged feet, his lean frame making him appear even taller. Amongst his fellow officers, he was disrespectfully known as 'Lofty,' but of course never to his face. Dressed in somber grey, and with the ever-present red carnation in his lapel he did not, on first meeting, command the immediate deference that a policeman of his rank was due, but all who knew him had to admit that he certainly produced positive results. In fact, he held one of the highest arrest records on the force.

Joining the Constabulary as a young man of farming stock, his rise through the ranks had been steady, if not spectacular, finally reaching the exalted heights of Inspector. He was a quietly spoken, taciturn individual but also a somewhat self-opinionated man. He had never married and lived alone in three rooms above a Haberdashers' alongside the cattle market in the center of Norwich city, a short walk from its famous Cathedral.

After speaking to the Baron at some length, the Inspector had suggested bringing together anybody remotely involved in the case. Sir Oliver had immediately volunteered to put the library at his disposal.

Rising from his seat behind the massive walnut desk, Sir Oliver held up a hand for silence, allowing a moment for everyone to finish clearing their throats and settle down.

"Let me begin by firstly thanking you all for coming here at such short notice. Most of you are aware of the purpose of this meeting and I trust that some good will come of it. My only concern at the moment is for the safe return of my dear wife, Felicity." The Baron cast his eyes down, as he mentioned her name, avoiding the looks of sympathy from the others.

"Now you all know Constable Townsend, here," (The policeman nodded acknowledgement), "but let me introduce Inspector Talbot, who has been sent here from Norwich to help get to the bottom of all this."

Inspector Talbot walked over and closed the library door, clearing his throat, politely.

"Thank you very much, m'Lord, and let me say how grateful I am for the use of your library. Constable Townsend and myself have been going over everything we know about this case, but there are still many questions that need to be answered. I will be speaking to some of you individually over the next few days, but because of the urgency of the situation I have called you all together here today." He paused, taking a dog-eared notebook from his inside pocket. "Now, it appears that a large part of this mystery seems to be hinging on a certain," he glanced at the notebook, "A Mrs. Victoria Black, whom I understand is employed as a cook here."

Lizzie and Bridget suppressed giggles at the revelation that the horrid Mrs. Black should have the same name as the late Queen.

"I have been doing some checking over our past records and I find that in the last few years there have occurred other deaths or disappearances, in what I can only describe as suspicious circumstances. Indeed, I am somewhat amazed with how quickly these events seem to have been resolved."

Talbot cast a critical eye at the constable, his action causing all present to do likewise. Edwin Townsend opened his mouth as if to speak, but thinking better of it simply looked down, self-consciously fingering the policeman's helmet held in the crook of his arm in the prescribed manner.

When the Inspector was sure that he once more had the full attention of the room, he continued, "As you are all no doubt aware, I refer to the violent death of," he glanced once more at his pocket book, "One Mrs. Elsie Patricia Heathcoat, midwife of the parish, and also the still unexplained disappearance of Sir Rupert Balmforth."

Oliver looked up at the mention of his father's name. "Surely you don't think there is any connection between this business and my late father?" he asked.

"May I ask why you refer to him as your late father, m'Lord?" responded the Inspector, "I was under the impression that Sir Rupert's body was never found, nor indeed was there any sign of foul play."

The Baron looked incredulously at the policeman, completely unaccustomed to being spoken to in such an authoritative manner, particularly in his own home.

"Just what is it you're trying to infer, Inspector?"

Without replying, he turned his back on the stunned Baron, the inspector now addressing the two men seated on the couch.

"Mister Noblet Swallow and Mister Thomas Morton," once more referring to his pocket book, "I understand that you were both present at the death of Lucille Burdett, Baron Balmforth's stable-girl, or should I say, groom? Is that correct?"

Both men nodded in agreement.

"Have either of you anything more to add to the statements that you have already given to Constable Townsend?"

Tom Morton shook his head. Noblet stared straight ahead obviously considering the questions.

"And you, Mister Swallow?" prompted the Inspector.

All eyes were now on the blacksmith.

Leaning forward, elbows on knees, Noblet once more related his story of Lucy's death, but now included the fact that he had heard two people running through the woods.

"It seems plain to me that he was chasing Lucy, and when she ran to Tom and myself for help, he watched from the trees as she ran under Tom's horses."

"That remains to be seen, Mister Swallow," answered the policeman, "When you say 'He' I take it you are referring to this 'Michael' who appears to be our prime suspect?"

"Our only suspect, surely?" interrupted Oliver.

"That too, remains to be seen. I'm afraid we have to deal with facts, your Lordship, not conjecture."

The animosity now flowing between the Baron and the policeman was self-evident. Everyone in the room remained silent, waiting for one of them to speak.

Inspector Talbot appeared to break first. Turning to Tom Morton, he asked, "Have you any explanation for the behavior of your horses on that day?"

"Well, Sir." responded the old farmer, "I've worked horses since I was a lad of twelve years old and I've never seen anything like it. Something terrified those animals and believe me, that young lady didn't run under their hooves. I know my horses and they wouldn't hurt a fly… something made those horses turn and trample her, but who… or what it was, God only knows."

At this, conversation broke out amongst the assembled company. All had their own theories as to what had happened that day.

Ignoring the disturbance, Inspector Talbot spoke to the Reverend for the first time. "I would like to ask you just one question for now, your Reverence, could you positively identify your attacker as being this Michael?"

James nodded slowly. "Without a doubt, Inspector."

"Even though, by your own admission you had never previously met him or even seen him at a distance?"

"I have had him described to me on numerous occasions." responded James, "Believe me when I say that his appearance is not one that you could easily confuse with any other, I recognized him the instant I observed him spying on Mrs. Christopher and Lady Balmforth and I think his reaction to being disturbed is proof enough as to his identity and his violent state of mind, don't you Inspector?"

Talbot said nothing, but looked at the Reverend for a long moment, before turning to speak to Gregory.

"I have noticed that Mrs. Christopher hasn't been able to join us Sir. May I ask you why?"

Gregory considered making some excuse of his wife's absence, but realizing the futility of such an act simply replied by saying, "I really think you'd best ask her that question yourself, Inspector."

Oliver Balmforth's voice rose above the others. "You all seem to have forgotten why we're here. My wife has been kidnapped. There's some mad bastard out there on the loose doing, God knows what to her and nobody seem to give a damn."

Moving from behind his desk he approached the Inspector, looked challengingly into the policeman's eyes and asked slowly, "What I would like to know is, when are you actually going to start doing your job and set about finding her?"

Before the policeman could respond there came a sharp knock on the library door. Talbot himself turned and opened it, speaking in hushed tones with the uniformed constable outside.

Turning back to the Baron he said, "I assure you, m'Lord, we are doing all we can to find your wife. Now, I'm afraid something important has come up and I really must bid you all good day for now. I will need to speak to some of you in more detail, so please try and make yourself available over the next few days."

Nodding to the whole room he thanked them for their time, and crooked a finger at P.C. Townsend as he left with his fellow officers.

James waited until all the servants had left the library, giving Margaret a wink as she passed in from of him. Bidding goodbye to Noblet Swallow and Tom Morton, he turned to Doctor Ellis, and informed him that he had some private business with Sir Oliver and Mr. Gregory. The doctor, happy not to get involved, nodded and said he would call by the Rectory tomorrow to change James's dressing. Shaking the Baron's hand, he departed, obviously pleased to be leaving.

Oliver poured three large brandies from the decanter on the long sideboard. Thinking abstractly that the level seemed to have dropped alarmingly over the last few days.

"Well Reverend, what's on your mind? he asked.

James accepted the proffered drink gratefully, downing half in one satisfying swallow; the fiery glow spreading upwards from his stomach helping to clear his somewhat drugged senses.

"Correct me if I'm wrong but from what I can gather," began the reverend, "It seems that your stable-girl, your cook, Lady Balmforth and…" He looked up at Gregory. "Katerina, seemed to have formed some sort of… " he paused, searching for the right words… "Some sort of sisterhood intent on a kind of quest to seek out… " again he hesitated, "To seek out… evil? Perhaps to find adventure, perhaps for a much deeper reason, who can say? But it seems they may have finally found it in this Michael fellow… or maybe he found them, we simply don't know? What's seems obvious though is that they are now in over their heads. Lady Balmforth undoubtedly realized the danger and as we now know, did in fact try to warn Katerina."

Oliver interrupted, "What you seem to be saying, James, is that you think that they have made some sort of… 'Pact with the Devil.'"

James pondered for a moment and considered his reply carefully before speaking.

"Well, m'Lord, that may be putting it a bit theatrically, but basically I believe you may be on the right lines."

Letting his response sink in, he continued, "It's too late for poor Lucy and it seems almost certain that Mrs. Black is completely under his sway. Now, may I suggest that our best hope of finding Lady Felicity is with the assistance of Katerina?"

"Yes, of course," agreed Oliver, "She must know more than any of us about the whole sorry business… Katerina will help us, won't she Gregory?"

Gregory finished his brandy, throwing it back with a jerk and poured himself another, filling the bulbous glass three quarter's full, still staring abstractly into the depths of the red gold liquid. His voice shook as he answered his friend.

"I'm afraid I really don't think she will help you in the slightest."

Oliver gazed at Gregory in astonishment, unsure at first if he had heard correctly.

"What in God's name do you mean, 'She won't help us?" he shouted, his face red with confused rage, spittle flying from his mouth. Gregory looked from Oliver to James but remained silent.

With an effort Oliver calmed himself, understanding that Gregory now had little or no control over Katerina's actions. In a gentler tone he continued, "But she simply has to help us… you have to damn well make her help us, she's your wife for Christ's sake!" His voice once more growing louder until finally he was shouting with rage.

Gregory was overcome with shame. He loved his wife dearly, but how much longer could he keep lying to himself about her?

"She's at home. Right now, up in the tower," he replied. "She refused to come here today and speak to the police. She just sits in that filthy room of hers, talking to herself." Gregory felt the tears swelling in his eyes; turning his back to the two men he sipped at his drink.

James rose awkwardly from the deep chair still obviously in pain and paced across the thick red carpet, putting a comforting hand on Gregory's shoulder as he spoke.

"When I had the honor of joining Katerina and yourself in matrimony, I knew then that you had a good, full life ahead of you both, and nothing has happened to alter my opinion of that. Her love for you was evident to everybody present that day and I simply refuse to believe so much has changed in so short a time."

Gregory turned suddenly, tears now streaming openly down his face, "James… I… " he could say no more.

The Reverend took the soldier's wet face in his two bandaged hands.

"Gregory, you must believe in yourself. When we first met, on the other side of the world, the name of Gregory Christopher was synonymous with bravery, with leadership, men were happy to follow you into battle no matter what the cost to themselves? Does that sound like the kind of man who would be defeated by circumstances that not only threaten to destroy his friends but are also beginning to tear at the very fabric of your love for your wife. Are you honestly telling me that you are prepared to sacrifice everything because of fear? You must trust in that love that brought you both together. You can bring her back, I just know it… let us three go and talk to her; this very minute, we can explain to her that Felicity is in great danger. Let us go now. I promise we won't pressure her, but I feel sure that with God's help, she will make the right decision. There is so much good in her I simply cannot accept that it's buried so completely."

Gregory was let into his home by Becky, the housemaid, who bobbed respectively, as the three men walked through to the drawing room.

"Where is my wife," Gregory asked her.

"I believe she's up in the tower, Sir. Would you like me to fetch her?"

"No. You attend to my guests. I'll fetch her myself."

He gave Oliver and James a look of determined resignation.

"Wish me luck, gentlemen, wish me luck," he said.

He walked slowly up the main staircase trying desperately to think of the best way to handle the imminent confrontation. As he stooped through the small arched doorway that led up the dismal spiral steps of the tower, he felt a cold shiver run up his spine; his wet palms were sticky on the wooden handrail.

This is ridiculous. He thought, how can I be so nervous about speaking to my own wife? He forced himself to recall James's recent speech, reminding himself that the bit about his bravery and his leadership were both true.

At the highest point of the old house he stood outside the tiny room, at a loss as to the best approach to take with Katerina. His breathing, heavy with the exertion of his climb, sounded loudly in the confines of the small landing. He looked long and hard at the thick, oak, paneled door separating himself from his wife, a dull, flickering light showed through the wide gap beneath it. Reflecting off the highly polished toecaps of his leather boots.

Without knocking, Gregory turned the door handle and tried to enter, not surprised to find it locked.

"Katerina?" he called, quietly, "can I speak to you… It's very important that we talk."

Her voice came back clearly through the heavy woodwork.

"Please don't disturb me, we have nothing to talk about. Now just go, and leave me in peace!"

With a sigh of defeat Gregory turned back towards the stairs, stopping after a single pace. Images of his dear wife flew through his memory. Her laughter on their long honeymoon voyage back from Africa, the joy they gave each other in their lovemaking.

What was wrong with him? There he was, a decorated officer in his majesty's forces. What kind of a coward had he become? How could he give in so easily to this evil that was stealing his wife from him? Once more he thought of James's words.

Turning on his heels he charged the sturdy door, the pain of the impact shooting agonizingly through his shoulder as the door flew back on its hinges, the ancient lock hurling across the room, torn from the wooden frame.

Katerina was on her feet in an instant, her fingers held like claws, lips drawn back over white teeth, her eyes wide, measuring inches. She moved slowly, a cat-like hiss coming from her throat as she stalked her husband.

Gregory was instantly reminded of the leopard he had once faced on a hunting trip in Africa.

"Katerina." He shouted, "What in God's name is wrong with you? Can't you see what's happening to you… to us? You've got to fight off this evil that's got a hold on you… Katerina! Please listen to me…"

As they faced each other, circling in the small space he braced himself for her pounce.

Slowly Katerina's face broke into a malicious grin, the smile in turn becoming a low throaty chuckle, the pitch of her laughter grew higher and higher until becoming a shrill scream echoing deafeningly in the confines of the tiny room.

Gregory's hands went instinctively to his ears, trying to shut out the terrible sound. In that moment she sprang, hurling herself at him, the force of their bodies colliding threw Gregory back against the lead-glazed stained glass window, his breath knocked from him.

Her small hands encircled his throat; their eyes inches apart, hers no longer the eyes of a beautiful young woman, but the eyes of some mythical beast; the whites had turned to black, the pupils burning like red balls of flame. Gregory tried to pull her hands apart, but the strength in those slender fingers was far superior to any normal person, man or woman. He felt himself being bodily lifted from the ground, her nails piercing the flesh of his throat. His lungs screamed for air. His vision grew dull. Even in the realization that the person he loved most in the world was slowly choking the life from him, he still could not bring himself to strike his wife, his hands fell away from hers, all strength abandoning him. His bowels, no longer under control, opened, spilling the waste from his body; he, incredibly, at the point of confronting death still felt a surge of embarrassment as the fetid smell reached him.

Without warning the door, which had been swinging, half open, was hurled back. Oliver leapt into the room, scattering the flaming black candles still burning on the floor. His forearm locked around Katerina's neck, forcing her to drop her husband in a gasping heap at their feet.

Turning her attention to the Baron, she wrenched herself free with ease, her unexpected strength catching him completely by surprise. Her left hand shot out, grabbing Oliver by his thick dark hair; her other hand forming a fist which she drove mercilessly into his face, the unexpected force of the blow sending him sprawling amongst the pools of black wax and rolling candles.

Desperately gulping lungfuls of precious air, Gregory slowly regained his feet, legs still weak and trembling, he leaned back heavily against the stained glass window behind him, feeling the small, diamond-shaped panes of colored glass move under his weight, the thin lead glazing bars beginning to sag.

Gregory struggled forward to get his weight off of the fragile window, holding his blood-soaked throat. Katerina, turning her attention from the dazed Baron, let out another scream and hurled herself once more at her husband. In that precise instant, whether out of a sense of self-preservation, or through his weakened legs simply giving way, Gregory plunged headlong to the floor.

Katerina was already in mid-flight through the air above him, her expression of malevolence turning to one of horror as she tried to stop herself crashing into the already weakened lead-light, the force of her pounce sending her through the window, tearing the thin strips of aged lead like a lace curtain. Her scream of rage becoming one of terror as she plunged earthwards in a shower of green, red and blue colored glass.

Gregory, stunned and bewildered, staggered to his feet once more, staring in open-mouthed disbelief at the gaping hole in the window. Small diamonds of colored glass still continued to crack and fall from their distorted lead mountings.

Supporting his weight against the wall, Gregory slowly sank back to the floor, his mouth silently forming his wife's name, his body numb with shock at the thought of her death.

Shaking his head to clear it, Oliver got heavily to his feet and leaned gingerly through the shattered window. Far below he could see the body of Katerina, bent double, slumped grotesquely face downwards over the cast iron railings surrounding the house, the ornate spear points impaled deeply into her stomach.

Ignoring Gregory, he ran down the winding stairs, taking the steps three at a time, a hand against his face trying to stem the flow of blood from his smashed nose. He reached Katerina at the same moment as James, the two men looked at the corpse in disbelief, her beautiful body broken so obscenely over the high black railings.

"We had better get her off before Gregory sees her," said James, going through the gate to lift her by the shoulders.

Oliver, blood still streaming from his nose, slid his arms under her hips in support.

Carefully, they manhandled the dead woman off of the cast iron spikes, carrying her past the horrified gaze of the housemaid.

Taking her into the drawing room, they laid her on the gold velvet chaise-lounge in front of the window.

Becky, trembling uncontrollably, stood gaping in the doorway staring down at her mistress, lying unmoving, one hand sprawled on the floor. Oliver ordered her to fetch a sheet to cover the corpse, repeating himself loudly as the maid stood transfixed in shock. Pulling herself from the spell she hurried to the linen closet.

"Your Lordship, would you come over here a moment, please?"

James's voice held a slight tremor.

Joining the Reverend the Baron looked down at the body of his best friends young wife. James lightly tugged at Katerina's torn clothing revealing the deep, vicious puncture marks in her white flesh; the dark wounds, round and vivid scarlet. Oliver and James looked incredulously at each other, the man of

God tightly gripping the crucifix that hung about his neck. Despite the horrific gaping holes, all but scything the woman in two, there was not a single drop of blood; her torn white bodice, soiled with dirt and rust held not a speck of carmine.

As they stared in stunned bewilderment, the holes in her flesh appeared to slowly pull themselves closed, to shrink. The shattered time beneath her torn flesh seemed to meld together… The tattered edges of her flesh growing and repairing itself before their stunned gaze. The lethal wounds appeared to go through months of healing in a matter of moments.

"Oh, my dear God!" Gregory's voice startled the two men as he stood in the doorway supported by Becky, the white sheet lying forgotten on the floor.

Four bewildered onlookers watched, spellbound, as Katerina's eyes flickered open. She looked around the room unsure for a moment of her surroundings.

Swinging her legs with great effort down to the floor she heaved herself upright, pulling her clothes straight, smiling up at her stunned husband.

"Please help me, darling. I feel so weak. We must hurry if we are to find Felicity."

Chapter 18

The bowler hatted Inspector Talbot joined the throng of villagers moving in a steady flow towards the hallowed portals of Saint Michael's church, acutely aware of the furtive glances in his direction.

As he moved among the Sunday morning church goers he picked up snippets of overheard conversation which in almost every case concerned the goings on up at the Hall and the appearance of a 'Special policeman' from Norwich, an Inspector, no less.

Striding on through the congregation he noticed a small group of people standing to one side of the arched entrance, to his surprise he recognized the profile of Sir Oliver Balmforth. Joining them he noted that he had met the previous day almost all of those present. He nodded a greeting to the domestic staff of the Hall before addressing Oliver and Gregory, "Good morning your Lordship… Mister Christopher, I'm glad to see you've taken time off from your search to come to church."

Oliver gave him a look of disgust. "We haven't taken time off, as you choose to put it. We happen to be here this morning because we believe it may help us to locate my wife."

Inspector Talbot replied, a sarcastic edge to his voice, "I'm afraid I don't share your confidence in the power of prayer myself. I've learnt over the years that man has to depend on himself to solve his own problems."

Gregory, sensing the animosity between the two men stepped hurriedly between them.

"Inspector Talbot, I don't believe you've met my good lady wife."

The policeman looked into a pair of sparkling eyes, Katerina's pretty face seemed to glow amongst the somber gathering.

"I'm very pleased to meet you at last Mrs. Christopher," he said, bowing gallantly, "I'm sorry you were unable to attend our impromptu gathering yesterday."

Katerina thrust out her lower lip in a childlike pout, "Yes Inspector, I'm very sorry about that, but I assure you I'm now completely at your disposal."

The thought of having this beautiful woman 'at his disposal' left him momentarily stuck for words. Suddenly aware of Gregory's knowing glare, he felt his face redden with embarrassment.

The bells above began to ring, the people around him taking it as a signal to enter the church. Pleased with the interruption, Talbot turned to join the queue filing into the cool of Saint Michael's, smiling a greeting to the still bandaged reverend as he passed.

Inside, the church felt damp, the yellowing, lime-washed walls of the ancient building flaking and in need of attention. The hushed voices and shuffling footsteps of the people echoed hollowly under the high, hammer beamed ceiling.

The Inspector settled himself at the rear. Turning to catch a glimpse of the 'interesting' Mrs. Christopher, he was somewhat amazed to see Edwin Townsend and Noblet Swallow among the band of bell ringers, the constable dressed in his civilian suit heartily tugging on the red and white 'sally' of the bell rope hanging from the tower above. Each ringer engrossed in the challenge of making the mighty bells sing their melancholy song.

Sir Oliver Balmforth sat in his usual pew, the same seat generations of Balmforths had used before him. Conscious of the absence of his wife, he glanced at the empty space beside him. He was reminded of his late father, so long before, seated next to that same empty spot. Having never remarried, the seat had remained vacant until Felicity had become Lady Balmforth but now once more, it was unoccupied. Oliver felt the tears starting behind his eyes. Trying to shake off his thoughts, he leaned forward to the next pew, where Gregory and Katerina were seated.

"Do you really think coming here today is going to help?" he asked, the doubt evident in his voice.

Katerina turned to the Baron noting his eyes still shining with tears.

"Oliver," she began in a whisper, "I know that you've never approved of me and that you blame me for all that's happened, not without some justification, I'm forced to admit, but you must understand, we are all pawns, Felicity, myself, Lucy, Mrs. Black, even Michael and perhaps even you, this whole thing began long before I ever came here, if it hadn't been me then somebody else would have helped her find him."

Oliver looked from her to Gregory, feeling more and more confused, "What do you mean help her to find him, surely you mean it was he who found her?"

"No! The four of us sought out Michael. We wanted a spiritual leader, someone to open our lives, to give us some purpose," Katerina looked embarrassed at her seeming naivety. "I admit now that there was some unknown force driving me on, controlling my actions as indeed it was controlling Mrs. Blacks, but I think Felicity herself was the real target of this force and I, being more receptive, was merely used to lure her into Michael's sphere of power. I don't honestly believe that even he is in full control of his actions."

"Poppycock!" burst out Oliver. "He's a cold-blooded killer and you're trying to make excuses for him." Gregory leapt to his wife's defense. "But he never actually killed Lucy, she ran under those horses and we don't even know for sure that he has Felicity, why… she could be with Mrs. Black somewhere."

Oliver looked at his friend in amazement. "I don't believe what I'm hearing, are you trying to tell me that you think this Michael is just an innocent bystander. What about Mrs. Heathcoat, you don't honestly believe that was an accident do you, and what about my… "

Oliver stopped short, aware that his voice had risen above a whisper. Looking around he saw all eyes on him; at the rear of the church Inspector Talbot sat with a sly smile on his face. Gregory turned to look at his ashen-faced friend. "What about your what? Oliver, what was it you were going to say?"

Katerina came to his aid. "Leave him alone darling." Reaching back she put her hand on Oliver's. "You must trust me Oliver, don't ask me how I know this is the right thing to do, because I have no answer for you, all I can say is that we must be in church this morning. Someone or something will help us find Felicity, of that I am perfectly sure."

The bells fell silent, and the ringers joined the congregation. Edwin Townsend giving the Inspector a nod of recognition as he joined him in the rear pew, Noblet Swallow sliding into the space next to Rachael, seated behind the staff of Sorrow hall, giving Margaret's shoulder a friendly squeeze as he did so.

James painfully mounted the four steps into the pulpit, feeling conscious of his bandaged face and hands.

Bidding the assembled congregation good morning, he instructed them to open their hymn books to Hymn number 155. Clearing his throat he began to sing.

'Be thou my guardian and my guide,
And heal me when I call; let not my slipp'ry footsteps slide,
And hold me lest I fall'.

Starting hesitantly the voices gradually swelled with increased confidence, the ancient building filling with song.

'The world, the flesh, and Satan dwell
Around the path I tread;
O save me from the snares of hell,
Thou quick'ner of the dead'.

High above, in the dusty bell tower the two women listened to the people below, the sound seeming to fill the small circular room.

'And if I tempted am to sin,
And outward things are strong,
Do thou, O Lord, keep watch within,
And save my soul from wrong'.

Mrs. Black sat, knees apart on the floor, biting at a hanging nail, her back to the bound and gagged Baroness. Felicity lay in a ball almost under the seven hundred-weight tenor bell, her wrists and ankles tied viciously tight with coarse Hessian rope, every movement causing agony where the flesh had been worn raw leaving ugly swollen welts staining the pale rope with lymph. In her mouth was forced a filthy piece of material held in place by a strip of her own petticoat, the taste of vermin filling her senses, the smell of her own urine on the floor about her making her nauseous. Around her neck, Michael had buckled his leather belt and tied it short around the base of the frame supporting the six bells, almost as one might tether a recalcitrant dog.

Laying there in the filth and the bat excrement she listened to the words of the hymn.

The words seemed strangely relevant, doubtless James had spent a long time with his selection of hymns; she found the thought strangely comforting.

'Still let me ever watch and pray,
And feel that I am frail;
That if the tempter cross my way,
Yet he may not prevail.'

She could clearly pick out the voices of people she recognized, undoubtedly Noblet Swallow, singing lustily. And of course Edwin Townsend's booming baritone? She concentrated hard, wondering if her husband was among the congregation, her hearing straining for the sound of his voice. Her head was throbbing violently after the deafening onslaught of the bells being rung. The largest almost above her head, Mrs. Black, being able to cover her ears, had watched unconcerned as Felicity had twisted and writhed against the mighty boom of the bells, trying with all her strength to free herself from the bonds cutting into her flesh so painfully.

She looked into the cooks eyes trying to detect a hint of compassion but found only a cold look of spite. *What had she ever done to this woman to make her treat her so?*

The singing stopped, the soft voice of the Reverend Underwood drifted up to the two women, they heard him lead the congregation in a prayer for the safety of Lady Felicity Balmforth.

Mrs. Black laughed quietly to herself, "You'll need more than their prayers to help you," she said maliciously. But Felicity wasn't listening. At floor level, supporting the timber framework above her, she had discovered a heavy wrought iron bracket. It's exposed edge worn rough with age. Forcing her ankles against the metal, she began to saw agonizingly up and down, the rope catching and fraying on the rusty metal.

After the prayers James revealed what most knew anyway, that the Norwich police had sent an Inspector to head the search for the missing Baroness, and he invited Inspector Talbot to stand up the for benefit of the villagers. On hearing this, Mrs. Black shuffled on her knees to the open trap in the floor, peering down cautiously to try and catch a glimpse of this new enemy.

Felicity, desperate to make good use of the moments that Mrs. Black had her attention elsewhere, gave a supreme effort; biting back the searing pain she forced the rope at her ankles again and again along the sharp edge of the iron bracket. At last, almost at the point of despair she felt the bonds give way, the pain shooting up her legs as the ropes clung to the congealed blood of her wounds, tugging viciously at the raw flesh.

Whatever sense alerted Mrs. Black at that moment, she didn't know, but as Felicity looked up the old cook was already turning from the trap door. Still on one knee she made a grab at Felicity's freed ankles, the young Baroness, in a surge of anger, forced all her remaining strength into the kick, she knew instinctively that she was near to collapse, she had but one chance. As their eyes met her right foot lashed out catching the old woman high on the temple. Mrs. Black staggered, putting a hand down to steady herself, but she felt only empty space as she overbalanced and tumbled headlong through the square opening.

The church reverberated with the scream of the falling woman as she plummeted downwards. Out of instinct, making a despairing grab at one of the bell ropes, the momentum of her decent causing the stout rope to jerk out a dull note above Felicity's head.

The church was in uproar, women screaming and trying to cover children's eyes. Men standing protectively over their families.

Inspector Talbot was the first there, removing his coat and spreading it over the dead woman.

James's voice called out, trying to calm the standing congregation, trying to hurry them outside. Looking up, he saw the Inspector disappearing through the trap door into the belfry, P.C. Townsend and Oliver Balmforth scurrying up the ladder behind him.

Chapter 19

Inspector Talbot followed the two uniformed policemen around the edge of the field of barley, his highly polished brogues sinking into the newly planted soil.

"If I've ruined my shoes on another wild goose chase you two are going to suffer," he shouted at their backs.

As they drew close to the furthest corner of the large field he could vaguely discern the outline of what appeared to be a small decrepit shed, its rotted, moss-covered timbers overgrown with ivy and brambles, and buried so far into the quickthorn hedgerow as to almost appear part of it.

Talbot's pulse began to quicken with the hunter's thrill of the chase. After nearly three weeks of fruitless searching in which his men had questioned hundreds of people, in a dozen villages, his instinct was finally telling him that he may have finally hit the jackpot.

The two constables stood to one side of the ramshackle building, which on closer examination turned out to be a long-abandoned shepherd's hut, it's four cast-iron wheels completely engulfed in the tussocky wild grass of the headland.

Talbot grabbed the rusty catch and pulled, letting out a curse as the sagging, rain sodden door crashed painfully onto his foot. Too late, he had discovered the absence of the lower hinge.

Ignoring the two smirking constables, he stepped into the damp interior, the air thick with the cloying smell of decaying wood, the rotten floor sagging under his weight. Along one side was piled a thick pad of dry bracken on top of which lay a crumpled heap of threadbare blankets. Stacked in the corner, next to a neatly folded 'long net' lay a pile of rusting gin traps and wire snares. Gaping holes in the wooden walls were plugged with old rags or bracken. Long strands of thorny briers grew through the woodwork and curled up the inside of the crumbling walls. Suspended on string from the ceiling, beside a soot-blackened oil lamp, hung three pheasants and a small paunched rabbit, its darkening pink flesh spotted with yellow clusters of flies eggs.

As the Inspector turned he kicked a battered, galvanized pail. He looked down with distaste at the greasy water within, containing an unwashed cook pot, tin plate and chipped enamel half pint mug.

One of the constables stuck his head inside, his nose wrinkling with the smell.

"Sir? P.C. Townsend is coming." Gratefully stepping back into the sunlight, the inspector watched the huge policeman hurrying towards them, his great loping strides carelessly flattening the young barley in his wake. Red faced and breathless he saluted the senior officer smartly.

"I think you had best come along, Sir. We've made quite a discovery back at the scene of the fire."

Arriving at the fire-blackened clearing that had once been Michael's cottage, the Inspector was greeted with a nod by his sergeant who led him over to a heap of freshly dug soil close to the Wood's edge, a spade sticking from the top of the mound.

Looking into the shallow hole, Talbot winced with shock at the sight of a partially mummified corpse; the decomposed flesh, shrunken and taught, giving it the impression of grey leather. Whether by some quirk of nature or perhaps by the chemical composition of the peaty soil, the hair was still clinging to the withered flesh. Standing out grotesquely at the genitals and upon the scalp sprung a thick plumage of what had once been flowing white hair. Between the hair-line and the earth-filled eye sockets ran a wide fracture, all but lifting the top from the skull, almost as one would remove the top from a boiled egg.

The inspector sensed P.C. Townsend at his side. He looked long at the constable.

"Well, Edwin," using the man's Christian name for the first time, "Have you any idea whom our friend here may be?"

"Yes, Sir, I'm very much afraid I have. It's Sir Rupert Balmforth."

Talbot nodded in agreement. "Yes, I guessed as much."

Turning to his sergeant he asked how the discovery had been made.

"Constable Townsend and myself were digging among the loose soil seeing if we could find anything of any help when I uncovered this."

He handed the Inspector a soil-encrusted pocket watch, the glass broken and the face full of dry soil. Talbot took the watch and studied it thoughtfully. Turning it over in his hand he wiped mud from the back with his thumb, revealing the inscription.

'To Rupert with all my love, Emma.'

It was dated July the fourth 1874.

"His Birthday?" asked Talbot.

Townsend nodded, "It would appear so... Would you like me to inform his Lordship?" he asked.

"No thank you, Constable, I think it's time I had a little chat with the good Sir Oliver Balmforth." Turning once more to his Sergeant, he instructed him to detail two men to keep a discreet eye on the old shepherd's hut that had been discovered earlier. "Constable Townsend will show you where it is. That's obviously where our man's been hiding up these past few weeks." He added as he hurried away, keen to have his confrontation with sir Oliver.

Felicity, legs curled beneath her as only a woman can, sat on the high-backed armchair beside her bedroom window looking out over the expanse of billowing green and gold that was Yarrow woods.

Three weeks after her ordeal the cuts and bruises had all but healed, yet she still could not sleep through a night without nightmares waking her and leaving her sobbing in her husband's arms until, finally, falling into a fitful sleep where the nightmares would return once more.

The door opened and Oliver entered. She was pleased to see him.

"What are you looking at?" he asked, following her gaze out of the window.

Before she could answer, Edward tapped politely on the still open door.

"I'm sorry to disturb you, m'Lord, m'Lady, but Inspector Talbot is here again Sir… Mister Owen has shown him into the library."

"Oh Hell!" snapped Oliver, "What does he want now? Tell him that her Ladyship has answered enough of his damn pointless questions and that she cannot be disturbed."

Edward cleared his throat self-consciously.

"Er… begging your pardon, m'Lord, he says he would like to speak to you, not her Ladyship."

At the news of the policeman's discovery, Oliver had felt his legs go weak, his heart beating so loudly he was sure Talbot could hear it.

Sitting on the corner of his desk he stared down at his trembling hands, only half listening to the Inspector's voice droning on in the background… 'found in a shallow grave in Yarrow woods'… Talbot, realizing that Sir Oliver wasn't paying attention, went across to the sideboard and lifted the whisky decanter.

"Do you mind?" he asked the Baron, who failed to reply.

Talbot poured two drinks and handed Oliver a large measure of his own fine whisky, before settling back on the chesterfield examining an even larger drink in his own hand.

"You seem rather upset by the news, Lord Balmforth," Talbot ventured.

Oliver looked down at him with evident contempt.

"What in God's name do you expect? You've just informed me that my father has been murdered! Of course I seem upset.... wouldn't you be?"

The Inspector leaned back in the deep, leather-buttoned upholstery, his arm lying comfortably along the back of the sofa.

"My Lord, please correct me if I'm wrong, but surely you already knew that your father was dead, and I assume that even you didn't suspect natural causes?" Talbot's voice was heavy with inferred sarcasm, secretly enjoying his oral jockeying with the Baron.

Oliver pondered for a moment and then answered, a slight tremor in his voice. "Yes... Yes obviously I guessed he was dead, but I had no idea he had been murdered by that evil little bastard, Michael... and that the killer would turn out to be my own half-brother!"

Talbot finished his whisky in a final swallow and put the heavy cut glass on a side table.

"You seem to be very sure of who the murderer is, m'Lord. We don't even know for certain if this... err...Michael fellow is definitely involved. I admit it's unlikely but it's even possible he has simply gone into hiding through fear... Or possibly that he too has met an unfortunate end, we are not in the position to discount any scenarios, no matter how implausible they may at first appear."

Oliver rose from the edge of his desk and stood menacingly over the seated policeman.

"What kind of a policeman are you? You are being absolutely ridiculous; of course he's involved. My father's body was buried in his garden for Christ's sake man, surely even you don't suspect old Mrs. Heathcoat."

Inspector Talbot allowed himself a wry smile.

"I wasn't aware that I'd said exactly where the body was found. All I said was, 'A shallow grave in Yarrow woods."

Oliver looked down incredulously at the Inspector's smug expression. He felt the color draining from his face. Slumping into his high-backed armchair, he gave the policeman a sickly smile.

"Bravo, Inspector, I suppose you feel very pleased with yourself."

Talbot lifted himself clumsily from the sofa. Pulling a notebook and pencil from his inside pocket he proceeded to become more formal.

"Right, my Lord, I think it's time you answered some questions... don't you? We can do it here or we can go headquarters in Norwich... Now, why don't you tell me exactly what you know about your father's unfortunate demise?"

Chapter 20

The young Oliver Balmforth sat tight-lipped on the steps of the terrace, still shaking with anger after yet another argument with his tyrant of a father.

"How dare he call Felicity a gold digger, a common tart."

Ever since Sir Rupert had met his son's sweetheart, the animosity between them had grown. All his life Oliver had been held responsible for the untimely death of his mother… and his father had treated him accordingly.

That morning Oliver had plucked up the courage to inform the Baron that he and Felicity planned to marry. The storm of rage that erupted from Sir Rupert proved excessive, even for him. Oliver tried to defend his actions, but his protestations were beaten down by a torrent of curses and accusations being hurled at him.

"If you think for one moment I'm going to let the pair of you get your hands on one farthing of mine, then you're very much mistaken," bellowed his father, "I'll change my will this very day and that whore can go on the streets where she belongs and you… you'll end up penniless."

He paused in his tirade, his eyebrows lifting as he was seen to consider something; something that evidently amused him, judging by the smug sneer that stretched across his face.

"Perhaps I'll leave everything to your bastard brother."

The Baron paused to let the words sink in.

"Yes, you heard me! You have a half-brother. Perhaps you and your trollop can live in his cottage and he can be the future Baron Balmforth. It seems I discovered his existence just in time."

Turning his back on his son he looked up at his late wife's portrait over the fireplace, placing his hands on the mantle piece he continued in the same hostile tone. "If you bring that woman into this house, I'll cut you off without a penny."

Oliver was stunned.

"Half-brother?" he questioned, "What do you mean, half-brother?… What half-brother… Where?"

Sir Rupert remained silent, enjoying his son's obvious discomfort.

"What do you mean my half-brother?" repeated Oliver loudly.

"Yes," snapped back his father. "Another freak that killed its mother. The two of you should have a lot to talk about."

Oliver turned his back on his father and strode outside onto the terrace, slamming the French doors behind him with enough force to crack one of the pains.

How long he had sat outside on the hard stone steps he didn't know, going over, again and again in his mind, what his father had said. How could it be possible? A half-brother? Who was he? Where was he? Had his father invented the whole thing?

Hearing movement in the room behind him, Oliver turned and peered through the French windows.

There, stood his father, counting five-pound notes into a neat pile on his desk, then placing them into a large buff colored envelope, sealing it, and slipping it into the side pocket of his tweed hacking jacket before finally leaving the room.

Oliver remained seated, pondering over what he had seen.

'*There must have been over two hundred pounds there. What on earth is that malicious old bastard up to now?*' Suddenly he jumped to his feet.

"I bet he's going to Felicity to try and buy her off. The stubborn old fool, doesn't he understand how much she loves me?"

Looking up at the sound of hooves on gravel he saw the Baron astride his chestnut hunter, cantering off in the direction of Yarrow woods.

It appears I'm mistaken, thought Oliver, noticing that his father was heading in the opposite direction to Felicity's home.

Hurrying to the stables, Oliver ordered his horse saddled and not bothering to change into riding gear galloped off in pursuit of Sir Rupert.

On reaching the border of Yarrow woods, Oliver reined in, standing high in his stirrups, he surveyed the surrounding fields.

"Not a sign of him, he must have taken the bridle path." he said aloud to himself.

Urging his mount between the trees he entered the cool shade of the woodland. Glancing down he saw what looked like very recent hoof prints in the soft mud.

This doesn't lead anywhere, he thought, *perhaps he's just out riding after all?*

Oliver rode on slowly, his ears straining for the sound of his father's mount on the path ahead. Rounding a curve he caught a glimpse of chestnut. Dismounting, he tethered his own horse and proceeded warily on foot.

Sir Rupert's hunter was tied to a small sapling, unconcernedly munching on the leaves of the young tree. On drawing level, Oliver noticed the tiny overgrown footpath disappearing into the thick of the woods. As silently as possible, he set off in search of his father, cursing himself for not changing into more suitable footwear.

After some time he was brought up short by the sound of his father's distinctive voice.

Moving with as much stealth as possible, he drew close to the edge of the clearing, crouching low amongst the undergrowth.

There, in front of a dilapidated wooden cottage, stood Sir Rupert talking to that freak that occasionally came into the village. Seeing the two together, he was immediately struck by the similarity of the long white hair, so different from his own.

"Oh my God," he whispered to himself, "That's him… that's who he was talking about… It's true… my half-brother."

He shuffled closer, his knees sinking deeply into the carpet of leaf-mold. He held his breath, their voices sounded clearly in the still air

"When will Mrs. Heathcoat be back?" demanded the Baron.

Michael looked up at him with obvious loathing, his bent body seemingly dominated by the upright, towering form of Sir Rupert.

"What do you want with her?" he spat with contempt.

The man and the boy eyed each other in silence. The Baron finally removing the envelope from his jacket pocket and throwing it at Michael's feet.

"When she returns, give her that, and tell her I will be back a week from today and I don't expect to find either of you here. There's enough money in that envelope for the pair of you to start a new life in another part of the county. If I set eyes on you again, I promise you, you'll both regret it."

"Go to Hell!" shouted the uncomprehending young man in a sudden burst of rage.

The Baron's hand shot out, his open palm slapping Michael hard across the face, the sound, like the crack of a whip, echoed loudly in the clearing. Michael was sent sprawling into the newly turned soil, his outstretched hand painfully striking the blade of a spade lying in the dirt beside him.

He looked up at the Baron's laughing face, resentment turned to rage, the anger welling up inside of him. Michael's hand closed about the shaft of the spade as he leapt to his feet.

Sir Rupert, sensing the imminent danger, was already trying to avoid the blow as the cutting edge of the spade arced towards him. He instinctively attempted to bring his arms up to protect himself, but his age and the excesses of alcohol slowed his reactions, and without a sound or any cry of pain, he felt the sharp steel slice into his temple; felt the coldness enter his brain, then darkness.

Oliver wanted to leap to his feet. His honor, his family pride, screaming at him to avenge his father, but caution seemed the safest choice, he remained in hiding, crouching in silence amongst the bushes, watching with morbid curiosity at the pool of blood spreading around his father's body. His emotions in turmoil… he felt outrage, but he didn't feel any pity, any remorse. The man lying in the dirt had made his life hell, had threatened to destroy his hopes of any happiness for the future. Lifting his eyes once more he watched as Michael threw the spade to one side, grabbed the dead man's heels and proceeded to drag him towards the edge of the garden.

As the corpse bounced over the rutted ground the top of the shattered skull lifted, spilling a steaming mass of grey-red brains and gore onto the loose soil.

Oliver felt a wave of nausea wash over him as his eyes followed the trail of carmine, his rising gorge making him vomit into his hands as he clasped them over his mouth, terrified of making any sound that may alert the killer to his presence… he had no wish to join his father.

Looking about furtively Michael retrieved the spade and began clearing a space among the rough grass skirting the vegetable garden.

Oliver watched spellbound as his father's killer laid the heavy turfs to one side and began digging with practiced ease.

Silently, Oliver stumbled back along the footpath, his mind reeling from the encounter with his father's death but clear enough to grasp the possibilities. By the time he reached the bridlepath he had already formulated his plans.

Obviously, his father hadn't been serious about leaving the estate to his bastard half-brother and he had tried to pay them to leave. Now, his father was no more; there could be no obstruction to his marriage to Felicity. There would be no talk of any half-brother and no waiting for his inheritance, plus there was the added bonus that he was finally free of the father he despised.

He would wait until next morning, then inform the village constable of his father's mysterious disappearance. There was bound to be an investigation, but what was there to find? His father had ridden off in a rage, Oliver had ridden after him but had been unable to find him… He had returned to the Hall. When his father still hadn't returned by the next morning, he had alerted the constable of his concerns.

Unhitching his father's mare, Oliver slapped it hard on the rump and watched the powerful animal gallop off into the distance.

Walking back along the bridlepath, he mounted his own horse and headed back towards the Hall, a smile of excitement adding a touch of fresh color to his grimy face.

Chapter 21

The ballroom of Sorrow hall was a hive of activity, almost all the household staff were bustling about, polishing glass and silverware, positioning furniture, checking every ledge and door top for a speck of dust, ensuring that the folds in the heavy brocade curtains hung with perfect symmetry. In one corner, Edward the Footman was busy setting up a small bar, arranging and rearranging the selection of spirits and liqueurs, his mind running through the many recipes and mixing instructions for the cocktails he considered himself so expert in.

From the bar, stretching to the French windows ran an unbroken line of folding trestle tables covered with snow-white Irish linen. Empty now, save for an enormous Georgian silver punchbowl, but soon to be groaning under the weight of the sumptuous finger buffet prepared for that evening; the platters of hot and cold meats, whole fresh salmon, the skin replaced with mock scales of paper thin cucumber, little pyramids of quails eggs inter-spaced with green olives, whole roast pheasant, the long tail feathers repositioned incongruously at the rear of the now inverted birds.

Meg and Bridget were busy placing silver trays full of champagne and sherry glasses onto a long sideboard next to the double-doors of the room, the two young girls standing to one side to allow a small gang of delivery men through, loaded down with everything Lady Felicity had considered so important for such occasions, ranging from a crate of 'Barnett and Fosters' soda siphons to a long wooden case of Windward Isles Bananas, outrageously expensive but *'absolutely essential'* to the massive fruit display planned for the center piece of the buffet.

Through one of the three sets of French windows entered Jock, the gardener, and at the moment, temporary Groom, his arms laden with fresh cut flowers, which he was ferrying in from the walled garden. Margaret was retrieving them and deftly breaking stems and arranging the blooms in a row of lead crystal vases, ready to be positioned to add a much-needed splash of vibrant color to the dismal oak-paneled room.

Alone in one corner, presiding over all, stood Felicity, a look of contentment on her pretty face as she watched everyone working together, each intent on their own chores, glad of the change of routine.

She was brought out of her reverie by the approach of Owen, informing her that Miss Divine was ready for her Ladyship to inspect the food prior to it being brought upstairs. Sighing happily to herself she started towards the kitchen, surprised at how eager she was to discuss such mundane matters as food with the new cook; perhaps it was because Mrs. Black's replacement was the only member of staff engaged by Felicity herself and not merely inherited when she had married the Baron.

Elsa Divine was as unlike her predecessor as was imaginable, a somewhat overweight, jolly, red-faced young woman with cheeks like two rosy apples. She was one of the new breed of domestic cooks, trained at the famous '*Marshalls School of Cookery*' in London's Regent Street. She had left the school clutching a fistful of diplomas and certificates testifying to her expertise in all matters culinary. No years of battling her way up from scullery maid for Elsa, she aimed straight for the top and in Felicity's opinion, quite justifiably.

Stopping at the head of the stairs leading down to the hot, steamy kitchen, Felicity paused, and leaning her weight against the newel post, allowed herself time to think back over the last few months since her ordeal in the church tower.

Slowly, life had returned to normality, her relationship with Oliver was now so much more satisfying; happy with each other for what they were, both intellectually and sexually. Oliver had even accepted Katerina as a friend now that she appeared to be content with her role in life, much to the relief of Gregory.

Perhaps because of the absence of Mrs. Black's undermining presence, or possibly from her newfound friendship with Margaret, Felicity was no longer treated with suspicion and disrespect by the staff who now seemed to speak to her with a smile, rather than a look of servility.

As her memory wandered back to that fateful day, the look of contentment slowly dissolved from her face, the tormented recollection of the horror that was Michael intruded on her happy thoughts.

She had never told Oliver about the obscenities carried out on her; about the appalling acts she had been compelled to endure. Even when Doctor Ellis questioned her on the matter during his examination, she had refused to discuss the horrid details. She could still recall the obscure, knowing look that the wise old doctor had given her.

Nothing had ever been found of Michael; the popular belief was that he was lying dead somewhere in Yarrow woods, waiting one day to be discovered. The official police opinion, however, was that he had left the area and was living rough somewhere.

The thoughts of Michael waiting until the time was right for him to return to Sorrow filled Felicity with a cold terror. She looked down at her hands as they began to tremble. Forcing the image of him from her mind she replaced it with an image of her husband's smiling face.

Sir Oliver Balmforth was still awaiting criminal proceedings concerning the circumstances surrounding his father's death, at one time things were beginning to look particularly bad for him. It was patently obvious that Inspector Talbot suspected Oliver of actually murdering his father himself, or at least to have been in collusion with Michael, but after certain 'pressures' were brought to bear on his superiors, the Inspector found himself taken off the case and ordered back to Norwich, this was in no small measure due to the intervention of the eminent barrister, Sir Wallace Hanwell Q.C. who, as well as being a close friend of the Balmforth family was acting on Sir Oliver's behalf and had assured the Baron that he was confident of clearing his good name.

Everything was beginning to work out fine. Felicity found herself actually enjoying the organizing of the Hunt ball and looked upon it almost as a celebration of her return to normality, the only cloud hanging over her was the uneasy feeling in her stomach that had been coming and going at irregular intervals over the last few weeks, sometimes affecting her enough as to make her physically sick. Oliver had suggested she mention it to Doctor Ellis, but she had assured him it was only the excitement of the forthcoming ball, and perhaps a delayed reaction to the trauma she had so recently experienced.

Rubbing her hand over her soft belly hoping to ease the nagging sickness inside, she set off down the dim staircase to the kitchen. After a cursory inspection of the magnificent spread laid out on the long pine table, she issued a few brief instructions to Miss Divine before returning to her room for a short nap, hoping that she would feel better upon awakening.

It seemed like only minutes after she had drifted into a deep sleep that Meg was waking her to help her dress and style her hair.

Standing in front of the full-length looking glass Felicity studied her reflection critically, turning sideways to examine her profile. Was she too thin? Too boyish? Facing the mirror she cupped her hands under her small breasts pushing them together in an attempt to increase the bulge of cleavage above the neckline of her black taffeta and lace evening gown.

"I think I could do with a bit of padding, don't you Meg?"

Meg grinned happily at her mistress, knowing that Felicity was only teasing her.

"You look beautiful m'Lady."

The sound of motor cars crunching up the gravel drive came through the open window, people were calling greetings to each other with familiarity, car doors slammed. Oliver's deep voice could be heard clearly as he greeted the first of the guests as they arrived.

Meg glanced down from the window. "People are starting to arrive m'Lady." She recognized Dr. Ellis as he drew up in his neat, horse-drawn cart. Beside him sat his wife, a thin, gaunt faced woman.

From the direction of Saint Michael's, taking a short cut across the close-cropped lawn sauntered the Reverend Underwood, resplendent in a black dinner jacket, a white silk scarf draped carelessly about his neck. Meg became aware of Lady Felicity standing beside her.

The Baroness felt a tingle of nervousness flow through her body watching all these happy, confident people arriving, knowing that she should be with Oliver to greet them, but also knowing that as soon as she made an appearance she would be the focal point of everybody's center of attention. All the guests present this evening knew of her ordeal and doubtless, many had come to their own conclusion as to what she had endured. Not all disagreed with the late Baron's impression of her.

"Is there anything else you would like me to do m'Lady?" asked Meg, noticing the look of sadness that had filtered into Felicity's eyes.

Putting her arm around Meg's shoulders, the Baroness smiled at the young maid.

"Just for a little while can we forget that I'm your mistress. Let's just sit together and talk. Let's just be two friends chatting together… can we do that?"

Meg felt the color rush to her cheeks, unsure of how to respond to the situation, but Felicity was now looking past her at the arrival of a canary yellow Lanchester motor car which ground to a halt with a crunch of gravel, the grey-uniformed chauffeur rushing smartly to the back door to open it. Out swept the elegant form of Lady Caroline Auburn, followed by a short, thickset man, sporting a bushy walrus mustache, the only man to arrive not wearing tails and black tie. Instead, he was clad in an outrageously gaudy brown and mustard checked three-piece suit, topped with a chocolate brown bowler hat balanced precariously on the back of his head. In his left hand he held a pair of kidskin gloves, in his right a silver topped cane. Meg was startled at how different he appeared from his exquisitely attired companion, now crushing Sir Oliver in an unladylike bear hug. She seemed to stand out like a beacon among all the other handsome women present, a tower of silver silk capped with pearls and topped by a billowing cloud of golden hair.

As her unlikely escort rushed to join her, he inadvertently stumbled on the gravel, falling heavily against Lady Caroline who turned on him with a withering look.

Meg stifled a laugh when she witnessed the strange couple's discomfort, aware that it was not her place to have opinions about his Lordships guests.

Felicity fixed her with a knowing look. They both started to laugh. For the first time in what seemed like an age, Felicity found herself really laughing, not the polite giggles expected in front of a servant, but open joyous laughter bubbling up from deep inside her.

Suddenly, the look of joy crumbled on her face. Clamping her hand over her mouth she stumbled to the pitcher and bowl standing on her washstand. A wave of nausea swept through her as she felt the contents of her stomach burning up her throat and through her spread fingers.

"My Lady, what's wrong? Whatever's the matter?"

Remembering the arrival of Doctor Ellis, the lady's maid ran from the room.

Chapter 22

Michael lay awake on the thick mattress of dry bracken that served as his bed. Outside he could hear the small night noises of the woods; the mice and shrews burrowing through the dead leaves; the sound of a hedgehog tearing at the bark of a rotten tree in its hunt for slugs, making far too much noise for so small a creature.

He shivered, despite the warmth of the night, pushing himself deeper into the bracken, he pulled an old army greatcoat up to his chin, now sporting a straggly excuse for a beard. Stifling a yawn, he reached out an arm to tug at a dusty, Hessian potato sack from a pile next to him and spread it carelessly over his feet, which were clad in two pairs of holed, filthy woolen stockings.

The late summer sun had slowly begun to set, the abandoned ice house seemed to attract what little light there was remaining in the day, illuminating the interior of the brick dome almost as if it were mid-afternoon. He cursed the light. He cursed the missing door. He had been tempted to make a cover for the opening but thought better of it. After all he was practically living in the back garden of Sorrow hall, he dare not take the risk of attracting any attention to the long-abandoned icehouse.

Laying there, searching for sleep, his mind began to wander back to the day he had first discovered his new home.

He had been living like a wild animal. Sleeping under hedges or in dry ditches, shunning anywhere that he may encounter people, living on what he could steal, trap or find growing wild. Frightened to return to the old shepherd hut for fear of discovery he had taken to slipping into outlying barns or remote farm buildings after the hours of darkness, always careful to never leave any sign of his nocturnal visit. In this way he had gradually amassed his few possession. The old overcoat and a battered tweed cap had come from a scarecrow, a rusty beet hook from Tom Morton's garden shed, now sharpened to provide him with a quite formidable weapon; the potato sacks he had found in a barn one evening while he had been raiding a fruit store. The slatted shelves full of paper-wrapped apples and pears, he had filled one of the sacks and had crept away to a quiet spot in the woods where he settled down in the darkness, his back against a tree to enjoy his illicit feast. After a night of gorging himself he fell into a contented sleep, his trousers loosened to accommodate his distended stomach, only to waken suddenly at first light, his insides twisted with pain. Stumbling to his feet he scrambled off in search of some fresh water. 'The finest cure for belly ache.' Mrs. Heathcoat had always said.

Clutching himself with pain, he headed towards the nearby church and the water pump in the churchyard. Through his fingertips he could feel the fruit fermenting inside him, his stomach heaving and bubbling like a witches cauldron.

Cautious, despite the early hour, he made his way to the hand pump that was fixed to a stout wooden post at the side of the gravel path leading to the side gate of Saint Michael's. After drinking his fill, he headed for the large copse of straggling trees and overgrown bushes that ran from the side of the churchyard and around the rear of the walled garden of Sorrow Hall to finally link with the outlying trees of Yarrow woods.

Relieving himself against an ivy-covered elm he glanced through the open archway leading to the Hall. His eyes came to rest on a moss-covered red brick dome standing out amongst the bushes and undergrowth. A smile crept across his face at the thought that had occurred to him. Clutching his still aching stomach, he slipped through the brick archway and pushed his way among the waist high nettles as quickly as possible, mindful of being so close to the Hall.

The soft red brick of the icehouse already felt warm to the touch, the morning sun beginning to climb steadily into the sky. He walked around the small, strange building carefully examining it from all aspects. The door was missing but its structure was sound. Looked at from the direction of the Hall, it seemed to rise out of the greenery like a huge moss-covered egg.

Hesitantly, he shouldered aside a spindly sapling to enter the derelict building. The interior felt cold, as was to be expected, the thick walls keeping out the suns warmth. The underground passageway looked like it had been purposely caved in several years ago, its stair-well blocked solidly with brick rubble and half rotted timber. The dome itself was some nine or ten feet in diameter with a ceiling height of about six feet, perhaps a foot more after the removal of the accumulated rubbish beneath his feet.

Stomach ache forgotten, Michael allowed himself a smile.

Now, wouldn't this make a cozy little home? Right in the back yard of the great Sorrow Hall; eating the vegetables from the Baron's garden; snaring his pheasants from under his very nose. Why! I've even got the church right on my doorstep.

He started to chuckle to himself, a coarse guttural sound, the spittle bubbling in his throat.

How long he had been hiding away there, he wasn't sure. How many days? Weeks? The year was moving on. The brambles surrounding the icehouse were bursting with great shining masses of blackberries, one of the best crops he had ever seen. He ate them until he was sick, his hands and chin purple with their juice.

Although the weather was still relatively warm, Michael was well aware that he would never survive through the coming winter in what amounted to little more than a red brick cave. He lay on his makeshift bed, eyes closed against the evening light, waiting for darkness and the oblivion of sleep. His tortured thoughts conjured up fantasies of himself living in the neighboring hall. Lying in a massive feather bed next to Lady Felicity; servants helping him to wash and dress, fetching him his food whenever he ordered it... why couldn't he live there?

Something inside him, something he didn't understand was trying to tell him that somehow it was right. He *should* be there. Felicity *should* be his.

Eyes screwed up tight, his thoughts drifted back to the church tower and to Lady Balmforth. His breath became short as he recalled the things they had done to each other. He let out a low moan as the familiar ache spread from his loins...

He could have her. He would have her!

In his twisted mind he had convinced himself that anything was possible, that all that stood in his way was Sir Oliver Balmforth himself.

Reaching out he drew a clumsily bound package towards him, unwrapping the stained canvas he removed a foul-smelling portion of meat and began to chew on the raw flesh of a young rabbit. Rarely daring to light a fire, he had forced himself to eat his meat uncooked. Now, after so many weeks he found himself relishing the rubbery sweetness of the flesh.

For some time he had been aware of the arrival of a stream of vehicles at the Hall, of carriages and motor cars; the late summer breeze carrying the sounds of laughter and friendly chatter. How long was it since he'd heard voices? How long since he had actually spoken to another human being?

Curiosity aroused, he licked the cold blood from his filthy fingers and heaved himself awkwardly from the pile of bracken. Cautiously, he began to pick his way through the shoulder high brambles towards the open gateway in the high brick wall surrounding the vegetable garden. Hurrying between the crowded vegetable beds, he exited near the front driveway of the Hall itself.

There he was, His Lordship... Sir Oliver Balmforth himself, laughing and smiling without a care in the world. Michael looked around for a glimpse of Lady Felicity. Something drew his gaze to one of the upper windows. Yes, there she was, Felicity and that young maid looking down, watching as the people arrived.

He could have her! He would have her. No more would he have to live like an animal, afraid of people, the police, the villagers.

This was his chance, he'd finally show them all the real meaning of fear.

Chapter 23

Oliver paced up and down outside the bedroom, waiting for the doctor to complete his examination.

Why was he taking so long? He'd been in there for nearly an hour.

Unable to stand the waiting any longer, he knocked loudly on the door, which was opened immediately. Dr. Ellis stepped from the room and closed the door quietly behind him.

"I've given Her Ladyship something to make her sleep. I'm very much afraid she won't be joining the party this evening."

Oliver was surprised to notice the beginning of a smile playing at the edge of the doctor's mouth.

"But can't you tell me what's wrong? Is it anything serious?"

Dr. Ellis took the Baron by his elbow and started to lead him back down the stairs. "I assure you, your Lordship, it's absolutely nothing for you to worry unduly about, but I really do think it would be better if her Ladyship were to tell you about it herself. Now come along, your guests will be waiting."

Re-entering the crowded ballroom, Oliver was immediately cornered by Lady Caroline Auburn waving a glass of champagne in his face as she spoke.

"Oliver, Darling," she gushed theatrically, thrusting her perfumed bosom at him. "And where's that gorgeous young wife of yours. Not poorly, I hope."

In a desperate attempt to change the subject, Oliver took the glass from her and disposed of it, before leading her by the hand onto the dance floor. A four-piece band on a makeshift stage in one corner were playing their own peculiar version of a waltz.

"Who's your escort? I don't believe I've met him before?" ventured Oliver.

"Oh! You mean, dear Robert? Robert Parker. Why, he's an actor, quite famous in London theatre land by all accounts… perhaps you've heard of him?"

Oliver admitted that he hadn't.

"Have you known him long?" he asked.

"Well, actually no. We only met last week at some charity fund-raising event or another. I know he dresses appallingly, but he's an absolute dear. Such fun. Not at all like the usual bores one meets at those bashes. Anyway, we got along famously, and he seemed to know that I was invited here tonight, so I just had to ask him to come along. You don't mind, do you?"

Oliver said he didn't. The dance ended, he made his excuses and began to play the host, mingling with his guests, gradually working his way towards Gregory and Katerina to explain Felicity's absence and who he hoped may possibly be able to shed some light on her sudden ailment.

"Pink champagne, your Lordship?"

Margaret stood before him, a silver tray expertly held aloft on one hand, the rose-tinted drinks balanced perfectly.

He took one gratefully, almost emptying the glass with a single long swallow.

"Pardon me for asking, my Lord, but I was just wondering if Lady Felicity was feeling any better?" ventured the housekeeper.

Before he could reply they were joined by James, perspiring slightly after a somewhat suffocating dance squashed in the arms of Mrs. Vaughn, the huge wife of a local, gentleman farmer.

Taking a glass from Margaret's tray and giving her a wink he turned to Sir Oliver. "Might I ask a favor of you, your Lordship? Do you think I could possibly steal your housekeeper away for a short moment?"

Sir Oliver chuckled to himself good-naturedly as he signaled Bridget to take the tray. Margaret bobbed politely to the Baron and turned to follow James across the crowded room, conscious of Owen's eyes looking at her with outrage at the desertion of her duties.

James led her through the French windows and out onto the paved terrace. She looked into his face impatiently.

"James, we shouldn't be doing this, I'm supposed to be working. Now what is it that is so important?"

Katerina and Gregory Christopher stood in front of the fireplace, chatting amiably to Robert Parker, a small bit of fire burned brightly in the huge grate, more for its aesthetic quality than for any real need of warmth on this mild late summer's evening. As the two men talked, Katerina's attention was taken by the way the flames flickered gaily in the breeze from the open French windows. Looking up she noted the red and yellow glow reflected a thousand times in the magnificent crystal chandelier hanging above the center of the dance floor. Something about the fire held her interest. It almost seemed to have a life of its own.

The Christopher's were surprised to find this strange friend of Lady Caroline Auburn's absolutely charming, not at all as they had imagined when he had first introduced himself. He seemed to be so interested in everything around him, his head constantly nodding as if with approval at all he was told.

He appeared to have a genuine curiosity about the village and the people in it, asking intelligent questions and listening attentively to the answers.

Suddenly becoming aware of the heat of the fire on their legs they took a single step backwards, simultaneously looking in wonder at the flames. A small fire no longer, before their astonished gaze, it was fast growing into a roaring blaze, filling the half-empty grate entirely. They looked at each other in puzzlement. No one had added any coal or logs, indeed, there was barely anything left to burn. Yet still the blaze grew, seeming to feed on the very air around it and fueled by nothing but its own self. In a matter of moments flames started to lick out of the top of the fireplace, lapping around the ornate granite mantle piece, stretching red flames like groping fingers up towards the heavy gilt frame of Sir Rupert Balmforth's portrait which hung above.

"Quickly… fetch some water!" someone shouted.

Music and conversation stopped. A woman screamed. As a body, the guests edged away from the flames now reaching out sideways along the oak panels flanking the fireplace. Within seconds the temperature of the room had begun to soar. Some guests retreated onto the terrace, men removing their jackets.

Unmoving, in the center of the dance-floor stood Lady Caroline, apparently unperturbed by the whole thing. She watched with amusement at their host in such a panic, Sir Oliver uselessly throwing water from an ice bucket onto the flames.

As she observed the mayhem around her, she became conscious of a sensation of heat at her fingertips. Glancing down at the glass of champagne that she held, she watched spellbound, as before her eyes the wine began to lightly bubble, a cloud of vapor rising from its surface. The stem of the glass grew hot between her fingertips. Still, she held it. The liquid began to boil, the hot wine splashing her hand. Unable to withstand the heat, the crystal glass shattered. A shower of boiling wine and splintered glass filled her vision. With a shriek, she felt the thin shards of glass cut deeply into the flesh of her face and chest.

All around people screamed. Bottles burst, exploding with showers of hot liquid, which seemed to stick to all it touched. Glasses steamed and ruptured, sending their scalding contents raining down on anyone near.

People ran into each other, clutching bleeding and scalded faces, cursing and shoving in a panic to reach the safety of the terrace.

In the center of the buffet, the huge George IV silver punchbowl, now tarnished gold by the heat, spewed its boiling contents high into the air, the hot red liquid gushing over the white linen tablecloth and dripping to the floor, people shrieked in pain as the shower of scalding fruit seemed to cling to their skin, taking the flesh with it as they clawed to remove it.

Amidst the running, crying, mayhem, Sir Oliver stood silent, the empty ice bucket still in his hand, heedless of the inferno around him, staring aghast at the burning portrait of his father, its gilt frame now fully ablaze, the canvas wreathed in flames, the thick oils starting to soften and run under the intense heat distorting the features of the late Baron. The canvas began to bubble and crack. The distorted face starting to blacken and smoke. Sir Oliver's mouth fell open as he looked into the flames. His father's features seemed to change with the melting of the oils, the harsh mouth drooping, giving the portrait the semblance of a mocking smile. He stood transfixed as to his horror, he recognized that grinning down at him was the lopsided smile of Michael.

With a sudden roar the painting was engulfed. The room shook with the noise of the conflagration. From far away, Oliver thought he could hear Gregory's voice calling to him. In a daze he turned, as with a horrendous explosion of glass the huge crystal chandelier crashed to the floor, plunging the room into darkness lit only by the raging fire which had now engulfed the entire end of the room.

He stared about him, it appeared like a vision of hell, a scene from his worst nightmare. The bottles continued to explode, spraying gouts of steaming liquid into the air, the reflection of the flames in the flying glass making it seem like some demonic firework party.

Somebody was tugging at his sleeve, pulling him back from the flames.

"Oliver? What's wrong? Snap out of it man!"

Coming out of his trance he realized Gregory was dragging him across the dance floor, his other arm held by the flamboyant Mr. Parker.

Between the two of them they pulled Sir Oliver unceremoniously through the open French windows and out onto the terrace to join the crowd of crying, frightened guests. The warm evening hit him like an ice-cold blast. He could see the red and gold parish fire pump being rushed towards them, cutting across the middle of the front lawn.

At once he took in the scene of carnage, his guests around him, burnt and bleeding, being frantically attended to by Doctor Ellis and his wife… His wife? A wave of nausea swept through him as in a flash of panic he remembered that Felicity was still upstairs laying in a drugged sleep. Screaming her name, he plunged back into the burning room, trying to make for the door before it too became engulfed in the flames.

Gregory watched helplessly as his friend seemed to make it, but as Oliver burst through the burning door leading to the entrance hall, a blinding spout of vivid blue flame leapt from the very heart of the fire, reaching through the open door and seemed to grab the running figure about the body and drag him screaming, back into the room. The flames gripped Sir Oliver like a huge fist of fire, holding him down, pinning his arms to his side. Gregory and Robert Parker ran back into the room pulling down the thick brocade curtains to smother the flames. They were soon joined by the many willing hands of others.

Suddenly, as if at the turn of a switch, the fire seemed to lose all its power. The raging inferno of seconds before had instantly dwindled to small areas of burning wood paneling and furniture smoldering and smoking. The black and curled canvas of the old Barons portrait drifted silently to the floor.

From near the French windows Margaret turned to James, a look of fear in her eyes.

"Lady Felicity… she's still upstairs."

The Reverend hurled himself through the smoke-filled room and ran for the stairs leading to Felicity's room. To his astonishment, the entrance hall was completely undamaged, save for a cloud of smoke drifting in the air, and the acid charcoal smell of burnt wood.

This was no ordinary fire, he thought as he mounted the stairs, taking them three at a time.

Felicity had awoken suddenly from her drugged slumber by the sound of screams and breaking glass and what at first sounded like gunfire. Sitting upright in the early evening darkness, she became aware of the strong smell of burning. From downstairs came a deafening crash of shattering glass, which shook the floor of her room. People were running, shouting, crying out in pain.

Leaping from her bed, she hurriedly threw on a silk dressing gown and tore open her door, coming face to face with the Reverend Underwood rushing down the passageway towards her.

Once again the library of Sorrow Hall was full. Felicity sat on the couch, still wrapped in her flimsy dressing gown, a woolen blanket draped about her shoulders. Head bowed she stared, red-eyed, into the untouched brandy glass held in her now trembling hands. Katerina and Margaret sat on either side of her, sheltering her from the gaze of others.

P.C. Townsend, leaving his duties of fireman to others, now resumed his position of policeman, albeit without his uniform and still filthy from the fire. Feeling strangely at a loss without his notebook and pencil, going over the facts with Gregory Christopher.

"And you say that you have no idea how the fire got out of hand," he questioned.

"I've told you all that I know. Now, couldn't this wait until tomorrow?"

Gregory gave a grimace as a spasm of pain shot through one of his blistered hands swathed in bandages, hastily applied by Doctor Ellis's wife whilst her husband did what he could to help the horribly burned Oliver Balmforth still lying unconscious on the floor of the ballroom.

With a sigh of resignation the policeman made his way across the room to the Reverend Underwood, who was standing against the door jamb of the open French windows, obviously deep in thought, peering out to the garden beyond. He looked up at the sound of P.C. Townsend clearing his throat.

"Well Reverend, have you anything to add to what's been said?"

With a sigh of impatience James drew himself up to his full height.

"Are all these questions really necessary, Constable? I understand that your superiors will be arriving at some time and doubtless they will be asking the same things."

"Well that's true enough Sir." he replied, "normally, this kind of thing wouldn't be of any interest to people like Talbot, you understand, but he left me strict instructions to inform him of anything out of the ordinary that was to occur concerning Lord Balmforth, and from what people are telling me, this was more than simply a house fire… Wouldn't you agree Reverend?"

James nodded, "Oh yes, this was so much more than that.."

Turning his back on the policeman he went to join some of the remaining guests gathered around the Baron's desk. He nodded politely to Lady Caroline, still exuding elegance, even with her face and chest covered with yellow ointment and pieces of lint, whom he noticed seemed to be handing the situation rather better than most, thanks, he suspected, to the ever-present glass in her hand, now changed from a champagne saucer to a brandy snifter.

"Ah! The new Reverend… Just the man," her voice sounded ever so slightly slurred, "I seem to have lost my escort, Mr. Parker. You must have noticed him. He was dressed… how should I say…"

James silenced her with a look. "I'm sure he's fine. I'll ask around for you. I don't suppose he's gone far."

Grateful for something to do he strode thoughtfully away, Lady Caroline calling after him.

"Someone said they saw him heading out into the garden."

James walked back towards the gutted ballroom, the acrid stench of fire hanging heavily in the air.

Passing through the entrance hall he noticed Owen and Edward busy showing the remaining guests to their vehicles. Meg stood by the front door handing out hats, gloves and furs, politely bidding the guests good night, almost as if nothing untoward had happened.

James entered the ballroom hesitantly, the air thick and damp. Puddles of dirty water lay on the charred dance floor. The three pairs of French windows were flung wide. Wedged halfway through one, stood the village fire pump, the brass gleaming against its red, black and gold livery. At its side Noblet Swallow was busy stowing the neatly rolled, canvas hose back into its compartment. Some of the other fire volunteers were also bustling about, stacking burnt furniture to one side, pulling down sections of wood paneling to ensure there were no hidden areas still smoldering, and dragging outside the water sodden piles of curtains and soft furnishings.

Seemingly ignored in the midst of all this activity lay Sir Oliver Balmforth, flanked by Doctor and Mrs. Ellis on their knees beside him.

James looked down helplessly at the horrific burns on the stricken man whom he had begun to regard as a good friend.

"Is he going to be all right?" James asked in a whisper.

Doctor Ellis turned, a look of dismay in his rheumy old eyes.

"We've done all that we possibly can. Thankfully, he's unconscious, so at least he's free of pain."

As they spoke, the Baron shook with a spasm of agony as Mrs. Ellis applied the yellow salve to the mass of weeping black and purple flesh that was Sir Oliver Balmforth.

Ashamed of his own weakness, the Reverend turned his head away. He had witnessed similar horrific injuries during the recent South African war. Indeed, he had often been called upon to perform the last rites on many burnt and disfigured victims. But somehow, in that faraway land, the atrocity of death and mutilation seemed almost normal… but here… here in the tiny hamlet of Sorrow in the peaceful green countryside of England, it was just too much to comprehend. Head bowed he silently headed out onto the terrace in search of the erstwhile Mr. Parker.

Robert Parker knelt lightly on one knee examining the area of flattened grass. Beside him in the rich, clay soil of the rose garden, standing out clearly in the bright moonlight, was the deep imprint of a heavy work boot behind which the concave depression of a knee pointed to the fact that somebody had been crouching next to the flower bed, careful to be concealed by the shadows of the rose bushes.

Abstractly tugging at his thick mustache, he tried to remember exactly what he had seen; exactly what had brought him to this very spot.

It was as the fire had got out of hand, he had been ushering people from the burning house, shouting to be heard, trying his best to calm the rising panic. He was outside, on the terrace when something caught his attention. Out of the corner of his eye he saw, quite plainly, across the expanse of the lawn, a shadow, dark against the light grey of the evening sky. There, moving fleetingly from the stand of elm trees lining the driveway, the figure was silhouetted perfectly by the rising moon. A crouching figure of a man, furtively rushing for the cover of the rose garden, dropping out of view among the dark shadows, Parker's curiosity was aroused. He had taken a step out into the garden, his eyes fixed firmly on the spot where the clandestine figure had disappeared. At that moment, through the French windows came the sound of shattering glass as the chandelier suddenly crashed to the floor. Turning back to the ballroom he had forced his way through the screaming guests, the room glowing red. Amid the wreckage stood Sir Oliver, seemingly oblivious to the danger as the flames flickered around him. Following Mister Christopher into the burning room, they had dragged the Baron out onto the terrace, only to have him turn and run back once more into the flames, calling his wife's name.

"Mister Parker, is that you?"

The kneeling figure was startled by the approaching James Underwood.

"Ah! Reverend Underwood, isn't it?"

He rose, brushing soil from his palms before extending his hand politely.

The two men shook hands firmly, looking suspiciously at each other.

James was surprised at the strength in the dry roughness of the man's grasp.

"You certainly don't have the handshake of a thespian, Mister Parker."

The silence hung heavy between them, the tension growing, only to disappear instantly as a warm smile spread over Parker's face, transforming his coarse features.

"You're very perceptive, Reverend," he said.

James let out an involuntary gasp as Parker suddenly reached inside his jacket, relieved when all that he produced was an expensive looking, crocodile skin wallet. He flipped it open to reveal his true identity: the Warrant Card of a Detective Sergeant in the Norfolk Constabulary.

Without warning, there came from the direction of the Hall the sound of a woman's high-pitched scream of anguish.

Rushing back to the ballroom, the two men were met by the sight of Lady Felicity sobbing uncontrollably, her face buried in Katerina's shoulder.

Doctor Ellis was standing above Sir Oliver, looking down with an expression of grief as Mrs. Ellis placed a discarded dinner jacket over the face of the dead man.

James crossed the room to Margaret. Taking her gently by the arm, she allowed him to lead her outside onto the terrace. Looking down sadly into sparkling blue eyes, wet with tears, he kissed her tenderly on her forehead.

Feeling herself starting to sag, she held on tightly to him, her face against his chest, eyes squeezed tightly shut, hoping to obliterate the horrors within the Hall.

The two of them stood silent and motionless as the sounds of grief drifted from the ballroom.

Slowly, the dark sky started to lighten as the first red fingers of morning began to clamber above the horizon.

"James, may I ask you something?"

He nodded, stroking the back of her hair.

"Earlier this evening, when you brought me outside, you said you wanted to talk to me, but we never got the chance…what was it you wanted to say to me?"

James stood back and took both her small hands in his and bringing them to his lips, he kissed her fingertips lightly.

"Can't you guess, my dearest Margaret? I brought you out here to tell you I loved you, and to ask you… to ask you to be my wife."

Chapter 24

Noblet Swallow moved through the familiar forest quickly but silently, his large feet clad in heavy hob-nailed work boots, treading almost daintily as he instinctively avoided the hundreds of dry twigs and other obstacles waiting to announce his presence.

Unslinging a stout canvas bag from his shoulder he laid it gently on the forest floor. Dropping down to crouch on one knee he examined a tunnel-like area of overgrown brambles; he fondled the broken stems, palming a flattened area of turf, carefully inspecting every minute sign which read like a book to the experienced eye of this extraordinary country-man.

Lifting a brass wire snare from his shoulder bag, he examined it quickly for any faults, before positioning it at the perfect height to claim the life of yet another unsuspecting rabbit. Making a mental note of the location, he moved slowly on, stopping now and then to set another snare, pushing the hardwood pegs effortlessly into the soft soil with the heel of his hand.

The shadows in the woods were growing longer as the sun, burning a flaming red, slowly set. Above his head, he heard the clap of wings as wood pigeons began to gather in their roosts in the uppermost branches of the surrounding beech trees. He looked through the treetops as the ball of fire sank behind the towering chimneys of Sorrow Hall. His mind drifting back to the previous evening.

Sir Oliver lay horribly burned, his face staring up from the dance floor; he had watched helplessly as the doctor's wife covered the Baron's face with somebody's dinner jacket; he remembered poor Lady Felicity sobbing uncontrollably… as if that poor woman hadn't suffered enough. His mind elsewhere, he was unexpectedly startled back to the present by the high-pitched scream of something in terrible pain. Pin-pointing the spot among the undergrowth he walked quickly towards the sound, his years of experience telling him exactly what he would find… a rabbit badly caught in a gin trap.

Sure enough, behind a knurled tree root lay the stricken animal, half out of its burrow under the tree, it's front leg and most of its chest gripped mercilessly in the blunt, interlocking teeth of the cruel trap. Noblet quickly dispatched the half-dead rabbit slitting open it's stomach with his pocket knife and with a practiced flick over his shoulder, sending the steaming paunch into the undergrowth.

Slipping the still twitching carcass into one of his many capacious pockets, he bent and picked up the gin trap, pulling the hazel peg from the ground as he did so. Turning it slowly in his hands he gave it a cursory examination, as he had suspected, it was one of his own. He was as familiar with his traps as any craftsman was with the tools of his trade, it had been crafted by his own hands in his own forge. Why, even the wooden peg that was still attached was one that he'd sat and carved on his own front porch.

Of late, Noblet had been aware that he wasn't the only person poaching the woods behind the Hall. He had accepted this philosophically, after all, everybody had a right to feed their family in any way that they could. He didn't for a moment object to sharing his hunting ground, but what he did object to was having his traps and snares stolen.

Over the last few weeks and months he had lost count of the number that had gone missing, and now the cheeky bastard was using them in the very place he had found them. Quickly,, he formulated his plans. Re-setting the trap in its original position he cursed himself for stupidly removing the ensnared rabbit. Better he had let it be, still... too late to worry about that now. Searching around he soon found what he was looking for. A shadowy hollow set deep beneath an overgrown mass of brambles. On hands and knees he shouldered aside the clinging, thorn-covered suckers and crept slowly beneath. Using his whole body he wriggled himself deeply into the accumulated leafmould, heaping it up around the depression. Satisfied with his efforts he then withdrew from his hiding place, carefully checking he hadn't left any visible evidence of his visit. He then headed quickly for home.

Returning before first light, Noblet knew he wouldn't have long to wait before his suspicions would be confirmed and the thieving bastard came to check his traps. Crawling once more beneath the thick brambles, he sat, cross-legged in his hiding place, coat collar pulled high, hat tilted forward concealing the white of his face. For over two hours he squatted among the leafy shadows, one thing a successful poacher had to be was patient.

The sun was now rising steadily into the sky. Birds were calling to each other, greeting what looked like being another glorious day, oblivious to the silent figure crouching amongst the blackberry bushes.

As if at a signal, the birds abruptly fell silent, save for the warning chatter of a blackbird as it whirred between the beech trunks.

Noblet remained motionless, his ears pricked for the anticipated footsteps. He braced himself, ready to spring, but forced himself to remain motionless when he saw whom his quarry was.

Michael came through the trees, a Hessian potato sack thrown carelessly over his shoulder. He swore out loud when he saw the gin trap remained unsprung. He reached down to retrieve the trap, hesitating, he noticed the torn grass, and the scratched soil at the burrow entrance. His hand jerked back from the trap almost as if it would burn him. Quickly springing upright he spun around, his eyes flickering nervously amongst the surrounding woodland. Noblet held his breath, knowing instinctively not to challenge the thief as he had at first planned.

For a long moment, Michael's eyes stared straight at the place, not daring to move, relying on the woodlands dappled shadows to keep him hidden from view. He had known at once what had alerted Michael. It was obvious from the ground around the gin trap that something had been caught, but more to the point, somebody had obviously re-set the trap. Noblet cursed his own stupidity.

'Why the hell didn't I just leave it be?' he thought pointlessly to himself.

He could see the drying entails still clinging to a distant bush, would they be spotted? Michael's eyes moved on, convinced there was no immediate danger. Looking suspiciously down at the rabbit hole, he picked up the sack and hurried off back in the direction he'd come, leaving the gin trap still untouched.

As soon as he was out of sight, Noblet exhaled loudly and withdrew quickly from his hiding place, setting off in quiet pursuit of the unsuspecting Michael, using all his experience and stealth to follow him.

Michael was moving fast, his fear of discovery over-riding his sense of caution. He knew it was time to move on, his shelter, so close to Sorrow Hall was no longer safe.

Moving stealthily, Noblet tried desperately to come up with some sort of plan. He was sure that he could get the better of Michael if it came to blows. After all, he was almost twice his size, but remembering Reverend Underwood's horrific injuries, he decided against confronting him unless it was absolutely necessary. Instead, he would just follow at a safe distance, find out where he was holed up, then hurry round and tell Edwin, who could get in touch with Inspector Talbot.

Noblet Swallow, Inspector Talbot, Sergeant Bob Parker, and four uniformed officers, including Edwin Townsend moved cautiously alongside the high red-brick wall enclosing the extensive vegetable gardens of Sorrow Hall. On reaching the open gateway Talbot raised a hand, stopping his followers. With a wag of his finger he sent Parker and two of the uniformed constables along the private path and into the churchyard, the constables hurriedly concealing themselves behind suitable headstones. Sergeant Parker himself continued on around the rear of the church to come up behind the overgrown spinney stretching around the rear of the Hall and thence to the blind side of the icehouse.

Talbot allowed his sergeant time to get into the prearranged position, before instructing the blacksmith to remain where he was and under no circumstances should he get involved. He then led Townsend and the other constable quickly towards the moss and lichen encrusted brick mound that was the disused icehouse, spreading widely in an attempt to cut off any possibility of their man escaping.

Noblet Swallow leaned against the warm red brick of the garden wall, watching with interest as the policemen closed in, completely encircling the crumbling icehouse, he was surprised to see the Inspector reach into his coat pocket and bring out a small hand gun. With a shout, Inspector Talbot leapt into the building, Bob Parker crowding in after him.

The distinctive voice of the sergeant could be heard clearly, even from where the blacksmith stood.

"Fuck! Too late," He snapped in bitter frustration. The two senior policemen slowly emerged into the sunlight, the pistol now back in Talbot's coat pocket.

"He can't have got far, Sir," continued Parker; "It's only a few hours since Mister Swallow spotted him."

Nodding agreement, Talbot turned to his officers.

"Well, don't just stand there, scratching your arse… find the bastard."

The constables dispersed in different directions, each of them wishing to get as far away as possible from the angry Inspector. Parker called after them, "keep within earshot of each other, and remember, he's a lot more dangerous than he looks."

With a jerk of his shoulder, Noblet pushed himself away from the wall.

"Slippery little fucker," he said under his breath as he set out to join the Inspector, stopping suddenly at the sound of a door closing quietly behind him. Spinning on his heels he stepped back into the walled garden, his acute poacher's senses straining for a sound or a movement. His eyes quickly scanned the large area of vegetables plots, brick paths, and muck heaps. Clustered in one corner stood a collection of small buildings, a long brick fruit store, a glazed potting shed and a large wooden hut, used for storing the gardener's tools. Leading from there, and stretching the entire length of the curved south wall ran a huge lean-to greenhouse, which had been erected by Sir Oliver's late father to grow grapes and exotic fruit.

In Noblet's mind he could still hear the door closing, there was something furtive about the way it was closed so quietly. Somehow the sound had held the quality of glass, a glazed door, the greenhouse door . . .

He looked back through the archway and could see that the two policemen were still busy searching through the icehouse. Noblet wondered whether to call out to them, after all, it may only be old Jock the Gardener. They had seen him earlier and he said he was going to repair a broken pane of glass in the green house. "Yes, that's who it was, probably only old Scotch Jock."

He walked over to the long, curved greenhouse.

"Best check," he said aloud to himself.

Pulling open the door, he peered inside. Despite the amount of glass, the interior was dull with the shade of thick grape vines growing up the walls and trained along stout wires covering the sloping ceiling, heavy with tapering masses of dark mauve grapes hanging low from the overhead vines.

He stepped into the stifling warmth of the heated vinery. Walking slowly, head tucked low to avoid the hanging fruit, he wondered once again whether or not to go back and tell Talbot? He'd already lost Michael once by going to fetch the police. Despite Talbots warning not to get involved he was determined not to risk making the same mistake a second time. Hardening his resolve, he quickened his pace, pushing through the trailing vines he hurried along the brick path stretching in front of him.

Due to the curve of the flank wall, he found he could only see a short distance ahead. He moved carefully, aware of how dangerous his quarry may prove to be if indeed it was Michael.

From ahead, the sound of smashed glass shattered the silence echoing back through the vines followed almost instantly by a piercing scream of agony. Noblet leapt forward, caution forgotten. Heedless of his own peril he ran head held low, towards the source of the scream, arms fending off the bushy foliage and hanging fruit. He rounded the final curve, stopping short in stunned disbelief.

Before him stood the hunched figure of Michael, his hand on the doorknob of the end door. He had a lopsided grin on his filthy, bearded face. At his feet lay the body of old Jock the gardener, his legs still twitching as the nerves settled into the final stillness of death. Where Jock's head met his shoulder protruded the curved blade of what looked like a sugar beet hook. Noblet felt the color drain from his face, he could not move. He wanted to put his hands around Michael's scrawny throat, but something kept him rooted to the spot, as his eyes fixed on the growing pool of blood spreading from Jock's impaled neck.

Michael placed his foot under the dead man's shoulder and with little effort callously rolled him over. Noblet felt a wave of nausea sweep over him. From the other side of the gardener's neck protruded the wooden handle of the beet hook. The bright arterial blood puddled over the broken pane of glass that the gardener must have been repairing when he was attacked. With a look of pure pleasure on his face, Michael opened the door and grinning widely at the blacksmith, stepped lightly outside. In that second Noblet felt his body become free; he felt the spell break, released from his trance-like state he hurled himself forward, his whole body trembling with rage. The greenhouse door slammed in his face. A noise like thunder boomed in his ears. His vision was filled with a thousand shards of glass, flying, falling as the glazed roof and walls shattered in an explosion of sound. Noblet instinctively dropped to his knees, covering his head and face with his forearms. He could feel the sting of the razor-sharp glass fragments slicing into his flesh, the air before his eyes seemed to glow silver with glass splinters, yet tinged pink with blood… his blood.

Sergeant Bob Parker was first to find him, still on his knees, covered in a mass of broken glass.

By the time Doctor Ellis arrived, Noblet was standing by the garden hand-pump washing the carmine from his face and hands, his hair now matted with dark blood.

Jock the gardener was still lying on his back amongst the shattered glass of the greenhouse, his blood-drained face now covered by the thorn-proof poachers coat, never before had Noblet been more grateful for that old waxed poacher's coat of his, without that he was sure he would have been cut to shreds.

Without exception, every single pane of glass stretching the entire length of the building was missing, the floor beneath some six inches deep in a carpet of glass fragments.

After treating the blacksmith's injuries, which incredibly proved to be only superficial and thanks to the protection of his thick coat were confined to the backs of his hands and to a lesser degree his head, face and neck. Doctor Ellis examined the dead gardener. Handing the completed death certificate to the Inspector, he called Sergeant Parker to join them.

"Now look here, Inspector Talbot. Something has got to be done about this man you're looking for, he's more than just a crazed killer. There are powers at work here which none of us understand. Only yesterday evening I had to write out the death certificate for Sir Oliver Balmforth. Now I'm writing one for his gardener." He indicated the folded paper still in the policeman's hands. "So far that's three members of the Sorrow Hall staff, not to mention his

Lordship. Why! it was only a matter of luck that Lady Felicity escaped with her life!"

Bob Parker spoke for the first time. "If you have any suggestions Doctor, I'm sure the Inspector would be happy to hear them?"

Talbot nodded agreement but remained silent.

"Well, might I suggest you both go and speak to the Reverend?" the doctor answered. "He's been involved in this whole business from the very start and I think even a sceptic like you, Sargent, will have to agree that the powers you're up against may well be more spiritual than criminal."

Talbot interrupted, not happy with the route this conversation was taking.

"All I know, Doctor Ellis, is that we have an obviously deranged man, seemingly with some sort of grudge against the Balmforth household going around killing innocent people, for what reason we have yet to discover."

From behind him came the voice of Noblet Swallow, who had been listening to the doctor's words.

"What about Lucy? What about the Baron?… What about me? Supposing I had an been killed by that glass. Are you saying they were just coincidences? The horses? The fire? Do you think all those hundreds of panes of glass shattered just because he slammed the door a bit too hard?" His question hung in the air, waiting for an answer… The four men now stood looking from one to another, searching for the logical explanation, which they knew did not exist.

Somewhat sheepishly, Sergeant Parker cleared his throat.

"You've got to admit Sir, there may be something in what he says."

Talbot was seen to ponder on his sergeant's words, abstractly tapping his prominent chin with the folded death certificate.

"Very well," he announced, "We'll go and have a word with the good Reverend Underwood… Perhaps he can enlist the assistance of the Almighty," he added sarcastically. "What's your thoughts on this, Bob?" he asked his colleague.

Parker didn't respond to the question immediately, unsure whether or not to voice an opinion in front of the doctor and Noblet.

"Well, Sergeant?" prompted the Inspector, "spit it out man, even the best policemen don't always agree with their superiors."

Parker considered his answer carefully before he replied.

"You know I'm not what you might call religious Sir, but perhaps it might be a good idea to enlist the help of the church. After all, as Mr. Swallow rightly pointed out some of the things that have taken place of late aren't exactly what you might call normal. Take the fire last night, for instance."

Talbot looked at his sergeant with a hint of skepticism, he had read Bob Parker's report earlier that day and couldn't help feeling that his colleague of many years may have had a glass or two of free champagne too much at the ball the previous evening… but had said nothing.

"I know what I saw, Sir," continued Parker, reading the expression on the inspector's face, "Those flames actually reached out for the Baron… nobody else, and when they had served their purpose and the man was as good as dead, they just died away like they had been turned off." He mimed the action of flicking an imaginary switch.

"That's a fact Inspector," added Noblet, Doctor Ellis nodding agreement. "By the time we arrived with the fire appliance, the fire was as good as out."

Talbot removed his spectacles and began to polish them with his handkerchief. Looking hard at his sergeant he saw a look on his face that could not be ignore, . He'd known Bob Parker for many years, had seen him rise through the ranks from constable to detective sergeant. Dismissing his previous misgivings, he now knew for sure that if things had happened the way Parker described, then it was undoubtedly true. For a brief moment the Inspector felt a touch of apprehension as he admitted to himself that he might, for once, be over-matched on this case. There was not a criminal mind anywhere which he would not engage, but here was something altogether new to his experience.

"Well?" asked the doctor. "Are you going to take the reverend's help seriously?"

The inspector nodded his head slowly as he replaced his spectacles.

Chapter 25

The day dawned unexpectedly cold for the funeral of Sir Oliver Balmforth. It was one of the few inclement days of what had been one of the hottest summers in recent years. The funeral was to be held at Saint Michael's but on the instructions of Lady Balmforth, Sir Oliver's body was not to be placed in the family vault as tradition dictated. The thought of her husband spending eternity lying next to the newly interred remains of his hated father was altogether too disturbing to contemplate. Instead, he was going to be laid to rest in a secluded part of the small churchyard, a cool, grassy spot overshadowed by a huge and ancient yew tree.

Upon the advice of Katerina, Felicity had agreed to the arrangements for the funeral to be made by Gregory, who with the help of James and Owen, had taken care of everything from the selection of a casket (the finest to be found in East Anglia), to the invitations of selected friends and associates, family being almost non-existent, Sir Oliver being the only child of an only child. The one arrangement Felicity was consulted upon was the design of the tomb and its inscription. After much consideration, finally deciding on a plain rectangular slab of white marble, largely unadorned save for the simple inscription:

SIR OLIVER BALMFORTH
1877-1904
LIFE IS SO PRECIOUS
TIME IS SO SHORT

Somehow, the overcast sky seemed to reflect the somberness of the occasion. Around the open grave were gathered almost the entire population of Sorrow, together with many of the residents of the neighboring villages of Swanton, and Handsthorpe to the south and Theydown Cross to the east.

The small church itself was full to overflowing. Most of those present at the fateful Hunt ball had felt compelled to pay their final respects, but many others had come purely out of curiosity, a look of expectant fear on their faces.

The rumors and stories of the strange events surrounding the Balmforth family had lost nothing in the telling.

The staff of Sorrow Hall were seated in their familiar pews, with the exception of Elsa Divine, Meg, Bridget and Lizzie who had remained behind in preparation for the arrival of the selected mourners invited back to the Hall for refreshments.

Felicity sat in the pew reserved for generations for the sole use of the Lady Balmforth. She felt strangely vulnerable with the absence of her husband. All eyes were upon her, she reached out a pale hand, searching for Katerina's, who was seated close by.

Gregory caught the movement, watching as the two women found comfort in each other's touch. He was deeply moved, but not too surprised to notice his wife's deep blue eyes fill with tears, her lower lip starting to tremble like a child's.

Although they had not discussed the matter, he understood that Katerina blamed herself for all that had happened; the deaths of Lucy, Mrs. Black and Oliver, even old Jock, the gardener.

As much as it hurt him, Gregory had to admit to himself that she was probably to some degree correct.

At the back of the church stood Inspector Basil Talbot, Sargent Bob Parker and P.C Edwin Townsend, the latter looking extremely uncomfortable in his best suit, the high starched collar chaffing painfully at his thick neck.

Talbot leaned over, his lips almost touching the constable's hairy ear as he whispered, "The moment this service is over with, I want you straight back in your uniform. I've a feeling that if we don't catch our man very soon, this won't be the last funeral we will be attending here." His gaze involuntarily went to Lady Felicity Balmforth.

After what seemed to those outside, like hours, the church doors finally opened. The gathered throng parting respectfully to allow the Reverend Underwood to lead the procession of mourners towards the waiting graveside. Following close behind strode the six pallbearers, Noblet Swallow, Edwin Townsend and Gregory Christopher among them. Next came Lady Felicity, her face hidden by a small black veil. Katerina Christopher supporting her by the arm.

Most of the others following were strangers to the villagers with the only exceptions being Doctor and Mrs. Ellis, Rachael Swallow and of course, the staff from the Hall.

James stood at the head of the open grave as the casket was lowered reverently into its gloomy depths, the sounds of weeping and embarrassed coughs punctuating his words as he read from the small leather-bound Bible held in his hands.

It seemed somewhat sad to James that most of the tears were shed by the villagers, the majority of whom had barely spoken a word to the dead man. He lifted his eyes from the Bible to look at the mourners surrounding him. Directly opposite stood the imposing figure of lady Caroline Auburn, still managing to look glamorous despite the small felt hat and veil concealing her injuries, giving her a look of mystery rather than one of mourning. Lined up respectfully were the staff from the Hall, Margaret stood by his side, her pretty face pale with grief.

On a cheap wooden chair sat Lady Felicity, flanked on her left by the doctor and his wife, and on the right by Katerina and Gregory Christopher. Her face hidden by a veil, she sat straight-backed trying to uphold the dignity of the Balmforth name. In a clenched fist she held a small lace handkerchief, her grip tightening as she nodded politely to the words of sympathy and proffered condolences. People introduced themselves as distant relatives or one-time friends of the deceased, some looking distressed when Felicity obviously didn't show any signs of recollection.

Inspector Basil Talbot stood well back from the gathering, feeling as though he had no right to be there. He couldn't pretend he had ever liked the deceased. In his opinion, if the Baron had reported his father's murder at the time it had occurred, then this Michael character would have been hung long ago and none of this would have ever happened. Indeed, the only reason he had attended was because he suspected this was just the sort of occasion that Michael would want to make his presence felt. Unbeknown to the mourners, Talbot's officers were placed amongst the villagers, dressed in civilian clothes in readiness for the Inspector's instructions.

Noticing the cold glare Lady Caroline directed at his Sargent, Talbot felt the start of a smile but quickly stopped himself before anybody had chance to notice. He nudged Bob Parker standing next to him.

"It seems that the romance has gone out of your relationship with the beautiful Lady Caroline."

Parker shrugged his shoulder in a gesture of disinterest.

"She did her job. She got me into the hunt ball, didn't she?"

Talbot nodded. "Just take a look at them. Like a flock of carrion crows." He indicated the mourners by pointing with his chin. "I doubt more than a handful of them even liked him, yet here they all are, crying and looking sad. Fucking hypocrites!" he spat.

Parker raise his eyebrows, surprised at the Inspector's profanity, it was one of the few times he had ever heard Talbot swear. 'This case is starting to get to him' he thought.

"It doesn't look like our man is going to show, Inspector," the sergeant ventured in a hushed tone.

The two policemen looked up as they suddenly became aware that the Reverend was already delivering his final words to the assembled mourners.

"This is indeed a sad day for us all. I have only been among you good people for a short while, but in that time I have found many new friends, not least of all the recently departed Sir Oliver Balmforth, taken from us so tragically."

The listening audience, nodding in puppet-like agreement with the Reverend's sentiments, whether they truly believed them or not.

Talbot looked sideways at his sergeant. "Hypocrites." he repeated.

James continued, eyes cast down at the now closed Bible in his hands.

"Today is made even more painful by the ungodly way our dear friend was taken from us. No illness. No fatal accident. No honorable death in the service of his King and country. Instead he met his end at the hands of the Devil himself."

The people around him looked alarmingly at each other, this was ridiculous. Everybody knew it was an accident. A fire had got out of hand in the Hall and claimed a victim, fortunately only one.

Sensing he may be losing his audience, the James lowered his voice. "Yes. I say the Devil, and by the Devil I mean… *The Devil…* in the form of some poor unfortunate wretch… In recent months we have tragically lost to many of our friends. And colleagues, even as we speak, the body of Jock Simkiss is laying in the Chapel of Rest, an innocent man, a sixty-year-old gardener who had never harmed anybody. The stable girl, or should I say groom, Lucy… A young woman who had managed to achieve what many would never had thought possible, a woman who had her whole life before her… and Mrs. Black, who had for many years been a faithful and loyal cook to Lord and lady Balmforth and indeed his late father before him… and of course the untimely death of Sir Rupert Balmforth himself.

"With what we now know, one would be forgiven for suspecting that the mysterious demise of old Mrs. Heathcoat was no longer such a mystery? Perhaps we will never know? How many more innocent people will I have to lay to rest?

"All of you here today are aware of the incidents I am referring to, and while I am assured that the police are doing all that is humanly possible to put an end to this abomination that is amongst us, I feel that we should all take it upon ourselves to join in prayers, not only to the memory of our departed friend, Sir Oliver Balmforth, but also to bring an end to the evil that has come into our midst. This man, if man we can call him, is still amongst us. He must be found and he must be stopped. It is an affront to God himself to allow this child of Satan to seemingly do, as he will. Why he should turn his wrath towards the Balmforth family is not important, but I tell you now, none of us are safe. He must be stopped!"

James drove his fist loudly into the leather-bound bible, startling the congregation, who were staring transfixed. His voice had slowly grown from a low growl to a shout of outrage. Attributing all the deaths to some sort of divine power was just too much for most of those gathered at the graveside. With embarrassed coughing and much shuffling of feet they slowly began to disperse, few attempting to feign politeness towards the young rector.

"James?"

He turned to comfort Margaret, her hand resting lightly on his sleeve.

"I… I apologize for my outburst." He called to the backs of the retreating villagers. He spoke self-consciously under the stern gaze of those still remaining.

For the first time, Lady Felicity spoke. Rising from her chair she swept the black lace from her face. Her eyes were dry but held a deep sadness. She spoke loudly, her voice steady, many of the dispersing mourners lingering to hear her words.

"Please don't apologize James. I'm very much afraid that what you say is entirely true."

She looked up to face the gathered villagers.

"My husband was murdered as surely as if he had been shot down. This evil that you speak of was brought about, albeit unknowingly, with my help, and it is up to me to put an end to this horror if I possibly can."

She looked steadily at the two policemen standing a little apart from the others.

"Inspector Talbot," she continued in the same calm tone, we are dealing with somebody much more powerful than you can ever imagine. One day soon he will come for me and when he does, I will be ready for him."

Katerina came to her side, taking her hand and squeezing it. Felicity stopped and bent down to pluck a white rose from the midst of one of the dozens of floral tributes spread upon the ground; throwing it into the open grave she turned back to James and gazed steadily into his eyes.

"Now, Reverend Underwood, if you would please say your final prayers and get this over with… I would be honored if you would join us all later at the Hall for some light refreshments?"

Still holding Katerina's hand, Felicity turned her back on the shocked mourners and headed towards the brick archway in the churchyard wall leading to the ancestral home of the Balmforths.

Chapter 26

Felicity sat at the end of the preposterously long dining table, the expanse of polished mahogany bare save for the small area in front of her containing a silver tray holding the cruet as well as a selection of various sized cut glass pots. The larger containing honey, raspberry preserve and thick cut marmalade, the smaller a choice of mustards, horseradish sauce and mushroom ketchup.

She pushed a kidney disconsolately around her breakfast plate. She had always had a meager appetite, as Owen was well aware of, but still, every morning, she went through the same ridiculous ritual. The long sideboard was laden with silver-lidded servers, oak smoked kippers from Cromer, new laid eggs, both poached and scrambled, crispy bacon, homemade pork sausages, mushrooms and kidneys.

Oliver had always insisted on a full traditional English breakfast, Felicity herself simply being content with a pot of Earl Grey and some lightly buttered toast.

Behind her she could feel the presence of Owen, waiting patiently for her to finish.

She knew it was time she stopped this façade but somehow she could not bring herself to change her husband's instructions to the staff, not yet, not so soon.

She pushed the still full plate away, dabbing her lips with the corner of a cotton napkin, more out of politeness than necessity. In an instant Owen was at her side, removing the plate and other accoutrements from the table, before ringing for one of the maids.

"I'm sorry, Owen, but you know I'm not a very big eater at breakfast."

As with every other morning, the apology was greeted with a polite bow from the diminutive butler. But she knew that tomorrow morning the same amount of food would be prepared. She was fully aware that none of the uneaten food would be wasted. Instead, it would be transferred to the huge oval china chafing dishes used by the household staff.

How she would have liked to join them, seated around the long, scrubbed pine table in the middle of the flagstone floor, the warmth of the kitchen, the relaxed conversation of people who know each other well enough to eat a breakfast together without all the pretense and pomp she had to go through each and every morning.

Owen's voice interrupted her thoughts.

"Would your Ladyship care to read this morning's newspaper?"

Taking it automatically she rose, nodding her thanks to the butler as she left the room, pausing to smile at the young maid as they passed in the fully aware that she would be eager to clear the sideboard and return downstairs for her own breakfast.

Felicity slumped heavily into one of the fireside chairs in the front parlor. The fire was made up but not yet lit. She sat looking down at the unopened copy of *The Times,* trying to make some sense of her life.

Every morning since the funeral she had gone through the same routine. Sat in the same fireside chair, a folded copy of the *Times* unread on her lap. With a slight shock she realized that it was a week to the day that Oliver had been laid to rest. How unfair life could be. Just as she and Oliver had discovered a new, more fulfilling love in each other, he had been so cruelly taken from her, leaving her life in ruins.

She had no interest in running the Balmforth estate. No interest in living in her husband's huge house with all his servants, his land, his worries.

Letting her head fall back, she stared up at the high, ornately corniced ceiling.

"I must make a decision, its time I took control of my life… After all, wasn't that what she had been trying to do when this whole Hellish situation began?" she whispered quietly to herself.

With a sigh of resignation, she grabbed the arms of her chair and pulled herself to her feet, the newspaper sliding to the floor. Picking it up, she tucked it under her arm and strode quickly towards the kitchen stairs, hesitating slightly before descending.

As she entered the large cluttered room she looked with envy at the happy band of servants seated casually around the long pine refectory table. All conversation stopped dead at her sudden appearance, the chairs scraping loudly on the flagstone floor as each of the servants nervously leapt to their feet, brushing crumbs from their fronts, wiping smears of egg yolk or butter from the corners of their mouth.

Owen, his mouth still full of half-eaten bacon, looking flustered at this unheard-of interruption, painfully forced the food down his throat and quickly replaced his calm, butler's mask, which had, to his embarrassment, slipped ever so slightly.

"My Lady. Is anything wrong? You have only to ring if you required us."

For some reason she felt intensely uncomfortable, as if she had no business here. She was a stranger in her own home, shut out, an unacceptable interruption to the morning ritual.

Realizing that she was behaving like a fool, she stammered an apology.

"I'm... I'm sorry to disturb you all at your breakfast... it's nothing important."

She turned as if to return upstairs. In an instant Margaret was at her side.

"Your Ladyship, please don't go."

Felicity looked into the pretty, open face of the housekeeper. Around the table all the staff were still on their feet, their mouths open in astonishment, wondering at Margaret's presumption.

Felicity felt her hand being taken, a wave of pleasure flowed through her at the words of the housekeeper.

"Please m'Lady, there's plenty to go around."

Hesitating, before replying, Felicity nodded, her cheeks reddening self-consciously.

"Yes, I think I'd like that. I'd like that very much."

Room was made around the table. Margaret piling a plate high with bacon, sausage, kidneys, scrambled eggs and mushrooms, before placing it in front of her Mistress. Owen stared, silent but wide-eyed, aware of the Baroness's frugal appetite, but remained silent.

That morning, seated with the others in the steamy atmosphere of the huge tiled kitchen, tucking into a breakfast the likes of which she hadn't sampled since her childhood, was one of the most agreeable Felicity could recall. The conversations between the staff had slowly grown as they relaxed in her presence. She found herself smiling with the others at the anecdotes of Miss Divine and actually laughing out loud when Edward described how Mr. Wharton the fishmonger had loaded his wagon the other morning only to find his horse had been stolen from between the shafts.

As she popped the last mushroom into her mouth she amazed the staff even more by carving herself a large chunk of bread from the crusty loaf being passed around the table, and proceeded to mop up the remnants of her breakfast, smacking her lips in a most unladylike manner as she swallowed the last morsel of crust. Aware that perhaps she had finally gone just a little too far, she felt all eyes upon her. 'To hell with it,' she thought, 'from now on I'm going to be myself, not pretend to be something I'm not.'

Wiping her mouth with the edge of her hand, she got to her feet.

"Thank you all so very much, I really can't remember when I've enjoyed a meal more. Now, I suppose I'd best let you all get on."

With a curt nod, she headed towards the stairs, picking up her still unread newspaper from the dresser.

As she walked slowly up the dim stairway her tongue ran lightly over her lips, still shiny with grease. Once again she tasted the mushrooms and the sausage. In her mind, the years rolled back. Once again she was seated at the breakfast table in a shabby terraced house in Stepney, in one of the poorer parts of East London. The smell of bacon frying, her mother, immensely fat and forever smiling, almost as it the two went together, her father taciturn, always dressed in black or dark grey, the aroma of tobacco clinging to his clothes...

With a new resolve she strode into the library, out through the French windows and headed towards the summerhouse.

The cold morning air made her shiver slightly. She almost turned back to fetch her wrap but somehow it felt like admitting defeat and that was something she could not bring herself to do.

With her back held straight she strode confidently across the lawn, her feet damp with the dew still clinging to the grass. She passed the rose garden noticing the drooping blooms turning brown now that the summer had drawn to a close. Indeed the whole garden would soon be in need of some attention.

Her mind conjured up a picture of old Jock, busy tending the flowers of which he was so proud, pushing his huge wooden wheel-barrow full of fruit and vegetables picked that very morning, trundling it around to the kitchen door for the cook to make her selection for the day.

Thinking of him, Felicity recognized that she would soon have to employ a new gardener, as well as another groom, as Jock had been doing both jobs since Lucy had died, and as willing as Edward was, he was no match for Lucy, or even Jock.

She glanced across at the ruined stable block, one more problem, she thought, her mare and Oliver's hunter were being housed temporarily in the barn but that was far from ideal. And the ballroom was still to be redecorated. So much to think about, so much to do.

The thought of the stable fire brought a picture of Mrs. Black to her mind, that image in turn bringing back the memory of Michael and her time in the church tower. What they had done. What he had done to her. Her hand stroked her abdomen. Thankfully the child growing inside was still too small to be noticeable through her clothing.

Arriving at the summerhouse, she sat on the cold wooden seat. It seemed every thought she had was linked to yet another horrific memory.

Her musing were distracted by a flutter of wings as a large song thrush landed on the grass less than a yard from her feet. Felicity instantly froze for fear of scaring it away. She watched spellbound at the capering of the bird, grateful for the distraction.

Hopping over the wet lawn hunting for food it stopped every foot or so, cocking his head to one side, as if listening for its quarry. Sure enough, with a sudden stab it plunged its beak into the soft ground, pulling a large earthworm from the soil. Gulping it down contentedly, it continued its hunt.

"Poor worm," Felicity whispered to herself, the thought bringing back the memory of a warm morning some months ago. She had been sitting in the same spot, chatting with Katerina when she had pointed out a tiny wren exploring one of the small box-hedges that bordered the rose garden. As they had both stopped their conversation to watch, amused at its acrobatics, a sparrow hawk had swooped down from nowhere and the wren was gone, nothing left save one or two tiny feathers drifting slowly to the ground.

Poor bird, she had thought to herself. Poor worm, poor bird… poor hawk.

It seemed people always pitied the victim, pitied the loser.

When Oliver had died, people had felt pity for his widow. When she had been kidnapped, pity. When she had first been introduced to Oliver's father, pity. Always pity, even that morning as she had sat around the servant's breakfast table she had seen it. In their eyes; pity, pity for the loser.

The word seemed to echo around her head.

Suddenly leaping to her feet, she called out aloud, "I will not be pitied." her voice breaking the silence of the morning. The thrush flying off towards the roses, calling noisily.

Lowering herself slowly onto the seat once more, she glanced self-consciously in the direction of the Hall, hoping nobody had heard her outburst.

"I will not be pitied," she repeated out loud, albeit this time in a whisper.

'Well, I always said I wanted to be my own master. Be in control of my own destiny. Answer to no one but myself. It seems I've got my wish. I'm a wealthy woman. I don't belong to anybody. It's up to me to make my life what I want it to be.'

Trying to forget the problems of her future for the time being, she picked up the still folded copy of the *Times* lying beside her on the bench. She slowly turned the unwieldy pages, which in her small hands seemed absurdly huge. Scanning the headlines with disinterest she came to *'Letters to the Editor.'* Folding the newspaper into four to make it more manageable, she settled back to read the comments about the growing force of Mrs. Pankhurst and the '*Women's Social and Political Union.*' It appeared that they were starting to make people nervous, people of course meaning *men*.

Her lip curled with distaste as most of the letters used the popular word 'S*uffragette*' as an easy term of derision.

Finally, she came to a correspondence from the eminent physician, Sir Almroth Wright, the pioneer of the recent anti-typhoid inoculation. He wrote explaining women's…"*unsuitability for making rational decisions,*" going on to proclaim that "*there are no good women, but only women who have lived under the influence of good men.*"

Felicity felt her blood pressure rising with anger.

"This is indeed too much!" she said out aloud.

Angrily, she crumpled the newspaper into an untidy ball and let it drop to the ground. Her mind had finally been made up.

"Thank you, Doctor Wright," she mockingly said to the crumpled-up newspaper, "You've made me realize just what I have to do."

Striding off back towards the Hall, she earnestly began formulating plans in her mind. So much to do. So much to organize. She headed directly to her room.

Standing in front of the full-length looking glass, she examined her reflection. Her skin looked pale against the somber black of her dress. Her hair was pulled back severely giving her face a drawn, almost gaunt expression.

"God what a mess I look," she said to herself.

Turning away from the mirror she went into the adjoining dressing room, the walls lined with racks of dresses, ball gowns, and coats, many of which she had never worn. On a series of shelves were lined up every conceivable kind of footwear, from elegant evening shoes and riding boots to white canvas tennis pumps. Facing the large window was a whole wall of pigeon holed shelving stacked high with neatly folded clothing, the uppermost section being full of round hatboxes.

Felicity let out a sigh as she pondered what would be suitable for a widow of only one week. Running her hand along the hanging garments she searched for something 'plain and sensible'; nothing too ostentatious. After rejecting one or two garments as being 'dull' her eyes came to rest on one of the dresses she had purchased on her last annual spring shopping trip to London.

"To hell with what people think. I will not begin my new life dressed as a dowdy old widow."

Grabbing the dress she re-entered the bedroom and rang for Meg.

While waiting for her lady's maid to arrive she quickly stripped off her 'widows-weeds,' dropping them in an untidy heap at the foot of her bed. Sitting down at her dressing table she began removing the pins from her hair.

It took over an hour but after much pinning and combing, arranging and rearranging, Meg finally came up with something that appealed to Felicity. Twisting her long blond hair into a large figure of eight and pulling it up to form the back of a high chignon, upsweeping the sides and allowing the hair to flow into a natural looking dip in the contour of the crown. At last Meg inserted the last clip, securing any stray strands neatly into place.

Taking the small hand mirror from the dressing table she held it behind Felicity's head, showing her the back view of her new coiffure.

Felicity's face lit up.

"Meg, you're an absolute marvel," she declared. Delighted with her new look, "You know, I honestly believe you could do this professionally," her voice lowering in tone as the germ of an idea invaded her thoughts.

"Oh! Thank you very much, m'Lady," gushed Meg feeling pleased with her effort, "It's been lovely having the chance to try out something new with your hair."

Standing once more in front of the looking glass, Felicity, with Meg's assistance, stepped into a dress of cornflower blue ninon over a foundation of fuchsia pink silk, the wide neckline dipping to a point in front of a 'Bertha' collar. A chemisette of ivory lace attached to the top, the material repeated on the tight lower sleeve. From shoulder to elbows the full sleeves were of fuchsia colored silk. The skirt falling from her small waist was edged with a double layer of frills in the same shade of pink.

Meg disappeared into the dressing room, returning moments later with a hat in each hand.

"Either of these would look lovely with that dress, m'Lady."

Trying first a high fronted, almost 'bonnet' like creation in shell-pink chiffon, Felicity looked at herself in the mirror for some time, her bottom lip sticking out with dismay before rejecting it as 'too old fashioned'. Throwing it onto the bed she tried Meg's second choice, a wide brimmed hat of ice-blue tulle over a silk lining, the crown and one side a mass of sapphire blue ostrich feathers spilling forward and over the front.

"Perfect," declared Felicity, smiling broadly at her reflection.

"Well? What do you think?"

The maid hesitated, unsure of herself. Felicity sensed her reticence immediately.

"What's wrong? Don't you like it?"

"No… no, m'Lady, it's lovely. It's just that…" Meg struggled to find the words, conscious that it was not her place to give an opinion on her mistress's taste in clothes.

"Just what?" asked Felicity, encouraging her with a smile.

Meg took a deep breath before replying, "It's just that I feel it needs something… something a little extra. Something like… "

Leaving the sentence unfinished, Meg picked up Felicity's jewel case from the dressing table.

"May I, m'Lady?" she asked respectfully.

Felicity nodded, an expression of amused interest on her face.

Selecting an item, Meg replaced the box.

Turning to her mistress she folded one side of the wide brim back onto the crown, forcing the blue feathers further to the front and causing them to hang low over Felicity's left eye, pinning the brim in place with an ornate diamond and sapphire brooch.

"There," she said simply, stepping from the line of vision.

Felicity stood and looked at herself in the long mirror. She was amazed at her maid's eye for detail.

"I must say, Meg, you really do have a talent for this sort of thing. You really are a natural. I truly believe that you're wasted here. Perhaps you and I should have a little chat about your future. About our future," she corrected herself.

Meg bobbed politely, not understanding at all the Baroness's choice of words.

Felicity put her hand on Meg's shoulder. A feeling of friendship seemed to pass between the lady and the servant.

"Now run along Meg, and ask Edward to bring the motor car around to the front, would you?"

Meg bobbed and turning to go, she noticed Felicity's crumpled black clothes still laying at the foot of the bed where they had been dropped. Stooping to pick them up she said "I'll take these and have them laundered, m'Lady."

Felicity turned, hand stroking her chin, deep in thought.

"No, there's no need for that. I shan't be requiring them anymore. You and I shall soon be taking a trip to London where we will choose a whole new wardrobe. As for those things, you may do with them as you please."

An idea suddenly struck Felicity.

"You keep them. They were very expensive, you'll be the envy of all your friends."

Meg stood open-mouthed, not knowing what to say.

Overjoyed at her maid's reaction and obvious pleasure, Felicity grabbed the pink hat, still lying forgotten on the bed and placed it lopsidedly on top of Meg's white lace cap.

"Stay right where you are" she ordered the stunned maid, hurrying into her dressing-room, she re-emerged some moments later with her arms full of clothes. Dumping them onto the bed she returned to fetch yet more. Soon the bed was buried under a mountain of evening gowns, dresses, underwear, shoes and hatboxes.

Meg still stood at the foot of the bed clutching the black clothes, the pink hat balanced precariously on top of her head.

Felicity started to laugh.

"Oh Meg! You do look silly." She took the mourning clothes and hat from her and added them to the pile. "Take them. They're all yours, with your skills with a needle and thread you will soon alter them to fit, you'll be the best dressed maid in the county."

Felicity sat in the back of the chocolate brown Wolseley Tonneau. The smell of the soft leather upholstery and the rhythmic throb of the powerful motorcar had always seemed to her strangely relaxing.

She was finally beginning to put her plans into practice. She already knew what her first steps were going to be. She was determined to set the wheels in motion before her child was born, yet was realistic enough to realize that she could accomplish nothing until the threat of Michael was resolved.

Her ambitions, her aspirations, would come to nothing while he still roamed free, and she knew that she was the only one who could solve that particular problem, but admitted to herself that help was needed.

Edward brought the Wolseley to a crunching halt in front of the Christopher's ivy covered home, he alighted and held the door open dutifully for his mistress, Katerina hurrying down the front steps to greet the Baroness.

As Felicity stepped from the back of the car's dark interior, Katerina stopped short, a look of astonishment on her face upon seeing her friend's flamboyant outfit.

"I see you're out of mourning," she said with an amused glint in her eye. "I was lead to believe that here in England you had to wait two years or so before you shed your widows black… and even then, aren't you supposed to go into grey?"

"Stuff and nonsense," responded Felicity, taking her friend by the elbow and steering her back towards the house, "Come Katerina, we have plans to make."

Chapter 27

Mrs. Stanton carefully placed the wooden tray onto the small table in front of the Reverend Underwood, poured tea from the willow-patterned pot into three matching cups and handed one each to Inspector Talbot, his Sergeant and the Reverend.

"There's some biscuits and some of my cheese scones…fresh baked this morning," she indicated the plates on the tray.

"Thank you, Mrs. Stanton, I'm sure we'll be fine." James cut his housekeeper short, knowing her fondness for inane chatter.

Sensing she was being politely dismissed, the housekeeper returned to her chores, closing the parlor door quietly behind her.

"Any progress, Inspector?" asked James, pouring milk into his cup and wincing as he sipped at the hot tea.

Talbot leaned forward, lifting his tea and helping himself to a biscuit. As he did so he spilt a generous portion of his hot tea into his lap, the scalding liquid soaking into the crotch of his trousers.

"Damn!" he let out the curse automatically, forgetting where he was.

"Sorry, Reverend," he apologized, giving the smirking Bob Parker a sideways look.

James laughed good-naturedly. "You've no need to worry Inspector. After all, I did spend many years in his Majesty's forces and I assure you I've heard expressions that would make even you blush. Now, Inspector Talbot, you were about to tell me if there's been any developments."

Talbot felt ill at ease, unused to having to report such little progress.

"Well, we've had a good think about what you said at our last meeting and we're all pretty confident he still intends to go after Lady Balmforth."

Bob Parker nodded his head in agreement, taking over from the Inspector. "We're planning to position some of our officers around the estate… plain clothes, of course," he added, spooning three heaped spoonfuls of sugar into his tea and stirring it slowly.

Talbot looked at him with distaste, aware of the Sergeant's sweet tooth.

“It appears that the Hall is in need of a groom and a gardener.” Continued Parker, “We intend to have a word with her Ladyship and propose that two of our lads temporarily take the jobs until we catch our man.”

James nodded his approval. “But how about Mrs. Christopher, she’s as deeply involved in this whole thing and I’m sure we must also fear for her safety.”

Talbot looked awkwardly from the reverend to his Sergeant and back again.

“I couldn’t agree more, but I’m afraid it’s a problem of manpower. I only have so many officers at my disposal and most of them are actively searching for our man, but I can assure you that we are aware of Mrs. Christopher’s possible danger and I’ve spoken at some length on the subject with her husband, and he assures me that he won’t let her out of his sight.”

“Of course Constable Townsend has been instructed to keep an eye on the… ” Parker interrupted.

“I was about to say that, thank you Sergeant,” snapped Talbot. This case was making him irritable.

The door to the parlor opened. Mrs. Stanton cleared her throat.

“Excuse me, your Reverence, Constable Townsend is here. He says he would like to speak to the Inspector.”

She stood to one side allowing the policeman to enter.

“Speak of the Devil and he’s sure to appear,” muttered Parker.

“If that were true this case would be a whole lot easier,” replied Talbot, “What seems to be the trouble, Constable?” he asked.

“Begging your pardon, Sir.” Townsend apologized as he stood stiffly to attention, his helmet held in the crook of his arm. “I just called in on the Christopher’s as you instructed, and Mr. Christopher informs me that his wife left in a motor car some time ago with Lady Balmforth. I was just on my way over to the Hall to check on them when I noticed your vehicle parked outside the Rectory so I thought I’d best let you know what’s going on.”

If at all possible, he stood even straighter, taking a deep breath. He was a man of few words and rarely had to report to a Senior Officer.

Talbot stood, placing his empty teacup back on the tray. Conscious of the wet stain on the front of his trousers, he wondered if he should explain it to the constable…

“You did well, Constable Townsend, I think we best join you. We’re just about finished here. I have one or two things to discuss with her Ladyship myself.”

James stood and shook hands with the Inspector and his Sergeant, walking to the door with them.

Thanking him for the tea, they bade him good day.

Parker drove, Townsend cycled, but Talbot decided to walk, following the path around the church and through the private gateway to Sorrow Hall. The Inspector arriving before the others, the road taking a circular route onto the main Norwich Road before coming to the gate of the Hall.

Trotting briskly up the steps, Talbot was surprised to find the heavy double doors being opened even before he rang the bell; Margaret stood in the entrance, wringing her hands, obviously distressed.

"Oh! Inspector. Thank God you're here."

Looking past her he could see Owen at the foot of the sweeping staircase talking animatedly into a telephone. Replacing the handset, he hurried over to the Inspector.

"I've just been trying to reach you, Inspector Talbot." his butler's calm completely overcome by his obvious distress, "It's Lady Felicity. You have to do something."

Talbot held up both hands, calling for silence.

"Now please calm down and tell me what's been happening."

Simultaneously, the housekeeper and the butler began to talk.

"One at a time… one at a time… please!" Talbot shouted.

Hearing his car pull to a halt on the gravel drive, he turned, calling through the open door, "Quick as you can, Bob," he called to his sergeant.

Leading Margaret down the steps he instructed Parker to question the housemaid while he himself spoke to the butler.

Taking his pocket book out, the Sargent licked the stub of his pencil.

"Now Miss. What exactly has been going on?"

Forty minutes later the two policemen sat in a quiet corner of the Wheatsheaf tavern, a tankard of Lacons Best Bitter in front of each of them.

Talbot tugged on the thick chain stretched across his front, pulling the heavy fob watch from his waistcoat pocket and checking the time.

"They should be here any minute."

Parker glanced up at the door as it opened.

"Here they are now, Sir," he said, standing to greet Gregory and James.

"Good of you both to come so promptly. Can I get either of you a drink?" he asked.

Minutes later they were seated, two more pints now crowding the small copper-topped table.

Gregory took a huge gulp of his beer and swallowed loudly. Wiping his lips with the back of his hand, he turned to the Inspector.

"I came as soon as I got your message. All I know is that my wife left at lunchtime with Felicity Balmforth. She said she was going to help her make some plans for the future. They drove off in the Balmforth's motor car. I assumed they were returning to the Hall."

Talbot pulled his pocket book out and folded it open on the table, more through habit than for any specific purpose. He knew exactly what was written on the pages.

"It seems… Mr. Christopher," he began in a hushed tone, "that your wife did indeed return to Sorrow Hall with Lady Balmforth, where it appears they both changed into outdoor clothing, boots, hats, that sort of thing."

"Yes, I do know what outdoor clothing is, Inspector." Interrupted Gregory impatiently, his concern for his wife growing by the second.

"Yes, quite," continued Talbot accepting the rebuff.

"It appears they left the Hall soon after, taking with them two of Sir Oliver's shotguns."

James put down his half-full glass and spoke for the first time.

"What exactly are you trying to tell us, Inspector?"

Bob Parker answered for Talbot.

"All we know is that they set out on foot in the direction of the main gate. Our people are searching the surrounding area. They haven't had time to get very far."

"I suppose it's just possible that they are simply out with the guns for some sport." added Talbot, "But we are of the opinion that this has something to do with our man Michael."

Gregory let out a low moan of anguish.

"Oh! my God! I doubt either of them has ever so much as fired a shotgun. Yet you're suggesting that they have gone off alone in search of this mad man. Surely, if they had any idea where he could be found, they would have informed you, they must realize the danger they are in."

Talbot gave Gregory a sympathetic look. "Mr. Christopher, we're not saying that is the reason for their actions. It is possible that they have located him, and have indeed set out in pursuit, but I think that highly unlikely. As you rightly say, they must be aware of the danger they are in."

Talbot hesitated, not wanting to admit his thoughts; even to himself; taking a sip from his tankard he continued, "You'll recall that on the last occasion Lady Balmforth disappeared, she left the Hall with Mrs. Black seemingly willingly, but from what we now know it seems she was under some sort of… influence… some kind of power, being used by this Michael… and from information I have received it appears that your wife too had been heavily under his influence at one time."

Gregory remembered that evening in the tower of his home. Katerina's incredible strength, her eyes, her grip on his throat… he had spoken to no one about the incident, swearing all those present to absolute secrecy. He could clearly recall her lying dead on the couch; her hideous wounds healing before his eyes. He turned, giving James a questioning look.

Talbot spoke, reading the signs,

"The Reverend hasn't told us anything."

"Who then?" asked Gregory, already guessing the answer.

"Sir Oliver told us the whole story," explained Talbot, "But I'm sorry to say we didn't altogether believe it… not until now."

Gregory squeezed his eyes tightly shut, trying to suppress the rising fear for his wife's safety. Taking a deep breath and trying to keep his voice calm, he addressed the Inspector, knowing this was not the time to panic.

"So am I to understand, that you are of the belief that my wife and Felicity Balmforth are once more under his control and somehow he has made them take Oliver's guns and… and do what?"

The question hung in the air, unanswered.

"May I say something?" asked James.

The three men turned gratefully to the Reverend, no one wanting to contemplate an answer to Gregory's question.

The Reverend took a sip of his beer, savoring the clean nutty flavor of the ale. "Between you, you have put forward two possibilities. Firstly, that somehow Katerina and Lady Felicity discovered where Michael is hiding and have gone there to confront him. But we all agree that's a most unlikely scenario."

The three nodded.

"Second," he continued, "is that he is using this '*mental power*' that we know he's capable of, to compel them to do his bidding… whatever that may be?"

Again they nodded but said nothing.

"Yet I believe there is a third possible option."

He lifted three fingers to emphasizes his point.

"We're listening," responded Talbot.

James took another sip of his beer to wet his mouth, before continuing.

"From what I know about this whole sorry affair, it seems that Katerina and Lady Felicity, with the assistance of the Balmforths stable girl and their cook, actually sought out this Michael. It was they that found him, not the other way around as you all seem to presume."

He paused, allowing his words to sink in.

"Now, somehow they managed to draw him out into the open, using his own powers to trace him to his cottage. Powers that even he may not have been aware of. If they could do it once, maybe they could do it again."

The table remained silent as each pondered the Reverend's words.

Gregory was first to break the silence.

"If you are right and if they do indeed plan to lure him out of hiding, then we have to find them, find where they plan to lure him to."

"Where indeed," remarked Talbot, stroking his jowls with concentration.

Felicity hesitated at the foot of the long iron ladder built into the flint wall of the church tower, the memories of her imprisonment still clear in her mind. She felt Katerina at her side.

"Felicity, we don't have to do this. There must be another way."

Felicity shook her head sadly.

"No, there is no other way. Until we're free of him we're going to live in fear. He'll destroy us both… you know that."

Katerina nodded, grim faced.

Felicity, hardening her resolve, began her ascent, pulling herself one rung at a time up towards the bell tower far above, the unwieldy shotgun banging noisily against the ironwork of the ladder as she ascended.

The two women heaved themselves awkwardly through the opening in the belfry floor, unused to such physical activity. They shuffled forward on their knees, crouching low under the bells. Felicity's eyes swept the interior of the circular room coming to rest on the scraps of filthy sacking and the frayed pieces of rope lying on the floor. She stretched forward, picking up a strip of white linen that had been torn from her petticoat.

Katerina's voice broke into her thoughts, the words echoing hollowly in the enclosed space.

"What a dreadful smell. I thought the bell ringers were supposed to keep this place clean?"

Felicity felt her face flush red with the embarrassed realization that she herself had contributed to the fetid smell. Glancing down at the spot where she had lain she noticed the oak boards stained by her urine and… and what?

She recalled Michael. The things he had done to her. His feel, his rancid breath, his taste, a shiver of revulsion ran along her spine. The memory only served to make her desire for revenge even stronger.

Katerina watched Felicity's back, guessing her friend's feelings. They had never really spoken about what had happened in the bell tower, but knowing what Michael was capable of, Katerina could conjure up her own images of what her friend had endured.

The two women sat with their private thoughts, neither of them really interested in bringing Michael to justice. So much could happen between capture and the hangman's noose. Who would believe them? Could either of them stand up in a court of law and explain the things they had done? Their naive plans… They would be branded as Heretics, they would be questioned as to why they had abandoned Lucy to her fate. There could be no justice, his death would be their only release.

If they succeeded, what then… how would Inspector Talbot react?

A frown of doubt spread over Felicity's face, "You don't think we could be charged with anything do you?" She asked Katerina, voicing her concern.

Katerina looked out of the slit like window of the tower, not wanting to meet Felicity's eyes, her voice was hesitant, unsure, realizing that they could be making a terrible mistake.

"Talbot is no fool," she began, "Why else would we be here with these guns," she picked up one of the unfamiliar weapons to emphasize her point. "If we do this it will be premeditated murder."

Felicity let out a gasp, her hand flying to her mouth. "No!' it's not murder, it's self-defense. Nobody is safe with him out there, everybody knows that."

"Self-defense or revenge?" asked Katerina, "We both know this is the right thing to do but think about the repercussions. There would have to be a trial, the whole thing will be in the newspapers. Do you think anybody is going to believe the things that have been happening to us? Do you think the Bishop is going to allow any of this to become public knowledge. We will be called Godless. Don't forget that Oliver was under suspicion of murdering his own father or at the very least having knowledge of his murder. All the victims have either been Balmforths or worked for the Balmforth family, and now you and I could be doing something that will result in us both facing a charge of murder."

"Stop… stop…" Felicity shouted, burying her head in her hands. "What are we going to do? I know that everything you say is true, but you do agree we have to do something?"

The two women sat in silence, each wondering about the danger of what they were attempting. Katerina looked up at the sound of Felicity climbing to her feet. The Baroness was biting her lower lip with concentration, a look of cunning coming to her eyes… "What are you thinking?" Katerina asked, a note of alarm in her voice.

Chapter 28

Cowering in the soft mud below the plank bridge, Michael held his breath as the heavy footsteps of the two police constables sounded loudly above his head.

He grinned to himself. The fools, if only they knew just how close I am. He closed his eyes as a dusting of dry mud fell between the planks onto his face, dislodged by the policemen's steps.

Waiting for them to pass, he hauled himself up the steep bank using the long, coarse grass as a handhold. Peering along the dirt track, he watched the policemen sauntering slowly into the distance, chatting together aimlessly, making the most of a pleasant duty, strolling in the sunshine and not particularly keen to encounter this dangerous young man they had been assigned to try and locate.

Waiting until they had disappeared around a turn in the track, Michael crossed the bridge and set off in the opposite direction, his eyes and ears straining for the sound of any more police in the vicinity.

He cursed himself for letting his concentration lapse, he was getting careless and realized that on no account could he afford to let that happen again… Allowing himself to become preoccupied with setting some fishing lines in the stream, the two constables had appeared on the track as if from nowhere. If not for his extraordinary sense of danger, they would surely have stumbled upon him, he barely had time to duck under the small plank footbridge before being spotted.

Hurrying back towards his present hiding place he stopped suddenly, looking around in confusion. Surprised to find himself walking in the wrong direction, walking towards Sorrow… The last place he wanted to go!

Shaking his head, as if to clear his mind, he turned and headed back towards the stack yard that had recently become his sleeping place.

Drawing close to the walled yard he stopped, his back against the high flint wall, his caution returning in full measure. Peering around a corner he cast a wary eye in the direction of the distant farm buildings. All was quiet. Crouching low he set off in a loping gait across the open yard, ducking behind any convenient cover at hand until reaching the dozen or so stacks of cut barley straw, each roofed with a heavy green tarpaulin, the thick canvas held in place by stout ropes pegged into the ground. Crawling beneath, he worked his way into the space he had formed among the densely packed straw.

The intense heat inside the stack would have been far more than any normal person could endure, but Michael found the suffocating temperature almost comforting. Quickly stripping off his garments he lay on his back in the darkness, hands locked behind his head, ankles crossed, perfectly relaxed. Within seconds the perspiration began forming on his body, tickling him as it ran down his sides. His breath came slowly, the heat seeming to drive the oxygen away. Somehow he felt safe, secure in this hot, airless nest, almost as if he had been there long, long ago. He felt as if he'd finally returned home after an arduous journey. With that comforting thought in his mind, he drifted into an uneasy sleep.

'Leave me be...'

Somebody was holding him, pulling him from the darkness and warmth. He could see a smiling face. His mother? No, his mother was dead. Mrs. Heathcoat? She was younger, younger than he could remember. She was taking him from his safe spot in the straw stack, dragging him against his will out into the light. She was too strong for him. He was weak, helpless.

It was bright, the light hurt his eyes. It was cold... Everything was so cold. Below him was a huge bed. A young girl, face flushed red, lying dead... No, not dead... She was sleeping... A noise, someone shouting. A man towering over him, a huge man, an evil man, shouting, shouting at his mother? Shouting at the sleeping girl... His mother? Shouting at her? Not stopping! There was the spade; he must stop him shouting. The blood... the man... the girl, both dead. His mother? Please let me go back, back to the dark and the warmth... Someone was calling him... calling his name. They needed him. He needed them. He needed her. He must go to her. The womb must wait . . .

He awoke trembling from his dream, trying to force air into his parched lungs. Grabbing his clothing he slid from beneath the canvas cover, the warm sunshine feeling like a blast of cold air on his sweat soaked body. Dressing quickly he ran from the stack-yard, not caring if he was seen, not caring about the police. His only purpose was to reach her. She was calling him... Asking for him to hurry to her... At last she would finally be his and no one would prevent it.

"He is on his way to us."

Katerina's voice held a slight tremor of fear. Felicity gave her a reassuring look but said nothing.

They sat below the great bells of Saint Michael's, cross-legged, facing each other, their hands linked together.

How long they had sat like this neither was sure. Katerina murmuring words to herself, sometimes quietly, sometimes almost in a shout. She called to Michael using those of her powers that remained strong, to transport Felicity's thoughts through to him, reaching out to him, calling in Felicity's voice, compelling Michael to come for them; to release them from their torments, praying he wouldn't suspect that only by his death could they truly be set free.

As her mind reached out to him, once more she relived the anguish of her plunge from the high window of her home. The agony as her body lay broken over the hard iron spikes… The woman who's life had become at one with Michael was no more. Katerina had struggled to resurrect her power. Slowly, she felt the connection reestablish itself. The draw of Felicity flowed through her. He was getting closer. She could hear his breathing loudly in her ears.

Michael flitted from tree to tree, keeping to the shadows, his sense of caution beginning to return. He was once again in the depths of Yarrow woods, his home for so long.

The force that was drawing him towards the distant church was now almost tangible. He accepted that it was preordained that the hated church of Saint Michael's had to be the place of their coming together, a re-enactment of the moment that had given him his ultimate pleasure.

Picturing Felicity's white naked body writhing on the floor of the tower stirred up the familiar hollow yearning in the depths of his stomach. The hint of sickness, of breathlessness that accompanied his strong, throbbing erection, his mind dwelt on the image of her soft flesh laying invitingly waiting for his touch, as a flower opens for the touch of the sun.

In the confines of the circular belfry the sound of Felicity's breathing grew ever louder, coming in short, sharp gasps. Her breasts heaved with each intake of air. Between her crossed legs she could feel herself growing moist, the fluids from her body soaking into her under-garments and creeping below her buttocks. Perspiration began to break out on her body, running down her forehead and jaw line, leaving glistening trails of dampness on her pale skin.

Letting go of Katerina's hands she slowly began to stroke her own breasts. Eyes closed, she fondled herself, oblivious to the presence of the other woman. Between her searching fingertips her small nipples grew hard and full, standing out through the fabric of her clothing. From deep in her throat came a low satisfying moan as her head fell back in ecstasy.

Michael was now running openly, desperate to reach the tower, his erection thrusting painfully at the course material of his trousers.

Finally, his heart pounding in his chest, he came to an abrupt halt. Unable to control his yearning any longer, he sank to his knees in the soft soil. Holding his head in his hands he felt his hardness subside, the warm stickiness of his emission clinging to the inside of his thighs. His mind reeled with erotic images of Felicity's lovely face, her lips, and her mouth. Once again he could feel the sharp edge of her gleaming white teeth.

Felicity's head shot forward as she gagged for air. Her body shaking in a fit of coughing as she tried to clear the choking foulness from her throat.

Regaining her breath she looked with embarrassment at Katerina.

"My God what just happened to me?"

Katerina tried her best to hide her embarrassment.

"Well, if I'm not very much mistaken, I would say you just had an orgasm! ...La Petit Mort."

Felicity eyes flew wide with shock at Katerina's answer. Even the very word wasn't uttered in polite society, least of all by a woman. She was silent for a long moment.

"He... He raped me, just now. He raped me... with his mind... it was just like when..."

Her voice fell silent, from outside came the sound of the heavy iron gate of the churchyard being opened, creaking loudly on its ancient hinges.

A look of terror past between them. They instantly knew who it was. Neither had suspected he would arrive so soon.

In a panic they scrambled to their feet, stumbling against each other in their frantic haste. The cramped space and low hung bells adding to their frustration.

Struggling to calm themselves they heard the church door open and slam shut, they could sense the vibrations of the wall ladder leading up from below.

As one, they made a grab for the shotguns leaning against the supporting framework of the bells.

Katerina, moving fast, slipped behind the huge tenor bell, her hands shaking fearfully as she struggled with the unfamiliar weapon. Using the bell-frame as a support, she pointed the double barreled 'Holland and Holland' at the head of the ladder protruding through the opening in the belfry floor.

Felicity stood in the small space next to the bells, the heavy gun held loosely in her two hands. She knew what she had to do, she had to destroy this thing that was coming for them, for the sake of her own future, her own survival, for the sake of her unborn child. She had to be the executioner.

Their plan was a good one. Once he was dead they would leave him at the bottom of the ladder with a discharged shotgun by his side.

Not the Holland and Holland but the old Purdy. Nobody would connect that gun with the Balmforth's, Oliver hadn't used it in all the time she had known him.

Even if Talbot guessed that the death had been no suicide she was sure he wouldn't want to pursue the matter. After all, as Katerina had pointed out, the facts would never be believed. Yes, Talbot would have a satisfactory conclusion to a difficult case… his reputation intact… everybody happy.

As Michael drew nearer with each rung of the ladder, Felicity could feel his power growing around her. She sensed him compelling her to once more submit to his will.

With a supreme effort she forced her mind to defy him. She knew that this was to be her one and only chance of release. With a trembling hand she slid her thumb forward, disengaging the Purdy's safety catch. The perspiration stung her eyes as she began to lift the heavy gun slowly to her shoulder, just the way Oliver had once taught her.

Her arms ached with the effort. The gun was heavy, enormously heavy. Its weight seem to grow by the second, forcing her down, down to the floor.

A filthy claw-like hand came through the trap door. Even as his white-haired head came into view Felicity was spinning on her heels, turning away from Michael, the gun now feeling light in her grasp, shooting from the hip she pulled the trigger. An explosion of sound filled the bell tower. The recoil of the powerful twelve bore making her stagger backwards.

At the moment of his appearance Katerina had begun to squeeze the trigger, but in the same instant she became aware of Felicity turning to face her. She immediately sensed what was happening, and instinctively dived behind the bell. Felicity's poorly aimed blast ricocheted around the small room, the sound of the gunshot merging as one with the dull reverberation of the protecting bell.

Felicity stood trembling, her back against the flint wall, the discharged gun held loosely in one hand and pointing down towards the floor. Eyes staring into space, tears streaming down her face.

Looking though the timber supports Katerina saw Michael step from the ladder, edging his way between the bells. He looked into her eyes, his back turned unconcernedly to Felicity.

He was smiling at Katerina with his strange lopsided smile that never seemed to reach his eyes, the whites of which were now tinted red, but holding none of the warmth of that color. Instead they seemed to reflect a cold hatred.

Katerina could feel the gun still in her hands, the smooth surface of the trigger hard against her finger. She was protected by the bells, he could not reach her without a struggle, all she had to do was aim and fire.

For some reason, the very thought amused her. She actually smiled as she slowly dropped to her knees, and crawled on hands and knees beneath the line of six bells. Brushing past Michael's legs she crept to the edge of the opening in the floor. Holding the shotgun by the barrel she let it fall. It seemed a long time before it struck the flagstone floor far below, the loud clatter echoing through the nave of the silent church.

James and Gregory walked slowly from the 'Wheatsheaf' leaving the two policemen finishing their drinks.

"Well, where do we go from here?" asked Gregory, feeling utterly helpless. "They could be anywhere."

Before James had a chance to respond they both looked up, hearing the unmistakable boom of a shotgun coming from the direction of the church. The dying sound turned into the hollow ringing hum of a bell as it blended with the raucous cawing of the rooks disturbed in the elms behind Sorrow Hall.

Above the rooftops the birds could be seen, a huge flock, black against the blue sky.

James reacted first, yelling to Gregory to run and fetch Talbot. The Reverend raced flat out towards the distant church. Breathing heavily, he pushed through the lynch-gate of the churchyard. As he did so he heard the loud clatter of something falling inside the church.

Shouldering open the ancient door he saw at the foot of the tower ladder a broken shotgun laying on the stone floor, its wooden stock split in two by the impact of the fall.

Heedless of his own peril he leapt onto the ladder, pulling himself quickly up the iron rungs. His mind racing, knowing his actions were foolish, knowing he could be heading into untold danger. One half of his mind praying for Gregory to arrive with the police, the other full of fear at the thought of what he might confront.

Michael sensed rather than heard the approach of the Reverend. Turning in the small space, he peered down the long ladder.

Their eyes met. James was overcome with a wave of hopelessness. He should have waited. He was unarmed. He had stupidly placed himself at the mercy of this monster. High above, Michael laughed quietly to himself. Behind him, with their backs pressing firmly against the wall stood the two women, eyes staring straight ahead as if in a trance. Felicity was still clutching the shotgun.

"The gun," Michael demanded, "Give it to me."

Katerina took the gun from Felicity and handed it to him.

James saw the twin barrels pointing down at him, the two black holes seemed to fill his vision.

Was this to be the final thing he ever saw?

A picture of Margaret flashed through his mind. He had so much to lose.

The click of the trigger sounded loudly in James's ears.

Michael hesitated for a moment as the hammer struck the empty chamber, his finger slipping automatically onto the second trigger.

The momentary delay was all that James had needed. Whether through bravery or sheer terror he instinctively threw himself from the ladder, his hands closing around one of the thick bell ropes hanging from above.

The explosion of the shotgun filled his senses. His body screamed with pain as the red-hot needles of lead shot tore into his back and buttocks. He felt himself falling, plunging towards the ground, the rope burning through the palms of his grasping hands as the recently healed skin was flayed from his palms.

Instinctively increasing his grip, he stopped with a jerk, his legs and feet scrabbling for extra purchase on the smooth rope.

He felt his body being lifted once again into the air. The momentum of the now swinging bell far above was pulling him skywards.

Michael realized that he had missed his chance. Dropping the empty gun he turned to mount the ladder. From the corner of his eye he caught a sudden movement. Behind him, the five-hundred weight 'tenor' bell swung forward, propelled by the weight of the man hanging below.

With one foot on the top of the ladder, Michael was already off balance. The lip of the massive bell caught him solidly in the chest. With a grunt of pain he felt his foot slip. Hands clawing at the empty air he fell through the opening.

The two men passed in mid-air. For a split second their eyes met. In that moment James could feel only pity for the strange young man, now lying broken on the flagstone floor below him.

Lowering himself painfully from the thick rope James stared in shock at the shattered body at his feet. Ugly in life, yet uglier still in death, the blood from Michael's smashed face was slowly crawling over the surface of the flagstones covering the stains made so recently by Mrs. Black.

Peering through the still open door of the church, James was relieved to see Gregory and the two police officers running along the gravel path towards him.

Opening his mouth to call to them, his voice was drowned by an ear-splitting crash of thunder, the noise loud enough to make the hurrying men cover their ears with their hands, even as they ran.

Almost simultaneously with the explosion of sound, the air outside seemed to turn crimson with an instant deluge of rain… if rain it was… dark… thick… red.

James stood open-mouthed with disbelief as he faced his companions. In a matter of moments the strange storm had given them the appearance of three survivors emerging from some horrendous explosion.

Oblivious to the downpour, Gregory ran into the church, leapt over the bloody corpse and onto the ladder leading to the bell tower, his concern only for his wife.

As Talbot bent to examine the smashed body of Michael, the voice of his sergeant sounded loudly behind him.

"Oh dear Lord save us!" sobbed Bob Parker. Dropping to his knees in front of the Rector he clasped both of James's hands tightly in his own. "In the name of God, what's happening?" he pleaded, looking at the Reverend with tear filled eyes.

Talbot, still crouching looked askance at his sergeant in confusion "What the hell's wrong with you?" he shouted above the noise of the storm raging outside.

Sergeant Parker looked silently at Talbot, his face a mask of anguish, the path of his tears showing clearly through the red wetness of his cheeks.

Reaching out, James ran his open hand over the sodden hair of the kneeling policeman and displayed his carmine covered palm to Talbot, he said just the one word… "Blood?"

As if in reply, the church was shaken by yet another almighty crash of thunder.

"Can someone help me up here?," Gregory's voice echoed from far above them as he called from the open trap door.

Talbot hurried up the ladder and disappeared into the belfry. Moments later, Gregory began leading the two shaken women down the high ladder, Talbot followed, calling encouragement down to Felicity and Katerina.

The descent was slow, both women silent… Listening to the Inspectors directions… Placing their hands and feet carefully on the unfamiliar rungs of the iron ladder.

As Felicity's feet were guided to the ground by the helping hands of Bob Parker she turned to look on the prone form of Michael, still laying forgotten on the cold stone floor. With a groan of horror, the ashen faced Baroness fell into a dead faint, James catching her as Bob Parker let out a cry and sagged unconscious to the ground.

Looking down from the ladder Talbot stared in disbelief. Michael's eyes opened as he reached out and took hold of the smashed shotgun by his side, swinging it in a vicious arc upwards into the back of Parker's skull.

Leaping from above the still descending Katerina, Talbot landed clumsily trying to avoid Parkers prone body, at the same time making a desperate grab at Michael, missing him by inches. In one movement, Michael had sprung to his feet and hurled himself through the open door, slamming it loudly behind him as he disappeared into the crimson deluge still falling outside.

Gregory, still helping his unsteady wife from the ladder, felt a shudder run through the sturdy flint walls flanking him, without really knowing why, he shouted a warning to the others, his voice going unheard as the huge stained-glass window at the far end of the church shattered into a cloud of a thousand multi-colored shards of ancient glass and lead ribbons.

The sixteen-foot-high arched opening seemed to suck the hideous storm into the building. The whitewashed walls turning pink with dripping, carmine tinted rain.

Talbot, leaping over the unconscious sergeant, struggled with the church door, heaving it slowly open.

Running outside he stood and looked about, completely disorientated by the obscuring horror of the abominable storm.

"Over there!" James shouted over the policeman's shoulder, pointing at a fleeing figure outlined in red by a sudden flash of lightening.

Slowly, the Reverend slid to the floor, finally succumbing to his injuries.

Running blind, Michael headed for the safety of Yarrow Woods, plunging among the familiar trees, grateful for the partial shelter from the storm.

He hurtled heedlessly through the wet undergrowth. His breath loud in his ears, the blood of the storm mingling with that of his own gaping head-wound and running into his eyes.

"YOU WILL STOP!" The voice was loud… commanding… familiar… the unmistakable voice of Sir Rupert Balmforth standing, immovable, blocking his escape. From out of the shadow of his father stepped Oliver, a shotgun held lightly in the crook of his arm… the same shotgun that was even now lying shattered on the stone floor of the church. Some way behind, an old woman knelt at the base of a huge oak, her head buried in her two hands, her shoulders heaving with silent sobs. Michael looked past the two men, he knew the woman though her face was hidden . . .

Michael, in a gesture of supplication, fell to his knees in the mud, his mouth opening in a moan of horrified resignation.

Was this real? It can't be real. It must be in his mind, had the fall done something to him?

The storm stopped as suddenly as it had begun, the sodden leaves of the trees dripping noisily in the otherwise silent woodland. With the lessening of the downfall the figures of father and son and the only person who had ever loved him seem to grow fainter by the second, dissolving into the moist air with the last of the raindrops.

Gulping air into his lungs he dragged himself to his feet and looked about him, fearful that the vision would reappear to him at any moment. At that point Michael, for the first time in his life, felt real fear. Behind him he could hear the people calling, people chasing.

With a bellow of defiance he hurled himself forward among the surrounding trees. Arms pumping, legs pounding in the sodden undergrowth, his ears straining for any sound of pursuit, the agony of his injuries causing him to screw up his eyes as each jarring step tore at his shattered jaw.

It came from nowhere…

The sledgehammer blow drove into his ruined face, it's power multiplied by the forward motion of his flight.

An explosion of light in his brain. The bunched fist of Noblet Swallow broke teeth and smashed bone as Michael fell into darkness.

Chapter 29

"I didn't mean to kill him," Noblet Swallow said to nobody in particular as he squatted, forearms resting on his bent knees, his back against a tree. "When that storm started, I knew something was wrong, I heard shouts and came running to help. I saw Michael run into the trees so I ran back down the bridle path and across to cut him off. I thought I had lost him, he was a lot further back than I expected. He must have got lost or snagged up or something, he was running straight at me as through I wasn't there... the look on his face, it reminded me of Lucy... that day... He just kept coming through the trees... so I hit him with all I had." He glanced down at the bleeding knuckles of his right hand, deeply gashed from the impact with Michael's teeth.

"I knew I'd only get one chance to stop him. I just hit him," he repeated in a half whisper. "I didn't mean to kill anybody."

Talbot put his hand comfortingly on the blacksmith's muscular shoulder, surprised at the look of shock on the big man's face.

"Nobody is going to blame you, Mr. Swallow, you did what you had to do. Just look on it as saving the hangman a job."

"And that must have been one hell of a punch," Bob Parker added, trying to ease Noblet's mind slightly.

Michael lay on his back, eyes open in his shattered face. His head turned unnaturally to one side, a trickle of thick blood running from the corner of his slack mouth.

Talbot was giving the wound on the back of Bob Parker's head a cursory examination, wiping away the congealing blood with his handkerchief.

"You'll live, although you've got a bump the size of a hard-boiled egg."

The three men turned to the sound of jogging footsteps approaching from the direction of the church. Gregory hurried through the trees, stopping short as he spotted the dead man lying curled in the undergrowth.

"You got him then?" He ventured needlessly.

"I only hit him once," Noblet spoke quietly. Gregory, for the first time, noticing the blacksmith still crouching in the shadows "Noblet! What are you doing here?"

"I didn't mean you kill him, I only hit him once..."

Gregory, realizing that the blacksmith was obviously still in shock over what he had done turned back to the two police officers.

"How are the women and the Reverend?" asked the inspector.

"They're surprisingly well" he answered," James is pretty badly cut up but physically Katerina and Felicity seem fine, and once they know our man here has finally been brought to book I'm sure they will both be right as ninepence!" He cast a glance at the prone body of Michael. "Shouldn't we cover him with something?" he suggested.

Nodding agreement, Talbot removed his suit jacket and threw it over the ruined face of the dead man. "We best head back, I have to report what's happened and I need to speak to the two ladies, are they still at the church?"

"When I left them, they were helping James back to the Hall, I should think somebody would have fetched Doctor Ellis by now."

"Good,"' answered the Inspector, "we will need him to come and officially declare our man deceased. Let's get moving, the quicker we get back with the doctor, the quicker we can get the body moved."

With a final look at Michael covered by the Inspectors crumpled jacket the four men set off through the woods, Noblet's head still bowed, his hand running through his wet hair.

Upon reaching Sorrow Hall they were met by P.C. Townsend, saluting smartly as he addressed the inspector. "Doctor Ellis is with her Ladyship and Mrs. Gregory. The Reverend is being driven to the Norwich hospital by Lady Felicities footman, Edward… Have you any orders for me, Sir?"

"Yes, Constable, would you ask the doctor to come and see me as soon as he is finished, I need you and Sargent Parker to escort him back to the body."

"Body?" questioned the Constable. Gregory put his hand on the policeman's shoulder.

"Come on, Edwin, I'll tell you what's happened, I want to see how my wife is." He entered through the double doors of the Hall followed by Townsend, eager to hear what had been going on.

Talbot sat in one of the high-backed armchairs that flanked the fireplace of the drawing room, on a small table next to him stood a china cup of Earl Grey. Gregory Christopher stood staring out of the French windows, his own teacup in his hand.

"Ok Inspector, so what happens now?"

Talbot leaned back in the comfortable chair and took a deep breath, "Well, if I had been allowed to take statements from her Ladyship and your wife I could now be thinking about heading home, as it is, thanks to the good doctor, I will now have to wait around until tomorrow to interview them. Once the doctor has returned from the woods we will have to organize the removal and storage of the body. I'm hoping that the Reverend will be prepared to make all the arrangements for the burial, although I don't intend to rely on it, considering the circumstances."

Gregory came and sat in the fireside chair facing the Inspector, depositing his now empty teacup on the side-table. "You seem very keen to speak to my wife and Felicity, surely it's just a formality, after all, we have our man at long last, what more is there to know?"

Before the Inspector could reply they were interrupted by the red-faced Edwin Townsend, struggling to catch his breath, "Sorry to interrupt Sir, it's just that Sargent Parker thinks you should come back with me straight away Sir. You see, Sir… He wasn't there . . .The body… It was gone… Sir."

Chapter 30

Michael opened his eyes. It was dark, he could smell sweat, sitting up the Inspectors coat fell from his face. He looked about him. He was sitting on the wet ground of the woods, his face throbbed, he spat something from his mouth, picking it from among the dead leaves he held it up… One of his teeth… He ran his tongue around the inside of his mouth, the pain shot through him like a hot knife. He put his hand to his jaw, was it broken? The metallic taste of fresh blood brought back the events of the last minutes. With no conscious thoughts other than to get away he lurched to his feet, and running at a low crouch he headed once more into the depths of Yarrow woods.

Every step he took seemed to jar his whole body with a shock of pain, his head felt like it was held in a vice, slowly tightening, squeezing his skull, forcing his eyes to close. He stopped, bent forward, his hand resting against the side of a tree, his head hanging down, pink tinted saliva dripping from his open mouth. Blocking the pain from his thoughts he forced himself to try and think clearly. His body was terribly damaged, his sight impaired, he needed food, shelter… At last the realization came to him that there really was nowhere for him to go. Nowhere he wanted to go. He now knew that he had lost Felicity forever but he *had* succeeded in destroying the Balmforths. He remembered the vision of the two dead men that had confronted him. Did that really happen? He remembered the huddled figure of his mother. No not his mother, he had no mother, no father, they had disappeared. Why did he hate the Balmforths? Why?

He had been running through the woods, he had escaped the policemen. Something had hit him, smashing his face…The poacher… The blacksmith… The man Swallow. He had been helping the Balmforths from the very start.

Racheal Swollow stood at the tiny window of her cottage watching the last pink drips of rain slide down the glass, she clasped her hands together in prayer, the terror of the ungodly storm still causing her heart to beat loudly.

Where was Noblet? She needed him, she was frightened. Walking through to the small entrance hall she took her walking cloak from the peg, wrapped it around her shoulders and fastened it at the neck. Opening the cottage door she stepped out into the wooden porch. Turning to close the door-latch behind her she heard the familiar sound of the heavy double-doors of the smithy slam shut. With a sigh of relief she hurried around the corner of the building, eager to speak to her husband.

Michael moved quietly behind the cottages that flanked the common, joining the sparse margin of Yarrow woods. Skirting the small but well-kept garden at the back of Noblet Swallow's cottage, he reached the untended area to the rear of the blacksmiths shop. He stood surrounded by a mass of flat iron strips and bars of rusty iron wired into bundles and stacked high against the rear wall. Various damaged items lay about, partially hidden by weeds, old cart wheels, long defunct machinery and many hundreds of rusting horseshoes. He put his ear against the clay-lump wall listening for any sound coming from inside the building.

Edging around the side of the adjoining loose-boxes he stepped into the shadows of the tiled lean-to that fronted the forge itself. Lifting the latch of the two-part stable door he stepped without hesitation into the warm interior, closing the door firmly behind him. The large brick-built furnace still glowed red, he doubted it was rarely allowed to cool completely. The glow from the fire and the dull light from the two cobweb shrouded windows was sufficient for Michael to see well enough. He had no plan other than to find someplace to hide from his pursuers long enough for him to carry out his newly formed plan. A plan that would make sure he would never be forgotten by the people of Sorrow, the fools that have always hated him. He smiled to himself as he thought about what he had done with Lady Felicity, the smile freezing on his face as he recalled his encounter in the woods.

The old Baron? It had been like looking in a mirror… was he his father? He had died by his hands, as had the Baron's son, his own half-brother? The Balmforth family that had treated him of no importance had learned to their cost that he was a force far stronger than they could have ever imagined. Three of their staff were now dead, the family was destroyed, the name of Balmforth would be remembered with foreboding, people would speak in whispers when they told how the young man from the woods had brought retribution down upon the hateful family that had treated him like an animal.

He knew this was going to be his final act, the Rector was probably dead, or at the very least badly injured, all that remained for him to do was to avenge himself on the man that had caused him to reach this point… Noblet Swallow would die screaming and he would be happy to die with him. Everyone had to die, but few could choose the place and the way they wanted to go, and who was to accompany them on that great journey.

He was brought out of his revelry by the small sound of the iron latch being lifted. The bright bar of sunlight growing wider as the door slowly swung open. Assuming it to be the blacksmith returning to his work, Michael dropped to his knees behind the central forge, his eyes franticly casting about for something to use as weapon, well aware that Noblet Swallow was a powerful man and would not be subdued with ease.

The voice came as a surprise, a woman's voice. She sounded afraid, and with good reason, he thought. His mouth twisted in a thin smile, breaking the newly formed crust of dried blood that coated his lips and gums.

Rachael Swallow stood in the doorway, she had called out her husband's name, her eyes searched the shadows, the feeling of fear was still with her. Suddenly, the room was filled by the leaping form of a blood-soaked creature appearing as if from nowhere. Reacting quickly she managed to get outside but lacked the strength to slam the heavy door into his face. Michael hit the half open door with a strength far greater than any would have believed possible, the door flew wide hitting Rachael squarely in the face, the sound of bone breaking sounded loudly in her ears as she felt herself falling.

Inspector Talbot, Sargent Parker, P.C Townsend, Noblet Swallow and Gregory Christopher stood in the clearing looking around foolishly. Talbot bent and picked up his coat from the ground, brushing leaf-mold from it with his hand. Noblet seemed more in control of himself, perhaps because he now realized that he hadn't after all killed somebody. Bob Parker began searching the surrounding area in the hope of some kind of clue to Michael's whereabouts, he looked up at the Inspector and was shocked at the look on Talbots face, if he hadn't known better he would have said it was a look of fear.

Talbot cleared his throat loudly, looking down at his hands he spoke quietly. "I examined his body. I have examined dozens of corpses, have I not?" he looked up at his Sargent for confirmation. "And I am telling you here and now that that man was dead. Not unconscious, but dead. He wasn't breathing, he had no pulse, no heartbeat. He was dead." his voice began to grow louder. "Do you hear what I said? He was stone dead, now either somebody took his body, or he just got up and walked away…"

The gathered men looked uncomfortably at each other sensing the Inspectors uneasiness. Gregory hadn't told the Inspector about Katerina's fall and her miraculous recovery but assumed Oliver had, he wondered if now was the time to bring it up? He was relieved when Bob Parker broke the silence.

"Well, nobody carried him away" proclaimed the Sargent examining the soft ground for footprints. He was interrupted by the voice of Noblet Swallow calling from among the trees.

"Inspector, I think I've found something," the experienced poacher could read the signs with ease, a broken twig showing a flash of white, a green leaf laying on the ground yet to turn dull. "He went this way." The blacksmith walked several steps before stopping and bending down to retrieve a fallen branch, showing it to his companions they could clearly see the line of blood, still tacky under the blacksmiths thumb.

With the guidance of Noblet they followed Michael's trail to the very edge of the woods, coming finally to the area of common land that lead down to the stream and the village itself.

"Why would he head back towards the village?" asked Townsend "I would have thought he would try and get deeper into the woods, he must know them like the back of his hand, after all he's lived there all his life."

"That's as far as I'm able to follow," said Noblet rubbing his hands together in frustration, "if he crossed the common he could have gone behind the houses and continued along the lane to Handsthorpe, but I wouldn't have thought he was in any condition to go very far."

"That's a good point," said Talbot, "the fall in the church should have killed him, actually I thought it had!"

They fell silent as they considered his words.

"Suppose it did kill him?" Suggested Parker. "Suppose Mister Swallow also killed him as we are all sure that he did?"

"Oh my God,"' Gregory squatted down on his haunches, his hands clasped together as if in prayer, "This is something unnatural, this isn't just some lunatic on a killing spree, this man is the Devil, perhaps he can't be killed. "

Talbot opened his mouth to dismiss Gregory's words but something stopped him, what alternative suggestion could he come up with? he accepted with a sense of doom that he had none.

"We need to organize a search party." he turned to the constable, "Edwin, get together as many men as possible, pull them from their work if necessary, explain that we need to cut off any exit from the village, but impress upon them that on no account are they to challenge him, if they spot him they are to raise the alarm, that's all, we don't want any heroics, the last thing we need is another death."

Edwin Townsend saluted smartly and turned to go, hesitating as he noticed Noblet disappearing across the common in the direction of the row of cottages on the other side, "Now where's he off to?"

"Looks like he's heading for his home," ventured Gregory, "probably checking on his wife, she would be finished at the school by now."

Michael finished dragging the straw bales from the loose-box, his sweat soaked skin coated with chaff and dust from the dry straw. Piling them around the inside walls of the blacksmith's shop he searched among the various drums and barrels of oil, petrol and lubricating grease that littered the room. Stacking them in a pile, he took armfuls of the kindling stored near the forge and began distributing it amongst the straw before dousing everything with the various inflammable liquids. The smell was strong enough for him to worry if the fumes would ignite on the glowing embers of the fire, eventually deciding to open the door to allow the air to clear. Taking a bundle of kindling he lay it alongside the furnace ready for use. All he had to do now was wait…

Noblet moved quickly across the common, his eyes focused on his home in the distance. Rachael would be in the kitchen preparing a meal, he could see her in his mind's eye, her face flushed from the stove, an apron protecting her clothes, hair tied back with a scarf.

Michael heard the blacksmith's heavy footsteps as he rushed along the short brick path leading to the cottage door, he quietly pulled the double door of the forge shut.

The acute hearing of the experienced poacher heard the small snick of the iron latch, he hesitated momentarily, was it a draft rattling the forge door? He entered the cottage calling his wife's name as he strode into the kitchen, then the scullery. Pausing only to glance out of the tiny window to check the rear garden before heading up the thin winding stairway that curled behind the chimney breast. Finding the upstairs empty, the sense of foreboding grew strong in his heart. Remembering the sound of the forge door closing, he hurried back down the stairs and headed for the neighboring smithy.

The smell of straw mixing unnaturally with the stench of oil assailed his senses as he burst in through the door. He looked about, confused by the straw bales and bundles of kindling lining the walls. He never got the chance to consider their implication. Waiting until the blacksmith had his back turned towards him, Michael stepped from behind a stack of bales and brought the heavy iron tongs down onto the blacksmith's head.

Michael looked down at the prone figure laying among the iron filings and rust that covered the stone floor. "That' for the punch in the mouth." Smiling, he drew back his foot and kicked the unconscious man in his unprotected face. Blood spurted from Noblet's shattered nose and mingled with the black puddle spreading from the open gash on the back of his head. Lifting his foot once more, Michael stamped down with all his strength, the heavy work boot edged with worn hob-nails tearing open flesh, the iron rim of the heel splitting the man's ear like it was rotten fruit.

"And that one's purely for pleasure..."

Taking the end of the one-inch thick chain hanging from the roof he dragged in across to the unconscious blacksmith, the wheel of the pulley spinning noisily as it rattled on its ceiling bracket, rolling him over onto his face he pulled Noblet's hands behind his back and began to loop the chain tightly around his wrists. Finding the chain was too thick to knot, Michael searched among the various trays and tins until he found what he was looking for. Pulling the chain tight he slipped the bolt through the links and twisted the nut home.

Satisfied with his efforts he pulled on the hanging loop of chain connected to the pulley wheel. Noblet's arms were forced back against his shoulder joints as the shortening chain slowly took up the slack and dragged him across the ground, Michael heaved on the chain, the slumped body rising up towards the roof until the bound wrists brought up hard against the pulley wheel, his feet hanging clear of the ground.

Standing back to admire his work, Michael heard a man's voice calling the blacksmith's name. Hurrying to the window he saw one of the policemen and Gregory Christopher standing at the garden gate, another policeman was banging loudly on the cottage door.

Knowing he had little time, Michael plunged the bundle of twigs into the red embers of the forge holding them until they burst into flames. Returning to the window he saw the three men walking towards the blacksmith's shop. Wedging the prepared length of iron under the door brace he opened the window and called out with a mocking laugh.

"Are you looking for me? Don't bother trying to reach me, I have the blacksmith and his wife and they will be dead before you could get through the door." He spoke clearly despite his smashed jaw and swollen mouth, the agony of his injuries were as nothing to him, as he taunted the men outside, smiling through a bloody mask.

Talbot, Parker and Gregory stopped short of the smithy door. Michael peered back at them through the grimy window. The policemen and the killer studied each other with interest. Without warning a whoosh of flame obscured his blood encrusted face. Michael disappearing from view as he leapt back from the fire inside the building.

Noblet could feel the heat on the lids of his closed eyes, the pain in his shoulder blades was growing stronger as he gradually regained consciousness. Lifting his head, the pain screamed through his brain, he could feel the wet crawl of blood creeping down inside his clothes and mingling with the hair on his chest.

He opened his eyes with difficulty, the lids stuck together with drying blood.

Michael was dancing around like a man possessed, a handful of burning twigs smoldering in his fist, he was calling out to somebody outside, laughing and shrieking, running from one window to the other.

The blacksmith looked around the familiar building, searching for his wife, he felt a sense of relief that she wasn't there, he made a supreme effort not to try and think of where she may be and if she was safe. Michael had not yet noticed him stirring, he knew he had to make the most of his opportunity.

Using his hips to gain momentum, he began to sway his body, little by little, increasing the arc of his swing, back and forth until he finally succeeded in stretching his leg far enough to reach the corner of the brick forge. Pushing off with a mighty thrust he increased the power of his swing, the pain in his head and back was growing to the point where he feared he might faint. After what seemed like an agonizingly long time but in fact was only a matter of seconds, he managed to wrap his feet around the large anvil that stood next to the long tool rack in the center of the room, hooking his ankle between the tools and tongs in the rack he edged himself slowly along towards his goal.

Michael had now built himself up to a frenzy, screaming obscenities through the flames that had now almost entirely encircled the two men. Noblet was acutely aware that he had barely seconds to act before Michael turned and became aware of his danger.

The small iron brake lever that locked the pulley wheel was bolted to one of the two timber supports that bisected the room, he knew he had only one chance, if he missed it he would swing back helplessly on the chain, even the prancing madman couldn't fail to notice what he was attempting to do.

Taking a deep breath Noblet tensed his muscles, launching his lower body upwards he lashed out with one leg, catching the brake lever. The pulley wheel spun free, Noblet, unable to bring his hands into play fell heavily onto the stone floor, the chain noisily cascading from the pulley above him.

Michael was on him in an instant. Snatched from his trance-like state of euphoria he leapt onto the stunned and injured blacksmith, landing with both knees in the small of Noblet's back knocking the breath from the man's lungs.

Noblet could feel the heavy pounding of uncoordinated blows rain down upon him, he tucked his head into his hunched shoulders, instinctively trying to protect his already badly injured head, his hands behind his back desperately fingering the bolt that held the chain about his wrists. Without the weight of his suspended body the bolt was no longer under tension, given time he could easily loosen the hand-tight nut, but time was something he had none of. Concentrating on the bolt he shut his mind to the punishment he was taking and the searing heat about him, the sound of crackling flames and falling woodwork goading him on even as he felt Michael's hands on his, pulling them away from the sweat slickened bolt.

Michael's laugh seemed to grow louder and louder, becoming more a shrill screech than any sound uttered by a human.

"There's no point struggling, you and I are both going to burn together in Hell, you, me and your pretty, young wife lying next door covered with dry straw listening to the sound of the flames getting nearer and nearer while those pitiful fucking policemen stand outside and watch."

He would never know where he summoned that extra ounce of strength from, but at the mention of his wife and her fate he seemed to shrug off the heavy blows and blinding agony of his injured head and face. Spinning his body onto his side, Michael was thrown heavily against the iron tool rack, Noblet, managing to get his feet against the anvil, used it as a firm base to give himself the impetus to hurl himself onto Michael's struggling body. The bolt was still gripped in his hand, but the nut rolled across the floor.

Even with his horrific injuries,, the blacksmiths years of working at the anvil had developed strength enough for him to contend with the inexplicable power of the screaming madman. Rolling together in the choking, smoke filled building, the burning embers falling about them, Noblet lifted his chain-wrapped wrists and brought them down hard on the back of Michael's head, managing at last to halt the torrent of blows long enough to free his hands. Still tightly gripping the chain he attempted to wrap it around the man's neck, Michael managing to get a hand to the chain to prevent it. Noblet wound loop after loop around the struggling Michael, ignoring the blows and scratches he was receiving. The flames were now so intense that the air was being sucked from the building,, He knew no matter what happened now he was going to die. Rachael was going to die. But Michael ? Could he die? He had to make sure that whatever the outcome, Michael must not survive yet again.

With his clothes beginning to singe and the old barn roof starting to collapse, Noblet let go of his foe and leapt upon the circle of chain hanging from the pulley. Throwing his weight against it he began to take up the slack. The unearthly screaming seemed to grow even louder, causing the pain in his skull to reach new heights. Looking up he saw the main supports of the roof begin to lean to one side as the massive roof trusses collapsed in on themselves and toppled towards him.

With a final surge of energy he lashed out, catching the pulley lock with his clenched fist… The burning post it was affixed to fell away from him, the ancient roof, no longer supported crashed down. Filling his parched lungs he screamed out the single word… “Rachael…”

Chapter 31

"We can't just stand here," shouted Gregory, "He's going to finish it, here and now, he knows his time is up and he intends to take Noblet with him."

Talbot turned to him, his face impassive, trying to look in control but failing badly. "Alert the firemen, we need the pump here and quick. Will you be able to find them?"

"That's Noblet and Edwin. I'll get Edwin and lend him a hand with the pump."

"Please be quick, and tell Edwin… P.C Townsend… To send over any help he's managed to recruit."

Gregory set off at a run. The flames of the old building were now gaining a hold, the face of Michael appeared at each window in turn, twisted into a grotesque mask as he taunted the policemen with words and gestures. Leaping into the air and shaking his fist at them while the fire raged through the building.

"Mad as a March hare." declared Parker.

Talbot nodded his head in agreement, "Mister Christopher's right though, we can't just stand and watch two men burn to death… Even if one of them does deserves it." he added as an afterthought. "Try and find something to break that door down"'

"But Noblet? if we interfere he'll be killed."

"He'll be killed if we stand here and do nothing. Now come on, let's get moving."

The policemen ran to the rear of the smithy, guessing correctly that there would be discarded ironwork or something heavy enough to be of use. The clay-lump wall to the back of the smithy was hot to the touch, the smoke already belching through the ill-fitting pan tiles of the roof. Searching among the rusty iron-work and rotten timber they came upon a thick wrought-iron gate post. With some effort they dragged it from the tenacious grip of the knee-high grass and weeds, taking an end each, they hurried back to the entrance noticing that the back of the smithy was beginning to bulge outwards and was getting close to giving way to the intense heat from inside.

Reaching the front of the building they saw P.C Townsend and Gregory Christopher hurrying towards them across the common pulling the parish fire-pump with the aid of a small army of villagers, both men and women.

Talbot and Parker held the long iron post like a battering ram, tensing themselves to charge the smoking door, their plan stopping abruptly by the loud shout of Noblet Swallow calling out his wife's name, followed immediately by the sound of the roof caving in, a great wall of flame bursting through the weakened barn which collapsed in on itself, supported only by the cottage and the burning loose-boxes at either end of the structure.

The gathered villagers stood in stunned silence next to the policemen, the parish fire-pump momentarily forgotten as the realization Hit home that nobody could survive such an inferno. As one they caught their breath in superstitious horror as the light breeze parted the billowing smoke, revealing a tilted, black smoldering post standing proud of the ashes, crossed at the top by one of the burning remains of a heavy roof beam. From the beam hung the blackened and flame wreathed body of a man, turning slowly on a thin chain in the rising flames. Nobody present would ever forget that image, people afterwards often described it as almost religious… the image of the cross and the body hanging like a sacrifice to the Devil.

Turning to the men by the pump, Talbot bellowed at them to snap them out of their stunned trance. "Get that pump working, play the water on that man," he lowered his voice to speak to his Sargent, "Do you think it could be Swallow?"

Parker looked ashen. "I very much fear that indeed it could."

The many willing hands worked the side-bars of the Parish pump, the jet of water slowly gaining power, Townsend getting as close as he dared to the flames with the brass collared hose. "Look out!" somebody shouted as the roof of the first loose-box finally succumbed to the flames and disappeared into the building with a mighty crash, the double stable door bursting open at the same moment.

From the flaming building stepped the smoking figure of a man. In his arms hung the lifeless form of a woman, her arms and legs hanging down limply as she was carried towards them through the thick billowing smoke. People backed away, unsure of what they were seeing… Gregory was the first to move. "Somebody fetch Doctor Ellis." he called as he ran past the gaping policemen, recognizing the smoke-blackened spectre as the village blacksmith.

The barely identifiable corpse of Michael lay wrapped in a shroud of dirty canvas in the porch of the church, many of the villagers had at first objected when the church was suggested, but compromising by allowing the porch to be used as a temporary shelter. Noblet Swallow and his wife were on their way to the Norfolk and Norwich hospital in the city. Doctor Ellis had accompanied them in the back of the Balmforth's Wolseley, leaving Talbot frustrated and keen to interview the blacksmith. Talbot himself sat with his sergeant in their now familiar spot at the bar of the Wheatsheaf.

"Well Inspector, I suppose that just about closes the case," said Bob Parker, "although I would love to know how Noblet managed to get the better of that crazy bastard."

Talbot nodded in agreement and took a gulp of his ale, "We'll be able to talk to him and Mrs. Swallow tomorrow I'm sure, but whatever took place in that room is going to make one hell of a fascinating tale, the villagers owe their blacksmith a huge debt and he's going to need all the help he can get. He's lost his livelihood after all, and who knows what damage this has done to his state of mind… and his wife's for that matter."

Noblet Swallow sat slumped in the back of the huge motor car, the soft luxury of the tan leather seating absorbing the bumps of the uneven roads. He opened his eyes and looked into Rachels. She smiled and squeezed his hand reassuringly, the darkening bruise on her jaw causing her to wince as she did so. Noblet lay back and closed his eyes, the agony of the burns seemed to cover his whole body. He attempted to close his mind to the pain, focusing on the events that saved his life… and Rachel's.

He remembered the roof falling in on them as he hoisted Michael up with the pulley and hit the brake to hold it in place. The burning timbers striking him across the shoulders as he let go of the chain and saw his only chance for survival. With a desperate leap he threw himself into the long metal trough of water he used to cool the red-hot ironwork. Holding his entire body below the surface he held his breath until he thought his lungs might burst. Lifting his face quickly for air he found himself staring up at the suspended body of Michael hanging above him wrapped in chains, his clothing burnt from his body, skin blistered and weeping, peeling off in cracked and blackened slabs of flesh, the hair on his head and body shriveled to nothing. The eyes of the two men met .Noblet was engulfed by a wave of terror he was never to forget. A memory that would keep him awake for many nights to come.

A wave of flame swept across him forcing him to duck his head once more below the surface of the water. Curled beneath the cold water the vision of Michael's grinning face, his teeth showing white in his black and swollen face was stamped forever on his mind. With a terrifying crash the main supports gave way, the entire roof crashing down, the strong iron-clad tank withstanding the heavy oak timbers as they crashed about him. Bursting up from the water he found himself in an inferno of heat, the roof had fallen in trapping him in the small triangular space against the burning wall to one end. With no other option, he rose from the water and ran head-down through the ankle-deep ash and crashed with every ounce of his remaining strength into the charred and flaming timber wall that separated the smithy from the adjoining loose-boxes. With an explosion of burnt timber paneling and flying hot sparks he burst through into the smoldering but still fire-free stable. Rolling on the floor to douse the flames engulfing his lower body he finally opened his eyes, his heart leaping as he saw his wife half concealed by loose straw, laying on a bed of straw bales, the straw beginning to catch and ignite even as he looked.

Closing his mind to the agony of his burns he staggered to his feet. Scooping his wife into his arms as he heard the roof collapsing about them. With his strength finally giving out he charged the flaming door .

Chapter 32

Felicity was awakened by a gentle knock. Meg entered, closing the door behind her.

"Doctor Ellis is here to see you m'Lady."

"Again?" sighed Felicity, still half asleep, "but he examined me yesterday. Why can't he just leave me in peace?"

The doctor could be heard coming up the stairs. Meg opened the door before he had a chance to knock.

"Good morning, Doctor Ellis, her Ladyship is expecting you."

Meg bobbed politely and quietly left the room, closing the door behind her.

The doctor placed his black leather bag on the foot of Felicity's bed.

"Just a final check over your Ladyship… Just to be on the safe side, that was quite an ordeal you and Mrs. Christopher underwent yesterday. A shock like that can have some strange side effects on a pregnant woman, we can't be too careful you know."

Felicity nodded, glad that Meg had left the room. Nobody but herself and the doctor knew of her condition.

"Doctor Ellis, I would very much appreciate it if you kept this to yourself. I'd sooner nobody knew I was expecting a baby… Not just yet, anyway," she added ,seeing the doctor's puzzled expression.

"But of course m'Lady," he replied, "but you do appreciate that you won't be able to hide the fact for much longer."

He left soon after, having given Felicity a cursory examination and pronouncing her "As well as can be expected."

After showing the doctor out Meg returned to help Felicity dress.

"Will you be having breakfast in the kitchen with us again this morning, m'Lady?"

Felicity thought back to the long breakfast table, the smell of bacon, the laughter, and the warmth. Was it only yesterday? It seemed like a lifetime ago.

Realizing that Meg was expecting an answer she put an arm around the young maid's shoulder and steered her towards the bedroom door.

"I'll be able to dress myself Meg. Now I want you to go downstairs and inform Owen that I'll be requiring a full breakfast in the dining room, and that I wish every member of the staff to join me as my guests."

Meg couldn't hide her expression of surprise.

"Why do you look so shocked?" Felicity asked, "I'm only returning an invitation."

She dressed quickly. "They had done it... She had done it. Only just, but with God's help she had brought about an end to this evil."

But, if it had not been for the unexpected intervention of the Reverend... She refused to contemplate that possibility any further.

Breakfast that morning was unlike any other ever held at Sorrow Hall. After the initial awe of being treated with such an honor the staff soon settled down, feeling as comfortable as they would have 'below stairs.' Helping themselves to second portions from the sideboard, offering the bread board to her Ladyship almost as if she were just one of them.

From outside came the sound of hooves on gravel. Craning her neck to look through the mullioned window, Felicity saw Katerina and Gregory dismounting and tethering their horses to one of the white marble lions flanking the front steps.

Owen stood, tugging the napkin from his collar, ready to attend to the visitors.

"Owen," Felicity called from the opposite end of the long dining table, "Please remain seated."

"But your Ladyship... the door?"

He motioned to the sound of the doorbell now jangling loudly.

"Let me," she said, obviously enjoying the look of confusion on the butlers face.

Dropping her napkin on the table she hurried from the room, leaving the servants in a stunned silence.

Gregory could not conceal his look of astonishment when the door was opened by Felicity. He only just stopped himself from automatically handing her his riding hat and crop.

"Gregory. Katerina. Do please come in." said Felicity, her smile growing even wider. She kissed them both fondly on the cheek.

"I hope you haven't eaten. We're just sitting down to breakfast. Do please come and join us."

Wordlessly, they followed her into the dining room. Spaces were made around the table and the eating continued in earnest.

Katerina, feeling she should say something asked Margaret how James was, knowing that he'd been taken to the Norfolk and Norwich Hospital to have his wounds attended to.

The housekeeper felt a little uneasy, talking to Mrs.. Christopher in such an informal atmosphere.

"I'm not really sure, Ma'am, I never got the opportunity to speak to him yesterday, and I won't be able to travel to Norwich until tomorrow when it's my day off," she explained.

"Nonsense," interrupted Felicity, overhearing their conversation, "You must go and visit him right away. As soon as you've finished your breakfast go and make yourself look pretty and Edward will drive you to the hospital."

After breakfast, Felicity informed Owen that she would like the whole staff assembled in the library that evening. She also instructed him to telephone Sir Wallace Hanwell and ask him to come as soon as he possibly could.

Gregory and the two women strolled in the garden, chattering casually about anything but the previous day.

Felicity slid her arm through his.

"May I ask a you huge favor, Gregory?"

"Of course, anything." He answered.

"Would you sell the horses for me?"

He stopped walking, totally surprised at her unexpected request, knowing her passion for riding.

"If it's because you're without a groom at the moment, and your stables still to be rebuilt… you know you're more than welcome to keep them at ours."

Felicity was silent. She looked sadly at her two friends, realizing for the first time just how much they meant to her.

"No it's not that… I've decided to sell the estate the… Hall, the land, everything. It's far too much for me to handle alone and I feel the need to devote myself to new things."

Katerina caught the familiar glint in her friend's eyes.

"You're planning something," she declared with a knowing smile.

"Nothing definite," admitted Felicity, "Just the seeds of an idea at the moment. I've decided to take a short holiday in London. Spend some time shopping and perhaps a night out at the theatre and hopefully when I return a buyer may have been found for the Hall.

"Why the rush?" asked Gregory.

Felicity took a deep breath, and paused, "I want to get everything sorted out before my baby is born."

The shock of the news was evident in their faces. Felicity felt a tingle of pleasure at their amazed expressions.

"I've known since the night of the Ball," she continued, "but I don't want anybody else to know just yet. That's part of the reason why I wish to move away."

Katerina hugged her tearfully, not sure whether to express joy or regret wondering despite herself about the unborn child's father, but not daring to voice her thoughts… Not yet, especially in front of her husband.

Gregory shook his head in confusion. "But the estate has been in the Balmforth family for generations. If you have a boy, he would be the next Baron."

A look of apprehension clouded Felicity's face. Her voice turned icy. "I'm sorry Gregory but my mind's made up," and with eyes brimming with tears she hurried off across the lawn in the direction of the Hall.

Gregory looked dumbfounded at his wife.

"What did I say?"

"Can't you guess?" she replied rushing after the retreating Baroness.

That evening, as instructed, the servants were gathered together in the library of Sorrow Hall, each wondering what new surprise the Mistress was going to spring on them.

Margaret was in good spirits, discussing with Meg her visit to the hospital. The lead shot had been removed from James's back, buttocks and thighs, and though painful, the wounds would soon heal. His main concern seemed to be the fact that he had to sleep on his stomach, apparently something he had always hated doing.

With the cloud of Michael no longer hanging over the community, they felt it was a good time to announce their forthcoming wedding. She had already informed Meg, who was overjoyed at the news.

"A wedding is just the thing we need to cheer everybody up," she said. The young maid couldn't help feeling excited at the opportunity of wearing some of her newly acquired finery.

All conversation ceased as Owen clapped his hands sharply, calling for silence.

Lady Balmforth and Mrs. Christopher entered the room. Katerina taking Oliver's leather swivel chair behind the massive walnut desk. Felicity, smiling a greeting to the staff, went straight to Margaret and Meg standing away from the others.

Margaret thanked her for the time off and for the transportation to Norwich. Reporting on James's condition, informing her that he would be allowed home in the morning. Felicity laughed out loud at James's concern about sleeping face down. Margaret had intended to tell her of their wedding plans but thought it may be better to wait until after this curious meeting had come to a conclusion.

Felicity took the center of the room, standing in front of the desk.

"Would you all, please sit down, those that can find seats. I'd like to keep this as informal as possible."

With much shuffling and throat clearing they got themselves settled, glancing at each other uneasily, not knowing what to expect.

Leaning her weight against the edge of the desk, Felicity looked down at her hands, toying with her wedding ring, waiting for silence.

"Well, I'm sure you have all heard various accounts of what's been going on recently." she began.

They nodded, but remained silent.

"And of course, you are aware that yesterday the culprit behind all these dreadful happenings was finally brought to book, thanks in the main to the courageousness of dear Noblet Swollow and of the timely intervention of the good Reverend Underwood... whom you'll be pleased to hear is making excellent progress and will soon be back among us, much to the relief of a certain someone," she added with a smirk, all eyes turning to Margaret, now blushing furiously.

Looking at the happy faces around her, Felicity felt a twinge of guilt as she contemplated how her actions might affect everyone present.

The staff seemed to sense her uncertainty and they too started to feel a nagging doubt about what was to come.

"Would you care for something to drink my Lady?" asked Owen, realizing she was wrestling with a problem that may well concern them all.

Felicity shook her head, annoyed with herself for allowing her weakness to be so obvious. Pushing herself from the desk she smoothed the front of her dress.

"Earlier today I spoke to the family Solicitor, Sir Wallace Hanwell, and I have instructed him to sell Sorrow Hall and the entire Balmforth Estate."

The reaction of her staff was more subdued than she had expected. The younger members began talking at once. Owen looked devastated, Meg sad. Miss Divine smiled, excited at the prospect of cooking for a 'proper' family. Margaret was grateful that she would be unaffected, as she had planned to leave the Hall soon anyway.

Felicity waited until the whispering and conversations died down before continuing.

"I assure you that I will recommend each and every one of you in the most glowing terms to the new owners and, of course, if any of you decide to seek employment elsewhere, I will be delighted to furnish you with most excellent references. I realize that the past months have been a trying time for all of you. The horrid deaths of Lucy, Mrs. Black, and Jock," She paused, eyes cast down, "And of course my own dear husband…"

She felt the tears burning behind her eyes. Katerina was at her side in a moment, a comforting arm sliding around her.

"Would you like me to dismiss everyone, my Lady?" asked Owen, sympathetic to his Mistress's feelings.

Katerina answered for her. "Yes… would you, please."

The servants filed from the room eager to discuss their future with each other.

Getting control of herself Felicity called to Owen, asking him to send Margaret and Meg back in.

Sitting in the middle of the long green couch she patted the seats either side in an invitation for them both to come and sit next to her. Turning first to Margaret she asked again about James, wondering if he had told her everything that had happened in the church. Felicity could tell by her manner that she wanted to say more.

"There's something you're not telling me isn't there?" she enquired.

Margaret sighed loudly and nodded her head, pleased to be able to share her exciting news at last.

"I intended to tell you earlier, but what with your meeting and everything else I haven't really had the opportunity."

Trying to guess what the mystery was, Felicity lowered her voice to a whisper.

"Would you like to tell me when we're alone?"

"Oh, no, it's nothing like that, m'Lady," laughed Margaret, "Meg already knows, it's just that… James and I plan to marry.'

The words tumbled out in a rush, not at all as she had planned to make her announcement. She realized that her news might create a bit of a stir, but she was completely unprepared for the reaction of sincere joy from her Mistress.

Felicity, throwing her arms around her, gave her a sisterly kiss on the cheek.

"Oh! That's absolutely wonderful news. I'm so happy for you… have you named the day?"

Margaret, overwhelmed by this uncharacteristic show of affection choked back the tears.

"Not yet, m'Lady, but we would both like to make it as soon as possible."

Embarrassed by the intimate atmosphere Margaret stood, her eyes beginning to moisten. "Nobody else knows yet, m'Lady, and I was going to ask Meg if she would be my Maid of Honor… with your permission. Of course." her nervousness making her ramble.

"Oh but of course. That's if I'm still the Mistress of Sorrow Hall when the time comes," replied Felicity, regretting slightly that she may not be there for the wedding.

"I'd best be getting back to my duties, m'Lady, Mr. Owen will be waiting for me." Margaret said, giving Meg a smile as she left the room.

Katerina rose from behind Oliver's desk and walked over to the sideboard and poured three sweet Sherries, bringing two of the tiny glasses over to the couch. Felicity took them and handed one to the lady's maid.

Meg looked horrified. "For me m'Lady?, but I…" Felicity raised her finger for silence.

Katerina picked up her own glass and returned to the desk, amused at the maid's expression of distaste at her first experience of the rich sweet wine.

"It's an acquired taste," laughed Felicity lightly.

Meg placed her glass on the side table and sat nervously with her hands in her lap.

Felicity, putting her drink next to Meg's, stood and resumed her earlier position on the edge of the desk.

"In a day or two Mrs. Christopher and I are taking a short trip to London. As you know I'm in desperate need of a new wardrobe, and I would very much like you to join us. I've booked three rooms at the Great Western Hotel. I was hoping we might have a night at the Theatre and perhaps sample some of the better restaurants. How would you like that?"

"Oh, m'Lady," Meg was beside herself with excitement. "London? That would be like a dream come true. It will be an honor to attend to Mrs. Christopher and yourself. I promise you, you won't be sorry."

Felicity and Katerina smirked at each other.

"There won't be any need for that, Meg. I don't intend to take you as my maid, I'm sure the hotel has ample staff to take care of our needs. I want you to help me choose my new outfits and also I intend to look into some exciting ideas I'm toying with." She stopped talking, noticing Meg's obvious confusion.

"I'll explain everything when we get there. Let's just say I'm making some plans for the future and I would like you and Katerina to help me. Both of you will be coming as my guests. I don't expect you to pack your uniform. After all, I don't believe you're short of something to wear." She grinned, "In fact, I'm forced to admit that you now own far more clothes than I do myself… I only hope they fit."

Meg sat up straight, the feeling of pride and achievement giving her a new confidence.

"Perhaps I could find a wedding present for Margaret while I'm there, m'Lady."

"Perhaps we can," agreed Felicity, "Oh and one more thing, when we are in London you are to call me Felicity." Meg look flustered. This was ridiculous…"Yes… Yes of course m'Lady." she stammered.

Chapter 33

Inspector Basil Talbot was shown into the front parlor by Owen, Felicity looking up, startled by the unexpected interruption.

She was seated as usual in the bulky fireside armchair, a small but efficient blaze flickering in the ornate grate. A copy of Tattler lay open on her lap.

"I do hope I'm not disturbing you, your Ladyship. I've had a word with Doctor Ellis and he informs me that you're up to making a full statement. I think I know most of it but if you could just tell it in your own words, I'm sure I won't have to trouble you any further.

He shuffled his feet uncomfortably. "May I sit down?" he asked.

"Please come and sit opposite me… here," she indicated the identical chair to her own on the other side of the fireplace.

"Would you care for a cup of tea? I was just about to ring for one myself?"

"That would be most welcome, m'Lady," he responded, dropping into the indicated armchair. He hadn't expected to be received so warmly and the thought made him slightly suspicious of Felicity's intentions.

"India or China, Sir?" enquired Owen, still standing unnoticed by the parlor door.

"India, please," answered the Inspector a bit too quickly, hoping he had chosen correctly.

Owen bowed respectfully and withdrew, closing the door quietly behind him.

Sliding her magazine into a brass rack next to the hearth, Felicity studied the Inspector as he got himself comfortable in the over-stuffed armchair. She watched with interest as he took out the now familiar pocket book and ridiculously inadequate pencil. Folding the shabby book back on itself, he rested it on his knee, licking the lead tip of his pencil.

She was amused. The policeman's ritual never seemed to vary. He opened his mouth to speak but was interrupted by the arrival of Mary with the tea things on what looked to him, like a silver tray with folding legs, which she positioned between him and Lady Balmforth. Obviously, the tea must have been ordered the moment the policeman had arrived by the efficient butler, even before being instructed to do so. Talbot was pleased to see the plate of biscuits. He had not eaten since a meager lunch of bread and cheese several hours earlier at the Wheatsheaf.

Mary poured the tea and left without a word being spoken.

"Now, Inspector, I assume you would like me to start at the very beginning?" asked Felicity, adding milk and sugar to her teacup.

She related all she could remember, starting with Katerina Christopher's arrival in England as Gregory's new bride. She explained how their friendship grew. Their mutual boredom at being two wealthy, spoiled young women.

Talbot wrote furiously, covering the small pages of his pocket book with his large scrawl. His head occasionally nodding as her story seemed to clarify events that had been troubling him. He listened in silence as she explained their search for a 'Spiritual Leader.' She elaborated upon the similar quest of Mrs. Black and Lucy, and the eventual coming together of the four women and finally the 'mental prayers' summoning Michael to the Church Tower; the realization that they weren't strong enough to defy his power, and the timely arrival of Reverend Underwood.

Curiosity aroused, Talbot asked how they had thought they would avoid prosecution if they had succeeded in the killing of Michael.

Looking a little sheepish, Felicity related her hurried plan feeling somewhat childish at its simplicity and her naive belief the people would agree it was the right thing and support her story.

Talbot looked uncomfortable, "You do realize of course, that the same question will be asked in court?"

Felicity nodded. "I'm aware of that Inspector. I take it you too have some believable answers prepared yourself, I suspect the truth is going to be a little difficult for the authorities to accept, don't you think?"

He hesitated, contemplating her words, the expression of concern on his face lending a certain amount of pleasure to the Baroness.

After discussing a few more minor points, Talbot finished scribbling, the point of his pencil worn flat. He was astonished to see he'd almost filled his entire pocket book. His thick fingers ached from gripping the tiny stub of wood.

"Thank you for your time, Lady Balmforth, that seems to be just about everything. I took Mrs. Christopher's statement earlier today and by and large your story tallies with hers."

Felicity glared at him angrily.

"And why shouldn't it? Are you inferring that I may be keeping something from you?"

He considered his reply for a moment, carefully closing his pocket book and replacing it in his inside pocket as he rose to leave.

"No, your Ladyship, I'm not inferring anything of the kind. It's merely that there seems to be one or two intriguing gaps in your account of things; your kidnapping for instance. When we found you, most of your clothing had been removed, and from what you tell us of this lunatic, I can't help finding it difficult to comprehend that he could compel you to do his bidding, yet you say he never forced himself upon you…sexually… I mean." He added, worried she may be unsure of his meaning.

She flushed red, remembering her time with Michael in the tower; the stench of his unwashed body, his breath, his touch, the feeling of helplessness , revulsion and… and pleasure, and Mrs. Black's leering face as she had watched…

Her thoughts were broken by Talbot's voice as he continued, the hard edge of accusation now replaced by a gentler, more sympathetic tone.

"Well, it's all academic now. What's done is done, he's gone for good and you seem well enough."

He looked at her, she seemed small and vulnerable, the rosy glow of the fire reflected on her pale skin, it's light sparkling in her wet eyes. He regretted his words and the obvious distress he had caused her. He walked to the door.

"I'll show myself out…" still she didn't answer.

He stood, shuffling from one foot to another, his hand on the door knob, his feelings of guilt growing.

"Lady Felicity?" His voice was loud, almost commanding. She turned her head slowly, looking at him through sad eyes. He lowered his voice once more.

"I'm so sorry… Do please forgive me, I had no right to say what I did. Perhaps some questions are better left unanswered. I'm afraid I'm just becoming a grouchy old policeman who tends to see the worst in everybody. This job has a dreadful knack of making you cynical."

She stared at him in silence. Opening the door he gave her what he hoped was a pleading smile. He made one last attempt at an apology.

"Please accept my apologies."

He felt his heart leap as she returned his smile. That was enough, no words were needed. Feeling cleansed of guilt he headed back to his room at the Wheatsheaf.

Entering the pub, Talbot was surprised to see Bob Parker sitting at the bar, a half-empty Pewter tankard held in his hand, a ridiculously large dressing covering the wound on the back of his head.

"Still here, Bob? I thought you'd be off back home by now."

He ordered himself a large whisky and a top up for his Sergeant.

"I've just come from Sorrow Hall. Her Ladyship's statement seems to be all in order." Parker sensed something in the Inspector's voice but thought better of pursuing the matter.

Paying for the drinks, Talbot pulled a high wooden stool along the counter and slid onto it, removing his bowler hat and placing it on the bar top.

Parker took a long draught from his replenished pint, the head of the beer leaving a coating of froth on his dark mustache.

"Christ. I'm going to miss the beer here. I swear it's one of the best pints I've ever tasted." Putting his tankard on the counter he stared down into its mahogany colored depths, almost as one would gaze into the eyes of a lover.

Talbot had worked with Bob Parker long enough to know when something was on his mind.

"Don't try and tell me you're staying around because of the excellence of the best bitter... Unless that bang on the head you got was worse than I thought."

Putting his drink down, Parker smiled at his superior. He never could hide anything from Talbot.

"I had a word with the Reverend earlier. He tells me that our man Michael's going to be buried later today. It seems the villagers want him six foot under as soon as possible."

Talbot nodded. "I'm not surprised... but I thought the Reverend was still in hospital?"

"Came out this morning," continued Parker, "Seems he's spent the whole morning arguing with the church committee about where exactly they're going to put the grave. Most of the locals were against using the churchyard, but in the end he got them to agree to a plot in the overgrown area among the trees, at the very back of the church. A right mess it is by all accounts. The gravediggers have got to clear a space among the nettles before they can even begin work."

Talbot looked surprised. "I didn't think the Reverend would have that much influence with the villagers. After all he's not been here that long."

Parker lowered his voice as if what he was about to reveal was a secret.

"Now that's the funny part, it appears they only agreed to it because of a note from Lady Balmforth. She says in it that this Michael character was simply another victim, just like herself. That really caused a stir, I can tell you."

"Strange," thought Talbot, "She hadn't mentioned any letter... but then, why should she?"

James walked stiffly, the pain of his injuries a constant dull ache. He moved slowly, following the cheap pine coffin held aloft by the four men.

Spread along the low flint wall of the churchyard the villagers looked on, feeling no remorse or regret at the demise of the man now being lowered into the dark earth.

The gathering at the actual graveside was small; the Reverend Underwood, Inspector Talbot, his Sergeant and the four pall-bearers, P.C. Townsend and Noblet Swallow, heavily leaning on a walking stick, every part of his exposed skin covered with a lint dressing, as indeed was much that was hidden. Two of the pall bearers removed their jackets and picked up their spades, keen to resume their job of gravediggers and finish the task as soon as possible.

James glanced down at the small Bible gripped in his hands. Leaving it unopened he began to speak.

"Michael is a simple name, a name taken from the Bible. It is said that this tragic young man that we now lay to rest was in fact named after this very church."

He raised his voice slightly, wanting the distant onlookers to hear his words.

"He lived amongst you for his entire life, yet he was a stranger, shunned by all. Living in isolation, uneducated, unloved, save for the love of one old lady… where did he come from? We all may have our own theories regarding that particular question, but what is undeniable is the fact that he didn't ask to be brought into this world, and when he was, he was just like you or I, innocent and helpless. Whatever evil infected him as he grew we can only guess at. But let each and every one of us be thankful that we ourselves were not chosen. That we ourselves were not selected by whatever evil is out there, to be the servant of its hate and its malice."

He paused for a moment watching the surrounding onlookers, giving them time to let his words sink in.

"No one among us has suffered such a loss as our dear Lady Balmforth. Yet even she asks us to look on this poor soul as a victim, a victim of the wickedness and evil that will always be present in this world of ours. His grave will be unmarked. Before the year is out the grass and weeds will spread unchecked and this mound of earth will disappear back amongst the undergrowth, to be hidden and forgotten. But I ask you, every one of you. Do not forget too easily, for none of us know how we ourselves would fare had we ourselves been in his place."

He nodded to the gravediggers, standing, spades in hand waiting to proceed.

The first spadeful of soil hit the coffin lid with a dull thud. They worked quickly, eager to bury this creature that had caused so much trauma in their quiet lives.

The villagers began to drift away, muttering angrily to each other about the Reverend's words.

James watched them go, knowing that his standing in his new parish was now too low to ever be restored. He could feel Talbot looking at him, reading his thoughts. With a last glimpse at the now half-filled grave, he headed back towards the Rectory. Talbot and Parker hurrying to join him.

"I don't think your little speech went down too well with the locals," said Bob Parker.

James shrugged his shoulders. "It's what I believe. Now if you'll excuse me, I have things to attend to."

He quickened his pace, leaving the policeman in his wake.

"Come on, Bob," said Talbot, "He's obviously not a very happy man… there's nothing more we can do here, let's get back to the station, I've got one hell of a report to write."

Talbot turned and headed in the direction of the church gate. His sergeant close behind.

At the graveside, Constable Townsend stood with Noblet, watching the inspector leave. "Why do you think they hung around for the funeral. Do you think they may have expected something more to happen?"

Noblet ran his bandaged hand through his thick black hair, thinking about the question. "All I know is that some funny things have been happening lately and the quicker they fill that hole in, the happier I'll be."

Chapter 34

The right honorable Sir Wallace Hanwell Q.C sat across the table from Inspector Basil Talbot, two pints of Bullard's best bitter between them. He looked around the crowded interior of the Adam and Eve, reputedly the oldest tavern in Norwich.

He was not at all happy with what he was about to do, but the Balmforths had been friends and associates of his own family for as far back as he could remember, and of course, Lady Felicity *was* paying him a considerable fee.

"Good of you to meet me like this Inspector, you understand of course that this conversation is strictly..." He hesitated, searching for the right expression.

"Off the record?" suggested Talbot, lifting his tankard and taking a long Swallow.

"Yes, quite... as you say, off the record."

Talbot continued supping slowly at his ale, happy to let the man squirm. He was pretty sure he knew where this unusual meeting was going and why the eminent Barrister insisted on meeting him here rather than at his chambers.

"This case involving my client is somewhat out of the ordinary, would you not agree Inspector?"

"Somewhat," Talbot replied.

"From what I can gather, the facts of the case are far from straightforward, in fact, I think it's fair to say that no court in the land is going to believe a word of it. I would go even further and suggest that a respected police officer such as yourself would accept that to publicly reveal the strange happenings that have occurred in and around the village of Sorrow over the last twelve months could very likely signal the end of your promising career..."

The two men faced each other, neither speaking. Talbot finally broke the silence, "I take it you have come up with some idea that is going to solve my dilemma." he replied with more than an edge of sarcasm in his tone.

"Well, the thing is this," continued the Barrister, "Whether or not I myself care to believe what Lady Balmforth has told me is of little consequence. My only interest in this matter is clearing the good name of the late Sir Oliver Balmforth. At the moment he remains under suspicion of colluding with the deceased murder suspect, named on record simply as Michael If not colluding then certainly being an eye-witness to his father's murder and actively concealing the fact, allowing the guilty man to evade justice for any years, and as we now know, go on to be responsible for the deaths of no fewer than five more people, Sir Oliver included, as well as various other serious crimes of which I needn't bother going into at this point."

"Talbot put down his tankard and spoke at length for the first time…

"Sir, I have been a member of the Norfolk Constabulary for more years than I care to remember, I have worked exceedingly hard during that time and have achieved no small measure of success. I am the first to accept that this has been no ordinary case, I also freely admit that the truth will probably never be accepted by the courts, or indeed by the church. I'm assuming that you would like me to drop the investigation into the late Baron and concentrate all my efforts solely on the issue of the murders themselves?"

"What would be achieved by dragging the name Balmforth through the courts?" Responded Sir Wallace, "The only person to suffer would be Lady Felicity. You may not be aware that she is selling Sorrow Hall and the entire estate and investing in some business or other, the publicity that a court case of this kind would attract would without doubt destroy any plans she may have for the future."

Talbot recalled the Baroness's tears at their last encounter. "I appreciate what you are saying and the last thing I wish to do is to cause Her Ladyship any more distress, Lord knows she's been through enough over the last year, but I will still be expected to stand in that witness box, under oath and relay the events as they happened. I will doubtless be asked about my findings concerning Sir Oliver's involvement in his father's death. Are you suggesting I should lie under oath?"

Sir Wallace allowed himself a wry smile, "I think that problem may not arise. I have recently met with Justice Prescott, who is to preside over the inquiry and the court case and he agrees that the resultant publicity, if these so-called facts were released, would be catastrophic. He has already been approached by the Bishop of Norwich, The Reverend Doyle, who understandably wants to keep all this as quiet as possible. The last thing he wants is talk of a madman being possessed by the Devil, people coming back from the dead, and biblical storms of blood falling from the sky!"

Talbot was intrigued by the thought of that conversation, "Did the Bishop believe what he had been told?"

"Strangely, he did. It seems he has been in close discussion with the Rector of Saint Michael's church, who it appears will shortly be leaving Sorrow and taking up a position somewhere out Cambridge way. Apparently a lot of the local people blame him for much that happened, even the church committee feel that the coincidence of the first relevant event, namely the stable fire, having occurred on the very day the Rector first arrived in Sorrow?… Anyway it seems that the Reverend Underwood has convinced Bishop Doyle that everything really did happen the way it has been reported. Apparently the Bishop even visited the church to see the damage for himself. By the way, did you know that Lady Felicity herself was footing the bill for all the repair work? Even replacing the stained-glass window. That must have come to a pretty penny."

Talbot held his hands up in the universal signal for silence. "I think we may be straying from the point. Are you saying that I am not to be asked any questions that could embarrass the church or the police."

"No, I'm not saying that. What I am saying is that Justice Prescott is making the necessary arrangements to postpone the case indefinitely. If you agree to accept his direction, the whole thing will become nothing more than an interesting report in the archives of the Norwich Police Force."

"What you really mean is that everything will be swept under the carpet! What about the families of the victims? Surely they deserve something? Some kind of justice to be seen to be done. And the blacksmith, what about him? He's lost his livelihood simply because he helped us, in fact, if it was not for him we could still be out there hunting a killer! "

Sir Wallace sighed and sat back in his chair linking his fingers in front of him. "I have taken the liberty to have the details of the people involved looked into by some of my team The Gardener, the Stable Girl, the Cook and the old Midwife all had no living family. Sir Rupert and Sir Oliver leave only Lady Felicity, so as you see it is a most fortunate situation, in fact it couldn't be better from our point of view."

"And the blacksmith and his wife? Mr. and Mrs. Swallow?"

"Ah yes, the blacksmith… Lady Felicity has offered to compensate him for his loss, as she feels his injuries and the damage to his property was caused primarily by her actions, also Justice Prescott has agreed to pay Mr. and Mrs. Swallow substantial damages out of the public purse. Subject of course to them keeping silent about the whole thing."

"A bribe, in other words, a payment to ensure that the facts stay dead and buried."

"That's an ugly word Inspector, but by and large true. It's thought that Lady Felicity is not very likely to choose to discuss the events, nor is it likely that Mr. and Mrs. Christopher will want people knowing about their involvement in all this. The same can be said for Reverend Underwood."

"What about the two maids, they were heavily involved, they must know all the details?"

“Ah, the staff. Well, it appears the young lady’s maid has been engaged by Lady Felicity to assist with her business plans, she will certainly keep quiet about the whole thing, the Butler? Well, I’ve known him for many years, I’m confident he wouldn’t do a thing that may besmirch the Balmforth name.”

“What about the Housemaid? Margaret.”

“Oh didn’t you know? She is to be married to the Rector, she will be living somewhere in Cambridgeshire, playing the little wife…”

Chapter 35

Lady Felicity Balmforth walked through the empty building, scribbling notes on a large writing pad. "This room I thought would be ideal for our Corsetière."

Meg hurried along in her wake, still struggling to take in the speed with which Lady Felicity's plans were coming to fruition.

Felicity continued with her tour of the building, "Over there we will have a proper beauty salon. That wall will be one huge mirror. We will have to order two large chandeliers for the main hall, where customers arrive."

She lead Meg up a wide staircase to a suite of smaller store rooms and a large workshop area. A second, narrower staircase lead up from there to a small apartment on the third floor where Felicity intended to live. Standing to one side of the landing, she invited Meg to enter first.

"This will be your domain, Meg. I'm relying on you to tell me exactly what you need and how you would like the room arranged… Why Meg… whatever is the matter?"

Meg stood in the middle of the dusty room surrounded by the flotsam and jetsam of its last occupants, balls of tears rolling silently down her cheeks and clinging to the point of her chin. "I'm sorry m'Lady… I mean Felicity… I mean m'Lady… it's just that this is all happening so quickly… I can't believe it's all true. "

Felicity gave her a reassuring smile and walked over to her, placing a comforting arm about her shoulder. "Times are changing Meg, women are finding their place in the world, soon we will have the vote, we will have a voice. I feel we are on the brink of something that will grow and grow. A year or so ago I felt that my life was one long bore. I had nothing to stimulate my mind. Nothing to occupy my time. Please don't misunderstand me, I loved my husband very much, but I have accepted that he is now gone forever… The estate is gone… the Hall. It's all gone for me, and it's gone for you too. This is your chance. I suspected long ago that you are worth so much more than being in service. Now dry your eyes and accept this opportunity for what it is, the start of a whole new life for you, just like Margaret."

Completing the tour of the building they stepped outside and examined the imposing entrance, pondering upon the exterior.

"I intend to have my name in black glass and gold leaf, done in fish-tail writing, rather like that shop over there," she indicated a large jewelers opposite, "And that one further down the road."

Meg tried to look impressed. "Have you decided on a name yet m'Lady?"

"Yes, I thought I would call it Balmforth's or possibly The House of Balmforth. Felicity could sense Meg's reticence.

Meg nodded her head but couldn't disguise her reservations.

Felicity looked sternly at her former maid. "Now listen to me Meg, I've told you before, you may be an employee of mine but you are not to consider yourself a servant, you must speak your mind, you know how much I value your opinion, why if it wasn't for your help I doubt any of this would be possible. Now please tell me what you really think, I promise not to be offended." Her somber expression was now replaced by a smile of encouragement.

Taking a deep breath Meg voiced her thoughts. "Well, if you look about us, every shop tends to be just the owners name, Jarrolds, Garlands, Bonds, even in London it was all names like John Lewis, Peter Robinson, Swan and Edgar, Boots, Harrods, and most of them tend to have that black and gold fish-tail writing. You said that you wanted it to be different from everybody else. Why not just let our shop window show what we have to offer and have your name displayed much more discreetly. I thought perhaps a nice brass plaque next to the door, and I also think it would be a terrible waste to not use your title. What would attract ladies of quality better than to be dressed by a Baroness?"

Felicity looked amazed at Meg's perception, at her knack of coming up with new and radicle ideas, "So you think a discreet brass plate simply saying Lady Balmforth's? Or were you thinking of perhaps Baroness Balmforth's?"

"Actually, I was thinking of something short and catchy.... Something like... *Lady B's*."

Lady B's opened its doors on the corner of Exchange street in the very heart of Norwich amid huge public interest. Local newspapers clamored for interviews and photographs, the reporters overjoyed when a deputation from the *Women's social and political union* arrived to congratulate Lady Felicity and to assure her of their patronage.

The very next morning Felicity open her copy of *The Norwich Mercury* with some trepidation, smiling as she was greeted by the banner headline... THE BARONESS SHOPKEEPER.

Chapter 36

The new Rector of Saint Michael's church stood with his back to the fully restored stained glass window, feeling strangely cheated that his first marriage ceremony in his new parish was to be such a high-profile affair as the wedding of the outgoing Rector who had had such a short but highly eventful time at Saint Michael's. The explanations of the events of the proceeding months were many and varied, and doubtless nobody would ever truly get to the bottom of things.

Meg felt strange entering the church. She had not been inside since the previous summer. Smiling across at the Hall staff still in their allotted pews, she noticed three or four new faces and wondered which of these was now doing her old job.

At the front of the crowded church she was seated on the first pew behind James and Gregory. The groom and best man awaiting the arrival of Margaret.

A murmur arose amongst the congregation as somebody entered. Meg turned expecting to see the bride, but instead was surprised to see Lady Felicity Balmforth striding confidently towards her, head held high, the glamorous outfit she was wearing doing nothing to conceal her obvious pregnancy.

People nodded their greetings to the Baroness as she passed, many doing quick calculations in their heads, figuring out the months since her husband's death.

She slid heavily into the pew next to Meg, glancing across at her former staff, returning their smiles. For a moment, she felt a slight pang of regret when she realized that the pew reserved for generations for the Balmforths was now occupied by Lady Caroline Auburn, still as willowy and as handsome as Felicity remembered her.

The two women nodded curtly to each other, strangers linked only by a time and a person, both sadly, no more.

Felicity looked around the familiar interior of the church. The new stained-glass window reflected the early spring sunshine onto the freshly painted white walls, the cost of which Felicity had been happy to meet from the sale of Sorrow Hall. James and the Bishop had discussed various themes for the new window but after many suggestions they had decided to let her make the final choice. Unable to choose she had decided to keep it just the same as the original; Mary holding the baby Jesus looking down on the altar below.

Felicity was brought from her musings as Katerina hurried down the aisle to join her.

"She's here," she gushed excitedly.

Margaret entered, a vision in Ivory silk and lace, her beautiful face hidden behind the long veil. At her side was the diminutive figure of Owen, looking resplendent in grey frock coat and top hat held stiffly in his hand.

"The gown looks gorgeous," whispered Katerina to Felicity.

"The first of Meg's wonderful creations. It was our wedding gift, perhaps we should think about including a range of wedding gowns to our collection."

Meg smiled to herself, overhearing the conversation. It had all happened so fast. In the quiet of the church she allowed her thoughts to slide back over the past few short months.

The day after Michael's funeral they had set off for London. She smiled to herself remembering the discomfort of being under Owen's gaze as he, stony-faced, held open the door of the motorcar for Felicity, Katerina, and herself.

The whole day had been like a dream, from the ride to Norwich in the luxurious car, to the exciting hustle and bustle of the railway station with its noise and steam, the sound of porter's whistles and carriage doors slamming. She had stood in a daze, the clouds of steam drifting up to the acres of glass arching high above her, the loud panting of the massive engines giving the impression of a wild beast, crouching low, waiting to spring forward and carry them on their adventure.

From the first jerking lurch of the journey Meg's mind had been bursting with possibilities, her thoughts seeming to keep time with the metallic gallop of the iron wheels beneath her, the distant melancholy whistle of the locomotive seemed like a promise of marvelous things to come.

And so it had proved to be, from that first unforgettable train ride, to the thrill of checking into the Great Western Hotel an ornately sculptured building strongly styled in a mixture of French renaissance and baroque, more reminiscent of a medieval palace than a modern hotel.

She had entered the opulent splendor of the 'Great Western' a shy, overawed and nervous young girl. She left, ten days later, a confident and assertive young woman, ready to take on the new challenges that were being offered to her.

She had shopped at the best stores in Knightsbridge, Bond Street and Piccadilly, she had dined in the finest restaurants, attended the theatre, the opera, seen sights she had only dreamed of, she had even traveled on a train that ran underground and on a moving staircase in Harrods, laughing and chatting with Felicity and Katerina as if they were older sisters.

On one memorable morning they had sat in the magnificent rooftop garden of Derry and Tom's, sipping tea beside the incongruous 'Flamingo stream' when Felicity had finally begun to expand upon her vision for the future, and in particular, Meg's future.

"Don't you think it ridiculous that in order to buy the finest clothes or the best jewelry one has to travel to London. Nowhere in our part of the country can a lady of breeding see the latest Paris fashions, or have her hair styled by an expert. Well that is all going to change."

She put her cup down on the table between them and rose to her feet, pacing to and fro in her excitement. "As soon as possible we are going to search Norwich for a property to rival the best stores in London. People will travel for miles to come there, why, we may even be able to design our own gowns! Something young Meg here was born to do."

That very same day they had visited various shops and suppliers. At Liberty's in Oxford Street they had been shown beautiful Japanese fabrics and Indian block printed silks. In St. James they had spoken to people in Lobbs, the Royal shoemakers and James Locks, who had made hats for Nelson and Wellington.

Felicity had talked business with confident authority to salesmen and proprietors alike, forcing them to forget she was a mere woman and making them accept her as a serious business opportunity by the sheer strength of her ambition.

The wedding over, Margaret and James ran the gauntlet of rice and confetti before putting themselves at the mercy of the photographer.

Felicity's face, aching from the forced smiling and polite social gestures took Katerina's arm.

"They're going to be some time yet. Let's have a stroll around the churchyard."

The two friends drifted away from the wedding party, stopping to look at the stone tomb housing the late Baron.

"Do you miss him?" asked Katerina.

After some moments Felicity shook her head, "No… does that shock you?"

They walked on around the church. Both conscious of the spot Michael had been laid to rest. It was now hardly recognizable, a slight hump amongst the docks and nettles of the unused corner of the churchyard.

Walking between the trees Felicity felt a wave of depression at the sight of the row, upon row of aged headstones leaning, tired and forgotten amongst the long grass and weeds, some so old as to be unreadable.

Trying to lighten the oppressive atmosphere, Katerina asked about the forthcoming birth.

"Have you decided on a name yet?"

Felicity brightened, "If it's a boy, it'll have to be Oliver…after his father!" She added hesitantly,

"What if you have a girl?" asked Katerina.

Felicity shrugged her shoulders. At that moment she stumbled slightly, the strap of her shoe caught by a thick brier growing over a small lopsided headstone.

Kneeling to free herself from the bramble she noticed the simple inscription carved into the discolored marble.

"Alice 1877"

Standing, she smiled at her friend, "Alice… what a lovely name."

Alice Balmforth was born just after midnight during a violent summer storm. Even in the pain of childbirth, Felicity was conscious of the sheets of rain lashing against the window of her bedroom, obscuring the familiar view of the nearby Norwich cathedral.

The midwife wrapped a blanket around the newborn infant and laid her in her mother's arms.

Felicity pushed the blanket back eager to see her baby. She felt her breath catch in her throat as she looked at the misshapen arm and hooked, claw-like hand.

Meg came rushing into the room at the sound of Felicity's scream, taking the sobbing mother in her arms.

In a small village churchyard, he awoke to the sound of a woman's scream. His eyes opened. He felt frightened by the total blackness surrounding him. It was dark… damp. Was he home? No, it was cold… so cold. He moved his hands with some effort to form a fist. His flesh felt wet, soft, like rotten meat. His nails cut into his palms yet he felt no pain. All he felt was the crushing weight of the raw, rain sodden soil about him. Running his hands over the interior of the pine box, he at last realized where he was. The last sound he made was a scream. A scream that nobody heard. A scream that lasted the rest of his life.

THE END